PENGUIN BOOKS

NEW PENGUIN PARALLEL TEXT: SHORT STORIES IN CHINESE

中国短篇小说集

JOHN BALCOM is a professor and the head of the Chinese program in the Graduate School of Translation and Interpretation at the Monterey Institute of International Studies, where he has taught translation for more than fifteen years. He has been translating Chinese literature for three decades and has won an NEA Fellowship for translation and two Northern California Book Awards. He has published and lectured widely on Chinese-to-English translation and is a past president of the American Literary Translators Association (ALTA).

New Penguin Parallel Text

Short Stories in Chinese
中国短篇小说集

Translated and Edited
by John Balcom

PENGUIN BOOKS

PENGUIN BOOKS
Published by the Penguin Group
Penguin Group (USA) Inc., 375 Hudson Street,
New York, New York 10014, USA

USA | Canada | UK | Ireland | Australia | New Zealand | India | South Africa | China
Penguin Books Ltd, Registered Offices: 80 Strand, London WC2R 0RL, England
For more information about the Penguin Group visit penguin.com

First published in Penguin Books 2013

All translations by John Balcom

Translations of "O, Xiangxue," "Plow Ox," "Lanterns for the Dead," "Greasy Moon," and "Receiving the
Precepts" are published for the first time in this volume. Copyright © John Balcom, 2013.

"O, Xiangxue" by Tie Ning. Published by arrangement with Tie Ning.
"The Ancestor" ("Zuzong") by Bi Feiyu. Published by arrangement with Bi Feiyu. Translation from
Chairman Mao Would Not Be Amused: Fiction from Today's China, edited by Howard Goldblatt.
Copyright © 1995 by Grove Press, Inc. Reprinted by permission of Grove/Atlantic, Inc.
"Dog" ("Gouzi") by Cao Naiqian. Published by arrangement with Cao Naiqian. Translation from *There's
Nothing I Can Do When I Think of You Late at Night* by Cao Naiqian. Copyright © 2009 John Balcom.
Reprinted by permission of Columbia University Press.
"Plow Ox" ("Gengniu") by Li Rui. Published by arrangement with Li Rui.
"The Mistake" ("Cuowu") by Ma Yuan. Published by arrangement with Ma Yuan. Translation of selection
titled "The Cap" published in Manoa, vol. 1, nos. 1 and 2, Fall 1989, University of Hawaii Press. Reprinted
by permission of the University of Hawaii Press.
"Lanterns for the Dead" ("Mingdeng") by Jiang Yun. Published by arrangement with Jiang Yun.
"Greasy Moon" ("You yueliang") by Jia Pingwa. Published by arrangement with Jia Pingwa.
"Receiving the Precepts" ("Shoujie") by Wang Zengqi. Published by arrangement with Wang Chao.

LIBRARY OF CONGRESS CATALOGING-IN-PUBLICATION DATA
Short stories in Chinese : new Penguin parallel text / translated and edited by John Balcom.
    p. cm.
    Text in English and Chinese.
    Includes bibliographical references.
    ISBN 978-0-14-311835-0
    1. Short stories, Chinese—Translations into English.   2. Chinese fiction—20th century—Translations
into English.   I. Balcom, John.
    PL2658.E8S56 2012
    895.1'30108052—dc23

                    2011044031

Printed in the United States of America
10 9 8 7 6 5 4 3

Set in Minion

For Yingtsih 黃瑛姿,
without whom this book would not be possible

Contents

INTRODUCTION

In the years since the end of the Cultural Revolution (1976)—the period of focus for this volume—writing in China has proliferated in a way that is beyond the powers of any one person to master. For this reason, any anthology of contemporary Chinese fiction will tell the reader as much about the interests and proclivities of the editor as it will about the contemporary literary scene. I have deliberately avoided stories by fine authors whose work is well represented in English translation—Gao Xingjian, Mo Yan, Su Tong, Yu Hua, Wang Anyi, and Can Xue, to name a few—and instead have opted for stories by less well-known, but no less worthy, authors. I have chosen stories by writers whose work I have enjoyed and translated over the years. In the course of time, some of these writers have even become friends.

The history of Chinese literature spans thousands of years, but coming to terms even with the literature of the twentieth century for the non-Chinese is an immense undertaking. The cultural, historical, and linguistic complexities of the country at times seem insurmountable. The New Literature movement of 1919 was directed against imperialism, the powerless Chinese government, and traditional culture, which were seen by students and intellectuals as responsible for China's woes. This meant replacing the classical language of imperial China with the modern vernacular.

Before the Yennan talks, a more experimental strain based on Western models coexisted with a more nativist approach in the social-realist mode with folk culture elements. Mao Zedong's Talks on Literature codified the dogmatic parameters of literature in China for the next four decades. Writers traveled or were sent to the countryside to learn from the peasants. Literature was to serve the revolution. The revolution and the revolutionary experience of soldiers, workers, and peasants were to be the subject matter of literature. This, of course, culminated in a cultural bureaucracy that produced the literature as propaganda that held sway for decades. Some good writing was produced within these parameters, but by the time of the Cultural Revolution, fiction seemed to be a dying art, with only two so-called literary magazines staying in print throughout the ten years of the Cultural Revolution.

After the Cultural Revolution, a new sense of freedom pervaded the cultural sphere, and unofficial publications appeared. For many writers, however, despite encouragement from Deng Xiaoping, the political atmosphere became more restrictive throughout the 1980s. Frustration with the political system culminated, in 1989, with the Tiananmen demonstrations and their brutal suppression. In the early '90s, the cultural sphere remained depressed, although there were hundreds of unofficial literary magazines. After 1993, when the current consumerist society really took off, literature became another commodity, freedom of expression was reborn, and writers who once wrote for an underground audience became mainstream and were published by state-run publishing houses.

Two thematic obsessions of the stories collected here are history and memory. These themes are not new to modern Chinese literature. Some of the writers collected here use subtle irony; some are more realist; some more allegorical. However, it is the interplay of memory—its fallibility and fragmentary nature—and history by which the writers grapple with issues of identity. Their vision is often dark and troubling, sometimes sadly lyrical, sometimes humorous, sometimes poignant. Yet it is their passionate, creative engagement with the times that makes their work so powerful.

Tie Ning was born in 1957 in Beijing and has written numerous short stories and novels. She is the first woman president of the Chinese Writers' Association. "O Xiangxue" is the story that first brought her to the attention of the reading public. A lyrical evocation of life in a remote mountain village, it describes the experiences of a girl whose encounters with people at the village railway station broaden her horizons. Its wide appeal to readers in China comes from the author's ability to capture beautifully a sense of youthful innocence in a simple, straightforward style.

Bi Feiyu was born in 1964 in Xinghua, Jiangsu Province. He has gained renown as a screenwriter (*Shanghai Triad*) and more recently for his novella *The Moon Opera*. Bi Feiyu's story "The Ancestor" is a dark tale about a period when China was undergoing immense change. Through the character of the grandmother and her relationship with her sons, the story represents an allegorical critique of China's relationship with its past. The old must make way for the new in often cruel and disastrous, if not superstitious, ways.

Cao Naiqian was born in 1949 and has a day job as a detective with the Public Security Bureau in Datong, Shanxi Province. He is a natural writer. His "novel" of thirty interlocking stories, *There's Nothing I Can Do When I Think of You Late at Night*, from which the story in this volume is drawn, is, to my mind, one of the finest pieces of writing China has so far produced this century. Cao's starkly lyrical work focuses on the disposable lives of some of China's poorest and most ignorant citizens, documenting their suffering and their joys. His writing is sometimes difficult for the general reader because of Cao's use of Shanxi dialect. The story published here, "Dog," is a sadly humorous tale of subtle irony. The main character is Dog, a humble, uneducated peasant who knows only the honor and dignity of work. He is often preoccupied by thoughts of food and sex, but he is also selfless and hardworking. Cao's depiction of the simple peasant, while being truthful as well as humorous and ironic, would have been ideologically unacceptable for most of the history of the People's Republic of China. Indeed, the very "backwardness" of the author's peasant characters is an indication of how things have changed in China. During the Cultural Revolution, writers were supposed to depict peasants as heroes of ideological purity who were leading the country toward a Communist paradise. Cao's character, fixated as he is on food and sex, and totally lacking in correct ideology, would have been unimaginable just a few decades ago.

Li Rui was born in 1950 in Beijing, but his family roots are in Sichuan Province. He has spent much of his life in Shanxi Province, having been sent to the countryside during the Cultural Revolution. He has written two historical novels set in Silver City, an imaginary city in Sichuan Province; two brilliant novels of the Cultural Revolution; and several volumes of short stories and essays. His story, "Plow Ox," in this volume comes from his collection *Things in Peaceful Times*. The collection was inspired by a late-Ming text on agricultural implements that Li Rui encountered in a used-book store. Each story revolves around an agricultural implement or, in the case of "Plow Ox," a draught animal. Like much of Li Rui's rural fiction, "Plow Ox" displays the honest simplicity of the Shanxi peasant.

Ma Yuan was born in 1953 in Liaoning, Manchuria, and was something of a literary phenomenon in the 1980s. I recall a huge conference at Fudan University on his writings when I was at the Shanghai Academy of Social Sciences for the 1988/89 academic year. Then Ma suddenly dropped out of sight and went into business. Some of his best-known pieces tend to be mysteries, and take place in Tibet or in Dongbei during the Cultural Revolution. "The Mistake" is no exception. From the get-go we are introduced to a narrator who exhibits an odd mix of the educated and low-register lingo one expects from an urban tough. The initial few paragraphs portray his mind as somewhat disorderly, switching randomly among topics and digressing. This mental pattern forms the narrative paradigm for the story—a perfect mystery in which the plot moves back and forth, revealing more and more clues until all things (almost) come together in the end. The story is a good example of how memory and incomplete understanding of events color our perceptions. In many of Ma Yuan's stories, there is plenty of mystery but often no final resolution.

Jiang Yun was born in 1954 in Taiyuan, Shanxi Province. A fine writer whose talent has not been sufficiently recognized, she is the author of several novels and collections of short stories and essays. She is married to Li Rui, and the couple has collaborated on one novel, a rewriting of the well-known White Snake legend dating back to the Tang dynasty. Jiang Yun's story "Lanterns for the Dead," as the title suggests, ostensibly revolves around the folk custom of setting lanterns adrift on water in memory of the dead during the Ghost Festival. The story is not plot driven or even character driven; rather, it is driven by its lyricism. The narrator recounts Fan Xilin's visit to a town along the Yellow River, where she witnesses an execution and later the folk custom of launching water lanterns. The narrative moves back and forth in time, with the contrasting and apparently random details from the days of revolution and the contemporary reform period setting up a pattern of resonance, which finally climaxes in the execution of a young woman.

Jia Pingwa was born in 1953 in Shanxi Province and is one of the most influential members of the "root-seeking" school of writers, who have a particular interest in rural life and sexual relationships. His story "Greasy Moon" is both a retrospective look at the horrors of the Cultural Revolution and perhaps a postscript to Lu Xun's famous story "The Diary of a Madman." In Lu Xun's tale, the madman has paranoid delusions that everyone is out to eat him. As he studies a historical text, he realizes that the history of mankind is the history of eating people, of cannibalism. In "Greasy Moon," You Yiren learns from growing up during the Cultural Revolution that preying on one's fellow man is the norm, if not something innate in mankind. His abnormally small size is symbolic of the stunting of the generation that grew up during the Cultural Revolution. You Yiren kills people for no apparent reason and then sells their flesh. One day he happens to eat in a well-known dumpling shop in the county town only to discover that the dumplings are filled with the meat he has sold. Sickened, he runs away. Later he is arrested, tried, and sentenced to death. His half-moon-shaped fingerprints stand as official testimony to the horrors bred by society, much in the way that Lu Xun's madman eventually finds himself awaiting an official position to join the cannibals.

Wang Zengqi (1920–1997) is the oldest writer included in this collection. His work is also the most culturally bound and, therefore, perhaps the most difficult. His story "Receiving the Precepts" is perhaps the finest example of his late fictional output, with its emphasis on customs and human feelings from an earlier day. It is also replete with the sights and sounds of the Jiangnan region of southern China. The story was written in 1980, but a note appended to the piece refers to it as a "dream of thirty years before." The plot is minimal, with the narrative focusing on a youth who leaves home to become a monk. In the course of describing the boy's removal to a temple, his life and new friends there, and his eventual receiving of the Buddhist precepts, the author provides detailed descriptions of temple life, rural life and custom, and the interpersonal relationships of his characters. The story appeared when scar literature and stories detailing the horrors of the Cultural Revolution were common. It was a welcome relief, but it, too, describes, in a lyrical fashion, much of what China has lost since the revolution.

By definition, literary translation is a compromise between being faithful to the author and to the reader. Needless to say, I have tried to be as faithful to each author as possible while at the same time attempting to create a readable English version that could be used as a crib for advanced language students. The pieces vary to some extent in the degree of literalness applied. As I have written elsewhere, bridging the gap as a translator between English and Chinese presents problems of the sort that most translators of Western languages could never conceive. That which is taken for granted by the reader of the source-language text is a matter of opacity for the reader of a translation. The cultural underpinning to a text is often completely lacking for, say, an American reader. What is to be done? Where necessary, I have provided notes, as is usual for the Parallel Text series, and have additionally worked explanatory notes into the texts themselves.

I have spent nearly thirty years reading and translating Chinese fiction. I am still learning about China, grappling with its immensity and the vastness of its culture. I would like to express my heartfelt thanks to a number of individuals who, over the years since I began studying Chinese, have been enormously helpful to me as a student and a translator. First of all, I would like to thank Howard Goldblatt, friend and mentor, who commissioned two of the stories here for earlier editorial efforts. I would also like to acknowledge the influence of Göran Malmqvist on my work translating Chinese fiction through our discussions and for his introducing me to such writers as Cao Naiqian, Li Rui, and Jiang Yun. Liu Jun of Nanjing University, a fine scholar of modern Chinese literature, whom I met at a conference on Taiwan modernism, suggested Wang Zengqi's challenging story. Thanks must go to Julia Han Qingyue of the Foreign Languages Press in Beijing, and a former student, for helping me secure author contacts. Lu Ye, my teaching assistant at the Monterey Institute of International Studies, was instrumental in preparing many of the Chinese texts for this book. I am also grateful to John Siciliano at Penguin for suggesting this project and for his support and editorial acumen. Last but not least, I would like to thank my wife, Yingtsih, who not only served as an editorial consultant in the present effort, but who also read and commented on every translation in this volume, saving me from many a blunder. It goes without saying that any infelicities that remain are my responsibility.

—John Balcom

O Xiangxue

哦，香雪

Tie Ning

如果不是有人发明了火车，如果不是有人把铁轨铺进深山，你怎么也不会发现台儿沟这个小村。它和它的十几户乡亲，一心一意掩藏在大山那深深的皱褶里，从春到夏，从秋到冬，默默的接受着大山任意给予的温存和粗暴。

然而，两根纤细、闪亮地铁轨延伸过来了。它勇敢地盘旋在山腰，又悄悄的试探着前进，弯弯曲曲，曲曲弯弯，终于绕到台儿沟脚下，然后钻进幽暗的隧道，冲向又一道山梁，朝着神秘的远方奔去。

不久，这条线正式营运，人们挤在村口，看见那绿色的长龙一路呼啸，挟带着来自山外的陌生、新鲜的清风，擦着台儿沟贫弱的脊背匆匆而过。它走的那样急忙，连车轮碾轧钢轨时发出的声音好像都在说：不停不停，不停不停！是啊，它有什么理由在台儿沟站脚呢，台儿沟有人要出远门吗？山外有人来台儿沟探亲访友吗？还是这里有石油储存，有金矿埋藏？台儿沟，无论从哪方面讲，都不具备挽住火车在它身边留步的力量。

可是，记不清从什么时候起，列车的时刻表上，还是多了"台儿沟"这一站。也许乘车的旅客提出过要求，他们中有哪位说话算数的人和台儿沟沾亲；也许是那个快乐的男乘务员发现台儿沟有一群十七、八岁的漂亮姑娘，每逢列车疾驰而过，她们就成帮搭伙地站在村口，翘起下巴，贪婪、专注地仰望着火车。有人朝车厢指点，不时能听见她们由于互相捶打而发出的一、两声娇嗔的尖叫。也许什么都不为，就因为台儿沟太小了，小得叫人心疼，就是钢筋铁骨的巨龙在它面前也不能昂首阔步，也不能不停下来。

I f no one had invented the train, if no one had laid the rails deep into the mountain, the small village of Tai'ergou would have gone unnoticed. The village of more than ten households was hidden in the folds of a huge mountain. With all their hearts, the villagers silently accepted whatever kindness or rudeness the mountain gave, spring, summer, fall, and winter.

However, two thin, bright rails stretched there; they wound bravely up the mountain, and again quietly advanced, sounding their way ahead, winding and snaking, until they finally arrived at the foot of Tai'ergou. Then they seemed to burrow into a dark tunnel and dash toward another mountain ridge, running far into the mysterious distance.

Soon the line began operating. People crowded at the entrance to the village, watching the long green dragon whistle on its way, carrying a strange and fresh wind from outside the mountain, hurriedly brushing past Tai'ergou and its poverty. The train sped by so quickly that even its wheels, as they rolled on the rails, seemed to say, Don't stop! Don't stop! That's right, why stop at Tai'ergou? Did anyone in Tai'ergou ever leave? Did anyone outside ever visit a relative or friend in Tai'ergou? Was any oil stored there? Was an old gold mine hidden there? Whatever might be said, Tai'ergou had no power to make a train stop.

But at some point, which no one can remember, a station at Tai'ergou was added to the train's scheduled stops. Perhaps the passengers had requested it. How many of them, who stood by their word, had kinship ties with Tai'ergou? Perhaps that happy male attendant discovered that there was a passel of seventeen- or eighteen-year-old girls who would gather together at the entrance of the village, their chins raised, greedily absorbed in looking up at the train as it sped by. One of them would point at the cars, and from time to time they would hit each other, pout prettily with displeasure, and scream once or twice. Perhaps it was simply on account of Tai'ergou being so small, so small as to make the heart ache. But the steel-and-iron-boned dragon could not stride forward, head

总之，台儿沟上了列车时刻表，每晚七点钟，由首都方向开往山西的这列火车在这里停留一分钟。

这短暂的一分钟，搅乱了台儿沟以往的宁静。从前，台儿沟人利来是吃过晚饭就钻被窝，他们仿佛是在同一时刻听到大山无声的命令。于是，台儿沟那一小变石头房子在同一时刻忽然完全静止了，静的那样深沉、真切，好像在默默地向大山诉说着自己的虔诚。如今，台儿沟的姑娘们刚把晚饭端上桌就慌了神，她们心不在焉地胡乱吃几口，扔下碗就开始梳妆打扮。她们洗净蒙受了一天的黄土、风尘，露出粗糙、红润的面色，把头发梳的乌亮，然后就比赛着穿出最好的衣裳。有人换上过年时才穿得新鞋，有人还悄悄往脸上涂点姻脂。尽管火车到站时已经天黑，她们还是按照自己的心思，刻意斟酌着服饰和容貌。然后，她们就朝村口，朝火车经过的地方跑去。香雪总是第一个出门，隔壁的凤娇第二个就跟了出来。

七点钟，火车喘息着向台儿沟滑过来，接着一阵空哐乱响，车身震颤一下，才停住不动了。姑娘们心跳着涌上前去，像看电影一样，挨着窗口观望。只有香雪躲在后面，双手紧紧捂着耳朵。看火车，她跑在最前边，火车来了，她却缩到最后去了。她有点害怕它那巨大的车头，车头那么雄壮地吐着白雾，仿佛一口气就能把台儿沟吸进肚里。它那撼天动地的轰鸣也叫她感到恐惧。在它跟前，她简直像一叶没根的小草。

"香雪，过来呀，看！"凤娇拉过香雪向一个妇女头上指，她

held high, but had to stop. In short, after Tai'ergou was added to the schedule, the train from the direction of the capital headed to Shanxi would stop for one minute every night at seven o'clock.

That brief minute disturbed Tai'ergou's normal tranquility. In the past, the residents of Tai'ergou would go to bed right after dinner, as if they had all heard the huge mountain's silent orders at the same time. Thus every little stone house in the village suddenly fell silent at the same moment, perfectly and profoundly silent as if recounting their piety to the mountain in a hush. Today, right after serving dinner, the girls of Tai'ergou lost their self-possession; distracted, they wolfed down a few bites, then put down their bowls and began to dress and put on makeup. They washed away the day's yellow dirt and dust, revealing coarse, ruddy faces; they brushed their hair until it shone black; then they competed to dress in the nicest clothes. One put on the shoes she wore only at New Year's; another stealthily applied rouge to her face. Regardless of whether the train arrived after dark, they still, each in her own way, painstakingly considered their clothes and appearance. Then they all set off for the entrance to the village, running to where the train passed. Xiangxue was always the first one out the door; Fengjiao, who lived next door, was the second, right behind her.

At seven o'clock, the panting train made its way toward Tai'ergou. After making a racket, it shuddered to a halt. Hearts aflutter, the girls pushed forward to the windows to look in as if they were watching a movie. Only Xiangxue remained behind, hands clutched to her ears. Seeing the train, she was always up front, but when it arrived, she always shrank to the rear. She was a little frightened by the huge engine and the way it fiercely belched white steam, as if it could swallow all of Tai'ergou in one gulp. Its whistle, which shook both heaven and earth, also frightened her. Before it, she was like a leaf of grass with no roots.

"Xiangxue, come here, look!" Fengjiao pulled her as she pointed

指的是那个妇女头上别着的那一排金圈圈。

"怎么我看不见?"香雪微微眯着眼睛。

"就是靠里边那个，那个大圆脸。看，还有手表哪，比指甲盖还小哩!"凤娇又有了新发现。

香雪不言不语地点着头，她终于看见了妇女头上的金圈圈和她腕上比指甲盖还要小的手表。但她也很快就发现了别的。"皮书包!"她指着行李架上一只普通的棕色人造革学生书包。就是那种连小城市都随处可见的学生书包。

尽管姑娘们对香雪的发现总是不感兴趣，但她们还是围了上来。

"呦，我的妈呀!你踩着我的脚啦!"凤娇一声尖叫，埋怨着挤上来的一位姑娘。她老是爱一惊一咋的。

"你喧呼什么呀，是想叫那个小白脸和你答话了吧?"被埋怨的姑娘也不示弱。

"我撕了你的嘴!"凤娇骂着，眼睛却不游自主地朝第三节车厢的车门望去。

那个白白净净的年轻乘务员真下车来了。他身材高大，头发乌黑，说一口漂亮的北京话。也许因为这点，姑娘们私下里都叫他"北京话"。"北京话"双手抱住胳膊肘，和她们站得不远不近地说:"喂，我说小姑娘们，别扒窗户，危险!"

"呦，我们小，你就老了吗?"大胆的凤娇回敬了一句。姑娘们一阵大笑，不知谁还把凤娇往前一搡，弄的她差点撞在他身上，这一来反倒更壮了凤娇的胆，"喂，你们老呆在车上不头晕?"她又问。

at a woman's head. She was pointing at a band of golden rings clipped around her head.

"What is it? I can't see," said Xiangxue, squinting.

"The one inside there with the big, round face. Look, she's wearing a watch that's smaller than a fingernail!" Fengjiao had made yet another discovery.

Xiangxue nodded silently, finally catching sight of the golden rings clipped around the woman's head and the watch that was smaller than a fingernail. But she quickly discovered something else. "A leather book bag!" She pointed at an ordinary brown student's book bag on the luggage rack. It was no different from the student bags that could be seen all over any small town.

Even though the girls weren't interested in Xiangxue's discovery, they still crowded round.

"Ow! You stepped on my foot!" Fengjiao shouted, complaining to one of the girls who had squeezed forward. She always liked causing a ruckus.

"What are you squawking about? Do you want that good-looking young man to say something to you?" replied the girl who had been scolded, not to be outdone.

"I'll tear your mouth!" threatened Fengjiao, unable to keep from looking in the direction of the door of the third car.

The fair, young male attendant actually did step off the train. He was quite tall and his hair raven black. He spoke beautiful Beijing Mandarin. Perhaps it was on account of this that the girls referred to him as "Beijing Mandarin." Beijing Mandarin, arms folded, stood nearby and said, "Hey, young ladies, don't press against the window—it's dangerous!"

"If we're young, does that make you old?" Fengjiao, who was a bit bold, replied tit for tat. The girls all broke into a fit of laughter. Someone pushed Fengjiao so that she almost collided with the young man. This just made Fengjiao all the bolder: "Don't you get dizzy always standing on the train?" she asked.

"房顶子上那个大刀片似的，那是干什么用的?" 又一个姑娘问。她指的是车相里的电扇。

"烧水在哪儿?"

"开到没路的地方怎么办?"

"你们城里人一天吃几顿饭?" 香雪也紧跟在姑娘们后面小声问了一句。

"真没治!""北京话"陷在姑娘们的包围圈里，不知所措地嘟囔着。

快开车了，她们才让出一条路，放他走。他一边看表，一边朝车门跑去，跑到门口，又扭头对她们说: "下次吧，下次一定告诉你们!" 他的两条长腿灵巧地向上一跨就上了车，接着一阵叽哩喔嘟，绿色的车门就在姑娘门面前沉重地合上了。列车一头扎进黑暗，把她们撇在冰冷的铁轨旁边。很久，她们还能感觉到它那越来越轻的震颤。

一切又恢复了寂静，静得叫人惆怅。姑娘们走回家去，路上还要为一点小事争论不休: "谁知道别在头上的金圈圈是几个?"

"八个。"

"九个。"

"不是!"

"就是!"

"凤娇你说哪?"

"她呀，还在想'北京话'哪!"

"What is that thing for on the roof that looks like a knife blade?" asked one of the girls, referring to the fan in the car.

"Where's the hot water?"

"What happens when you get to a place where there are no tracks?"

"How many meals a day do you city folks eat?" asked Xiangxue from the rear.

"This is hopeless!" grumbled Beijing Mandarin, surrounded by the girls.

Only when the train was about to depart did they let him go. He looked at his watch as he ran toward the carriage door. At the door, he turned and said to them, "Next time I'll tell you, next time!" With one step, he nimbly jumped aboard the train. After the train made a racket, the green car door closed silently in front of the girls. The train plunged into the darkness, abandoning them beside the cold tracks. For a long while, they could sense the lessening tremble of the train.

The quiet returned, a saddening quiet. The girls walked home. On the way they argued continuously about one small thing: "Who knows how many gold rings were clipped on her head?"

"Eight."

"Nine."

"No."

"Yes."

"Fengjiao, what do you say?"

"Her? She's still thinking about Beijing Mandarin!"

"去你的，谁说谁就想。"凤娇说着捏了一下香雪的手，意思是叫香雪帮腔。

香雪没说话，慌得脸都红了。她才十七岁，还没学会怎样在这种事上给人家帮腔。

"他的脸多白呀!"那个姑娘还在逗凤娇。

"白? 还不是在那大绿屋里捂的。叫他到咱台儿沟住几天试试。"有人在黑影里说。

"可不，城里人就靠捂。要论白，叫他们和咱们香雪比比。咱们香雪，天生一副好皮子，再照火车那些闺女的样儿，把头发烫成弯弯绕，啧啧! '真没治'! 凤娇姐，你说是不是?"

凤娇不接茬儿，松开了香雪的手。好像姑娘们真的在贬低她的什么人一样，她心里真有点替他抱不平呢。不知怎么的，她认定他的脸绝不是捂白的，那是天生。

香雪又悄悄把手送到凤娇手心里，她示意凤娇握住她的手，仿佛请求凤娇的宽恕，仿佛是她使凤娇受了委屈。

"凤娇，你哑巴啦?"还是那个姑娘。

"谁哑巴啦! 谁像你们，专看人家脸黑脸白。你们喜欢，你们可跟上人家走啊!"凤娇的嘴巴很硬。

"我们不配!"

"你担保人家没有相好的?"

不管在路上吵得怎样厉害，分手时大家还是十分友好的，因为一个叫人兴奋的念头又在她们心中升起：明天，火车还要经过，

"Up yours! If you say so, you must be the one thinking about him." She pinched Xiangxue's hand, indicating that she wanted her to help out.

Xiangxue said nothing. Flustered, she blushed. She was only seventeen and didn't know what to do in this matter.

"His face is so fair!" the girl continued to tease Fengjiao.

"Fair? That's because he is covered inside that big green room. See what happens if he stays in our Tai'ergou for a few days," said someone in the shadows.

"Of course, city folk are always under a roof. If you want to talk about fair, you should compare him to our Xiangxue. Our Xiangxue was born with a nice complexion. And look at the appearance of those girls—they permed their hair into a tangle of curls, whew! Hopeless! What do you say, sister Fengjiao?"

Fengjiao didn't reply and let go of Xiangxue's hand. The other girls seemed to be belittling the young man as if he were her somebody. She felt a little outraged by the injustice done to him. Not knowing why, she decided that his skin was white not because he was under a roof all day but because he was born that way.

Xiangxue stealthily touched Fengjiao's hand, indicating that Fengjiao should hold her hand, seemingly asking Fengjiao to forgive her, as if she were responsible for her plight.

"Fengjiao, why are you so quiet?" said the same girl.

"Who's quiet? Who's like you checking to see if a person is fair or dark? You can go with him if you like."

"We're not a match."

"You guarantee there isn't someone he fancies?"

Regardless of how terribly they quarreled as they walked, when they parted, they were always on the best of terms, because another exciting thought had entered their minds: The train would pass by

她们还会有一个美妙的一分钟。和它相比，闹点小别扭还算回事吗？

哦，五彩缤纷的一分钟，你饱含着台儿沟的姑娘们多少喜怒哀乐！

日久天长，这五彩缤纷的一分钟，竟变得更加五彩缤纷起来，就在这个一分钟里，她们开始跨上装满核桃、鸡蛋、大枣的长方形柳条篮子，站在车窗下，抓紧时间跟旅客和和气气地做买卖。她们垫着脚尖，双臂伸得直直的，把整筐的鸡蛋、红枣举上窗口，换回台儿沟少见的挂面、火柴，以及属于姑娘们自己的发卡、香皂。有时，有人还会冒着回家挨骂的风险，换回花色繁多的沙巾和能松能紧的尼龙袜。

凤娇好像是大家有意分配给那个"北京话"的，每次都是她提着篮子去找他。她和他做买卖故意磨磨蹭蹭，车快开时才把整蓝地鸡蛋塞给他。又是他先把鸡蛋拿走，下次见面时再付钱，那就更够意思了。如果他给她捎回一捆挂面、两条沙巾，凤娇就一定抽回一斤挂面还给他。她觉得，只有这样才对得起和他的交往，她愿意这种交往和一般的做买卖有区别。有时她也想起姑娘们的话："你担保人家没有相好的？"其实，有没有相好的不关凤娇的事，她又没想过跟他走。可她愿意对他好，难道非得是相好的才能这么做吗？

香雪平时话不多，胆子又小，但做起买卖却是姑娘中最顺利的一个。旅客们爱买她的货，因为她是那么信任地瞧着你，那洁如水晶的眼睛告诉你，站在车窗下的这个女孩子还不知道什么叫

again the following day and they would have a wonderful minute. Being at odds over trifles was, by comparison, nothing.

O, what a colorful minute, you contained so much joy, anger, happiness, and sadness for the girls of Tai'ergou!

In the course of time, that colorful minute became even more colorful. For that one minute, they started a business by standing by the windows with rectangular osier baskets filled with walnuts, eggs, and dates, grasping the moment to sell these items to the passengers in a friendly manner. Standing on tiptoe, arms stretched forward, they lifted the baskets of eggs and dates to the windows in exchange for the fine dried noodles rarely seen in Tai'ergou, matches, and things for the girls themselves, such as hair clips and perfumed soap. Sometimes someone would risk a scolding at home and trade for a great variety of gauze and elastic nylon stockings.

The girls seemed to have the intention of matching Beijing Mandarin to Fengjiao, and every time the train arrived she would take her basket in search of him. In dealing with him, she was intentionally slow-going. Only when the train was on the point of departing would she thrust an entire basket of eggs at him. He would take the eggs first, and the next time they met he'd pay her, in this way making things more interesting. If he gave her a bundle of fine noodles and two strips of gauze, she'd always return a *jin* of noodles to him. She felt only in this way could she feel worthy of dealing with him. She was willing for this kind of exchange to be different from ordinary business. Sometimes she would think of what the girls said: "You're sure he has no one he fancies?" Whether he had someone or not wasn't her business—she had never thought of going with him. But she was willing to treat him nicely. Did a person have to be the one he fancied to do so?

Xiangxue normally didn't talk much. She wasn't very bold, but she was the most successful of the girls in doing business. The passengers liked to buy her things because she looked so reliable. Her crystalline eyes told you that a girl like the one standing below the window didn't know

受骗。她还不知道怎么讲价钱，只说："你看着给吧。"你望着她那洁净得仿佛一分钟前才诞生的面孔，望着她那柔软得宛若红缎子似的嘴唇，心中会升起一种美好的感情。你不忍心跟这样的小姑娘要滑头，在她面前，再爱计较的人也会变得慷慨大度。

有时她也抓空儿向他们打听外面的事，打听北京的大学要不要台儿沟人，打听什么叫"配乐诗朗诵"（那是她偶然在同桌的一本书上看到的）。有一回她向一位戴眼镜的中年妇女打听能自动开关的铅笔盒，还问到它的价钱。谁知没等人家回话，车已经开动了。她追着它跑了好远，当秋风和车轮的呼啸一同在她耳边鸣响时，她才停下脚步意识到，自己地行为是多么可笑啊。

火车眨眼间就无影无踪了。姑娘们围住香雪，当她们知道她追火车的原因后，遍觉得好笑起来。

"傻丫头!"

"值不当的!"

她们像长者那样拍着她的肩膀。

"就怪我磨蹭，问慢了。"香雪可不认为这是一件值不当的事，她只是埋怨自己没抓紧时间。

"咳，你问什么不行呀!"凤娇替香雪跨起篮子说。

"谁叫咱们香雪是学生呢。"也有人替香雪分辨。

也许就因为香雪是学生吧，是台儿沟唯一考上初中的人。

台儿沟没有学校，香雪每天上学要到十五里以外的公社。

what cheating was. She didn't know how to bargain and would say, "Whatever you want to pay." Looking at her clear face, which looked as if it had just been born a minute ago, looking at those red lips soft as red satin, a pleasant sensation would arise. You wouldn't have the heart to trick such a girl; even those who liked to haggle would become openhanded.

Sometimes she'd take a moment to ask them about things outside, such as whether the universities in Beijing wanted people from Tai'ergou, or what were "poems recited accompanied by music." (That was something she saw by chance in a book on her shared desk at school.) Once, she asked a middle-aged woman in glasses if there was such a thing as a pencil box that opened automatically and how much it would cost. But before she received an answer, the train had already started to move. She followed it at a run for quite a distance, until the autumn wind and the squealing wheels sounded in her ears and she stopped, aware of how silly she was.

The train was gone without a trace in the blink of an eye. The girls gathered around Xiangxue. When they understood why she was chasing the train, they all thought it was funny.

"Foolish girl!"

"There's no reason to ask that!"

Clapping her on the shoulders, they all seemed to treat her like a child.

"It's my fault for dawdling and not asking sooner." Xiangxue didn't think it was something she shouldn't ask about. She was just upset with herself for not grabbing the moment.

"Huh. What's wrong with asking about that?!" said Fengjiao, picking up Xiangxue's basket for her.

"Our Xiangxue is a student," said one of the girls, also defending Xiangxue.

Perhaps because Xiangxue was a student she had been the only person in Tai'ergou to pass the junior high school exams.

There was no school in Tai'ergou. Every day, Xiangxue went to the commune school fifteen *li* away.

尽管不爱说话是她的天性，但和台儿沟的姐妹们总是有话可说的。公社中学可就没那么多姐妹了，虽然女同学不少，但她们的言谈举止，一个眼神，一声轻轻的笑，好像都是为了叫香雪意识到，她是小地方来的，穷地方来的。她们故意一遍又一遍地问她："你们那儿一天吃几顿饭？"她不明白她们的用意，每次都认真的回答："两顿。"然后又友好地瞧着她们反问道："你们呢？"

"三顿！"她们每次都理直气壮地回答。之后，又对香雪在这方面的迟钝感到说不出的怜悯和气恼。

"你上学怎么不带铅笔盒呀？"她们又问。

"那不是吗。"相雪指指桌角。

其实，她们早知道桌角那只小木盒就是香雪的铅笔盒，但她们还是做出吃惊的样子。每到这时，香雪的同桌就把自己那只宽大的泡沫塑料铅笔盒摆弄得哒哒乱响。这是一只可以自动合上的铅笔盒，很久以后，香雪才知道它所以能自动合上，是因为铅笔盒里包藏着一块不大不小的吸铁石。香雪的小木盒呢，尽管那是当木匠的父亲为她考上中学特意制作的，它在台儿沟还是独一无二的呢。可在这儿，和同桌的铅笔盒一比，为什么显得那样笨拙、陈旧？它在一阵哒哒声中有几分羞涩地畏缩在桌角上。

香雪的心再也不能平静了，她好像忽然明白了同学对她的再三盘问，明白了台儿沟是多么贫穷。她第一次意识到这是不光彩的，因为贫穷，同学才敢一遍又一遍地盘问她。她盯住同桌那只铅笔盒，猜测它来自遥远的大城市，猜测它的价值肯定非同寻常。

Despite not being talkative by nature, she always had something to say to her sisters in Tai'ergou, but the commune middle school didn't have that many sisters. Although she had quite a few female classmates, their manner of speech, a glance, a quiet laugh, all seemed to be directed at reminding Xiangxue she was from a poor and insignificant place. They intentionally asked her again and again, "How many meals a day do you eat where you're from?" She didn't understand what they were getting at and each time would reply in all sincerity, "Two." Then, in a friendly fashion, she would look at them and ask, "And you?"

"Three!" they would reply with self-assurance. Later, they would feel an inexpressible sorrow or sullenness about her slowness of mind.

"Why don't you bring a pencil box to school?" they asked.

"Isn't that one?" she'd reply, pointing at the corner of her desk.

Actually, they all knew that the little wooden box in the corner of her desk was her pencil box, but they would all act surprised. Always at that point, her desk mate would start noisily opening and closing the lid of her large plastic pencil box. It was the sort of pencil box that snapped closed on its own. Only much later did Xiangxue learn that it shut automatically because enclosed within was a magnet, neither large nor small. What about Xiangxue's little wooden box? Even though it was made by her carpenter father when she tested into middle school, it was unique in Tai'ergou. But in school, compared with the pencil box of her desk mate, why did hers look so clumsy and old? Amid the clicking, it recoiled with shame in the corner of the desk.

Xiangxue never again felt at ease. She seemed suddenly to understand why her classmates kept asking her questions and she understood how poor Tai'ergou was. It was the first time she realized that it wasn't an honor and that her classmates kept asking her questions because she was poor. She stared at her desk mate's pencil box, guessing that it had come from some far-off big city, guessing that it hadn't been cheap.

三十个鸡蛋换得来吗？还是四十个、五十个？这时她的心又忽地一沉：怎么想起这些了？娘攒下鸡蛋，不是为了叫她乱打主意啊！可是，为什么那诱人的哒哒声老是在耳边响个没完？

深秋，山风渐渐凛冽了，天也黑得越来越早。但香雪和她的姐妹们对于七点钟的火车，是照等不误的。她们可以穿起花棉袄了，凤娇头上别起了淡粉色的有机玻璃发卡，有些姑娘的辫梢还缠上了夹丝橡皮筋。那是她们用鸡蛋、核桃从火车上换来的。她们仿照火车上那些城里姑娘的样子把自己武装起来，整齐地排列在铁路旁，像是等待欢迎远方的贵宾，又像是准备着接受检阅。

火车停了，发出一阵沉重的叹息，像是在抱怨着台儿沟的寒冷。今天，它对台儿沟表现了少有的冷漠：车窗全部紧闭着，旅客在黄昏的灯光下喝茶、看报，没有人像窗外瞥一眼。那些眼熟的、长跑这条线的人们，似乎也忘记了台儿沟的姑娘。

凤娇照例跑到第三节车厢去找她的"北京话"，香雪紧紧头上的紫红色线围巾，把臂弯里的篮子换了换手，也顺着车身不停的跑着。她尽量高高地垫起脚尖，希望车厢里的人能看见她的脸。车上一直没有人发现她，她却在一张堆满食品的小桌上，发现了渴望已久的东西。它的出现，使她再也不想往前走了，她放下篮子，心跳着，双手紧紧扒住窗框，认清了那真是一只铅笔盒，一只装有吸铁石的自动铅笔盒。它和她离得那样近，她一伸手就可以摸到。

一位中年女乘务员走过来拉开了香雪。香雪跨起篮子站在远

Could she exchange thirty eggs for one? Or forty? Or fifty? At that moment her heart sank: why was she thinking about all this? Her mother didn't save egg money so that she could devise a plan. But why was that attractive clatter snapping shut in her ears?

In late autumn, the wind gradually grew cold and it got dark earlier. But Xiangxue and her sisters would, as usual, never miss the train. They would wear padded cotton jackets. Fengjiao wore several decorative pink plastic hair clips, and some of the other girls tied their braids with rubber and wire hair ties. These were all obtained by trading eggs and walnuts with the train passengers. They armored themselves by imitating the city girls on the train. They lined up in an orderly fashion alongside the tracks as if they were welcoming a guest from afar, or as if they were lining up for inspection.

As the train stopped it released a great sigh, as if complaining about the cold in Tai'ergou. Today it seemed to treat the village a little distantly: all the windows were tightly closed and the passengers were drinking tea and reading the paper under yellow lights; no one even glanced outside. Those familiar people who always rode this line seemed to have forgotten the girls of Tai'ergou.

As usual, Fengjiao ran to the third car to find her "Beijing Mandarin." Xiangxue wore a purplish-red cotton knit scarf tightly around her head and switched the basket from the crook of one arm to the other while running along the side of the train. She stepped as high as she could on her toes, hoping that the passengers might see her face, but no one on board noticed her. On a small table heaped with food, however, she discovered the thing she had long desired. Its appearance made her stop with no thought of continuing on. She put down her basket and, with her heart pounding, grasped the window frame with both hands, clearly recognizing a pencil box, one with a magnet and that closed on its own. It was close enough to reach out and touch.

A middle-aged female attendant came over and pulled Xiangxue away. Xiangxue picked up her basket and examined the pencil box

处继续观察。当她断定它属于靠窗的那位女学生模样的姑娘时，就果断地跑过去敲起了玻璃。女学生转过脸来，看见香雪臂弯里的篮子，抱歉地冲她摆了摆手，并没有打开车窗的意思，不知怎么的她就朝车门跑去，当她在门口站定时，还一把扒住了扶手。如果说跑的时候她还有点犹豫，那么从车厢里送出来的一阵阵温馨的、火车特有的气息却坚定了她的信心，她学着"北京话"的样子，轻巧地跃上了踏板。她打算以最快的速度跑进车厢，以最快的速度用鸡蛋换回铅笔盒。也许，她所以能够在几秒钟内就决定上车，正是因为她拥有那么多鸡蛋吧，那是四十个。

香雪终于站在火车上了。她挽紧篮子，小心地朝车厢迈出了第一步。这时，车身忽然悸动了一下，接着，车门被人关上了。当她意识到眼前发生了什么事时，列车已经缓缓地向台儿沟告别了。香雪扑在车门上，看见凤娇的脸在车下一晃。看来这不是梦，一切都是真的，她确实离开姐妹们，站在这又熟悉、又陌生的火车上了。她拍打着玻璃，冲凤娇叫喊："凤娇！我怎么办呀，我可怎么办呀！"

列车无情地载着香雪一路飞奔，台儿沟刹那间就被抛在后面了。下一站叫西山口，西山口离台儿沟三十里。

三十里，对于火车，汽车真的不算什么，西山口在旅客们闲聊之中就到了。这里上车的人不少，下车的只有一位旅客，那就是香雪，她胳膊上少了那只篮子，她把它塞到那个女学生座位下面了。

在车上，当她红着脸告诉女学生，想用鸡蛋和她换铅笔盒时，

from a distance. When she determined that it belonged to the girl who looked like a student sitting by the window, she decided to run over and tap on the glass. The girl turned and saw the basket in the crook of Xiangxue's arm and waved her hands apologetically. She didn't seem to have any intention of opening the window, but for some reason Xiangxue ran toward the car door. When she stood in front of the door she grasped the handrail with one hand. If she ran with any hesitation, the warmth and the atmosphere unique to the train only gave her more self-confidence. In the manner of Beijing Mandarin, she leapt nimbly up on the carriage step. She planned to enter the car with all quickness and trade her eggs for the pencil box as quickly as possible. Perhaps she had been able to decide to board the train in a matter of seconds because she had so many eggs: forty.

Xiangxue finally stood on board the train. Clutching her basket, she took the first step in toward the car. At that moment the train moved and the door closed. By the time she figured out what was happening, the train had slowly begun to depart from Tai'ergou. Xiangxue pressed against the door and saw Fengjiao's face go by in a flash. This was no dream; everything was real—she was leaving her sisters, standing in this both familiar and strange train. She pounded against the glass and shouted to Fengjiao: "Fengjiao! What am I going to do? What am I going to do?"

The train mercilessly sped off with Xiangxue; Tai'ergou was left behind in a flash. The next stop was Xishankou, which was thirty *li* from Tai'ergou.

For a train or an automobile, thirty *li* was nothing. Xishankou arrived as the passengers chatted. Quite a few people boarded the train there; only one passenger disembarked: Xiangxue. The basket was missing from her arm; she had placed it under the girl student's seat.

On the train, as she blushed telling the girl student she wanted to exchange the eggs for her pencil box, the girl student also blushed.

女学生不知怎么的也红了脸。她一定要把铅笔盒送给相雪，还说她住在学校吃食堂，鸡蛋带回去也没法吃。她怕香雪不信，又指了指胸前的校徽，上面果真有"矿冶学院"几个字。香雪却觉着她在哄她，难道除了学校她就没家吗？香雪一面摆弄着铅笔盒，一面想着主意。台儿沟再穷，她也从没白拿过别人的东西。就在火车停顿前发出的几秒钟的震颤里，香雪还是猛然把篮子塞到女学生的座位下面，迅速离开了。

车上，旅客们曾劝她在西山口住上一夜再回台儿沟。热情的"北京话"还告诉她，他爱人有个亲戚就住在站上。香雪没有住，更不打算去找"北京话"的什么亲戚，他的话倒更使她感到了委屈，她替凤娇委屈，替台儿沟委屈。她只是一心一意地想：赶快走回去，明天理直气壮地去上学，理直气壮地打开书包，把"它"摆在桌上。车上的人既不了解火车的呼啸曾经怎样叫她像只受惊的小鹿那样不知所措，更不了解山里的女孩子在大山和黑夜面前倒底有多大本事。

列车很快就从西山口车站消失了，留给她的又是一片空旷。一阵寒风扑来，吸吮着她单薄的身体。她把滑到肩上的围巾紧裹在头上，缩起身子在铁轨上坐了下来。香雪感受过各种各样的害怕，小时候她怕头发，身上粘着一根头发择不下来，她会急得哭起来；长大了她怕晚上一个人到院子里去，怕毛毛虫，怕被人胳肢（凤娇最爱和她来这一手）。现在她害怕这陌生的西山口，害怕四周黑幽幽的大山，害怕叫人心惊肉跳的寂静，当风吹响近处的小树林时，她又害怕小树林发出的悉悉萃萃的声音。三十里，

She wanted to give the pencil box to Xiangxue and said that she ate at the school cafeteria and couldn't even take the eggs with her. She feared that Xiangxue might not believe her, so she pointed at the school pin on her chest on which was written, "Mining Management Institute." Xiangxue thought the girl was fooling her. Didn't she have a family? Xiangxue was thinking about what to do as she fiddled with the pencil box. No matter how poor it was in Tai'ergou, she never took anything for free. As the train shuddered in the seconds before it came to a stop, Xiangxue quickly thrust the basket of eggs under the girl's seat and rushed away.

The passengers tried to persuade her to spend the night in Xishankou before returning to Tai'ergou. The enthusiastic Beijing Mandarin told her that his wife had a relative living near the station. Xiangxue had no place to stay? But she certainly wasn't going to go looking for some relative of Beijing Mandarin's. His words made her feel bad. She felt bad for Fengjiao; she felt bad for Tai'ergou. She had only one thought: she had to hurry and walk home because tomorrow she had to go to school with self-assurance, open her book bag with self-assurance, and place "it" on her desk. The people on the train neither understood why the train whistle left her frightened like a deer and at a loss, nor knew about the ability a mountain girl had in the face of the huge mountain and the dark of night.

The train quickly disappeared from Xishankou, leaving Xiangxue with a vast emptiness. A cold wind blew over her thin frame. She pulled the scarf that had fallen over her shoulders and tied it around her head and, shrinking, sat down on the tracks. Xiangxue had suffered from all sorts of fears: she was afraid of hair when she was little, and if one strand stuck to her and she couldn't brush it away, she'd begin crying. When she got older, she was afraid to go out into the courtyard alone at night; she was afraid of caterpillars; she was afraid of being tickled (Fengjiao really liked tickling her). Right now she was afraid of Xishankou, which was unfamiliar, afraid of the mountain in darkness all around her, afraid of the frightening silence, and when the wind blew in the trees nearby, she was afraid of the rustlings of the small wood. Walking back over thirty *li*,

一路走回去，该路过多少大大小小地林子啊！

　　一轮满月升起来了，照亮了寂静的山谷，灰白的小路，照亮了秋日的败草，粗糙的树干，还有一丛丛荆棘、怪石，还有满山遍野那树的队伍，还有香雪手中那只闪闪发光的小盒子。

　　她这才想到把它举起来仔细端详。它想，为什么坐了一路火车，竟没有拿出来好好看看？现在，在皎洁的月光下，它才看清了它是淡绿色的，盒盖上有两朵洁白的马蹄莲。她小心地把它打开，又学着同桌的样子轻轻一拍盒盖，"哒"的一声，它便合得严严实实。她又打开盒盖，觉得应该立刻装点东西进去。她丛兜里摸出一只盛擦脸油的小盒放进去，又合上了盖子。只有这时，她才觉得这铅笔盒真属于她了，真的。它又想到了明天，明天上学时，她多么盼望她们会再三盘问她啊！

　　她站了起来，忽然感到心里很满意，风也柔合了许多。她发现月亮是这样明净。群山被月光笼罩着，像母亲庄严、神圣的胸脯；那秋风吹干的一树树核桃叶，卷起来像一树树金铃铛，她第一次听清它们在夜晚，在风的怂恿下"豁啷啷"地歌唱。她不再害怕了，在枕木上跨着大步，一直朝前走去。大山原来是这样的！月亮原来是这样的！核桃树原来是这样的！香雪走着，就像第一次认出养育她长大成人的山谷。台儿沟呢？不知怎么的，她加快了脚步。她急着见到它，就像从来没有见过它那样觉得新奇。台儿沟一定会是"这样的"：那时台儿沟的姑娘不再央求别人，也用不着回答人家的再三盘问。火车上的漂亮小伙子都会求上门来，火车也会停得久一些，也许三分、四分，也许十分、八分。它会

how many woods, big and small, would she walk through?

A full moon rose, shining over the silent valley and the ash-white path, shining on the withered autumn grass and the coarse tree bark, the brambles and the strange rocks, the massed trees spreading over the mountain, and on the small shining box in Xiangxue's hand.

Only then did she lift it to examine it closely. She wondered why she hadn't taken a good look at it while riding on the train. Right then, under the bright moonlight, she saw that it was light green with two white calla lilies on top. She carefully opened it and, in the manner of her desk mate, carefully closed the lid, tightly, with a *click*. She opened it again, thinking she ought to put something inside. She pulled a small jar of face oil from her pocket and placed it in the box and closed the lid. Only then did she feel that the box really belonged to her. Then she thought about the day to come, how tomorrow at school she hoped they would keep asking her!

She stood up, feeling suddenly very satisfied. The wind had died down considerably. She noticed how bright the moon was. The mountains were enveloped by the moonlight, like her mother's dignified bosom. The autumn wind blew the dry leaves of every walnut tree; they were curled up, resembling small golden bells. It was the first time she had heard them rattling and singing, incited by the night wind. No longer afraid, she strode ahead, stepping on the wooden railroad ties. So this was what the huge mountain was really like! This was what the moon was really like! This was what the walnut trees were really like! Walking, Xiangxue seemed to recognize for the first time the valley that had nurtured her. And Tai'ergou? For some reason she quickened her pace. She was anxious to see it, possessing the novel feeling that she had never seen it before. Tai'ergou must be "this way": at that time, the village girls would no longer have to beg; nor would she have to answer those repeated questions. The handsome young fellows on the train would come to her door begging to visit them, and the train would stay a bit longer, for perhaps three, four, even eight or ten minutes. All its

向台儿沟打开所有的门窗，要是再碰上今晚这种情况，谁都能丛从容容地下车。

今晚台儿沟发生了什么事？对了，火车拉走了香雪，为什么现在她像闹着玩儿似的去回忆呢？四十个鸡蛋没有了，娘会怎么说呢？爹不是盼望每天都有人家娶媳妇、聘闺女吗？那时他才有干不完的活儿，他才能光着红铜似的脊梁，不分昼夜地打出那些躺柜、碗橱、板箱，挣回香雪的学费。想到这儿，香雪站住了，月光好像也黯淡下来，脚下的枕木变成一片模糊。回去怎么说？她环视群山，群山沉默着；她又朝着近处的杨树林张望，杨树林悉悉萃萃地响着，并不真心告诉她应该怎么做。是哪来的流水声？她寻找着，发现离铁轨几米远的地方，有一道浅浅的小溪。她走下铁轨，在小溪旁边坐了下来。她想起小时候有一回和凤娇在河边洗衣裳，碰见一个换芝麻糖的老头。凤娇劝香雪拿一件汗衫换几块糖吃，还教她对娘说，那件衣裳不小心叫河水给冲走了。香雪很想吃芝麻糖，可她到底没换。她还记得，那老头真心实意等了她半天呢？为什么她会想起这件小事？也许现在应该骗娘吧，因为芝麻糖怎么也不能和铅笔盒的重要性相比。她要告诉娘，这是一个宝盒子，谁用上它，就能一切顺心如意，就能上大学、坐上火车到处跑，就能要什么有什么，就再也不会被人盘问她们每天吃几顿饭了。娘会相信的，因为香雪从来不骗人。

doors and windows would be open to Tai'ergou, and if her situation that night ever arose again, the person would be able to leisurely step off the train.

What happened in Tai'ergou that night? The train had carried off Xiangxue. Why was she recalling it now in such a humorous light? She had lost forty eggs. What would her mother say? Didn't her father wish every day that someone would come for a daughter-in-law, for a fiancée? He worked constantly, his copper-colored back bare day and night, making cupboards, beds, and trunks in order to pay Xiangxue's tuition. Thinking of this, Xiangxue paused. The moonlight seemed dimmer and the ties at her feet fuzzy looking. What would she say when she got home? She looked around at the mountains; they were silent. She looked at the poplar grove nearby; the leaves rustled but didn't truly tell her what to do. Where did the sound of flowing water come from? Looking about, she discovered a small stream flowing a few meters from the tracks. She stepped off the tracks and sat down beside the stream. She recalled how once she and Fengjiao had gone to wash clothes in the river and had run into an old man bartering sesame candy. Fengjiao tried to persuade Xiangxue to exchange a sweaty shirt for some candy and to tell her mother that she had not been careful and the river had swept away the shirt. Although she really wanted the candy, she had not exchanged the shirt for it. She recalled how that old man had sincerely waited ages for her to make up her mind. Why had she remembered that insignificant incident? Perhaps this time she should trick her mother; after all, sesame candy couldn't in any way compare with a pencil box. She was going to tell her mother that it was a valuable box and everything would go smoothly for whoever used it. Whoever used it would be able to go to university and ride the train anywhere and would get whatever they desired and never ever be asked again about how many meals she ate each day. Her mother would believe her because she had never lied.

小溪的歌唱高昂起来了，它欢腾着向前奔跑，撞击着水中的石块，不时溅起一朵小小的浪花。香雪也要赶路了，她捧起溪水洗了把脸，又用沾着水的手抿光被风吹乱的头发。水很凉，但她觉得很精神。她告别了小溪，又回到了长长的铁路上。

前边又是什么？是隧道，它愣在那里，就像大山的一只黑眼睛。香雪又站住了，但她没有返回去，她想到怀里的铅笔盒，想到同学门惊羡的目光，那些目光好像就在隧道里闪烁。她弯腰拔下一根枯草，将草茎插在小辫里。娘告诉她，这样可以"避邪"。然后她就朝隧道跑去。确切地说，是冲去。

香雪越走越热了，她解下围巾，把它搭在脖子上。她走出了多少里？不知道。尽管草丛里的"纺织娘""油葫芦"总在鸣叫着提醒她。台儿沟在哪儿？她向前望去，她看见迎面有一颗颗黑点在铁轨上蠕动。再近一些她才看清，那是人，是迎着她走过来的人群。第一个是凤娇，凤娇身后是台儿沟的姐妹门。

香雪想快点跑过去，但腿为什么变得异常沉重？她站在枕木上，回头望着笔直的铁轨，铁轨在月亮的照耀下泛着清淡的光，它冷静地记载着香雪的路程。她忽然觉得心头一紧，不知怎么的就哭了起来，那是欢乐的泪水，满足的泪水。面对严峻而又温厚的大山，她心中升起一种从未有过的骄傲。她用手背抹净眼泪，拿下插在辫子里的那根草棍儿，然后举起铅笔盒，迎着对面的人群跑去。

The stream purled pleasantly as it flowed ahead, striking the stones, constantly creating little waves. Xiangxue had to hurry on her way. Cupping water in her hands, she washed her face and with her wet hands smoothed her hair, which had been mussed by the wind. The water was cold, and she felt invigorated. She said good-bye to the stream and returned to the long, long railroad tracks.

What was that lying ahead? A tunnel stood there distractedly like the dark eye of the mountain. Xiangxue stopped but didn't go back. She thought of the pencil box she clasped to her breast and her classmates' looks of surprise and envy, which seemed to flicker in the tunnel ahead. She bent down and plucked a stalk of dry grass and stuck it in her short braid, telling herself that in this way she could avoid evil. Then she ran toward the tunnel. In fact, she rushed toward it.

Xiangxue got hotter and hotter as she walked. She took off her scarf and hung it around her neck. How many *li* had she walked? She had no idea. The katydids and crickets chirruping in the grass kept her awake. Where was Tai'ergou? She looked ahead and saw black dots moving on the tracks. Only when she was a bit closer did she see that it was a person, a group of people coming toward her. In front was Fengjiao and behind her were her sisters from Tai'ergou.

Xiangxue wanted to run to them, but her legs suddenly felt heavy. She stood on the wooden ties and looked back at the straight rails clearly illuminated by the moonlight, calmly marking the route she had traveled. Suddenly she felt her chest tighten and for some reason she began weeping, weeping tears of joy and satisfaction. Facing the huge mountain, stern yet kind, she felt a pride she had never experienced before. She wiped away her tears with the back of her hand, removed the stalk of grass from her hair, held up her pencil box, and ran toward the group of people.

　　山谷里突然爆发了姑娘们欢乐的呐喊，她们叫着香雪的名字，声音是那样奔放、热烈；她们笑着，笑得是那样不加掩饰，无所顾忌。古老的群山终于被感动得颤栗了，它发出宽亮低沉的回音，和她们共同欢呼着。

　　哦，香雪！香雪！

The valley suddenly exploded with the happy shouting of the girls. They called Xiangxue's name; their voices were ardent and unrestrained. They laughed, simply and freely without dissembling. The ancient mountains were finally moved and emitted a deep resonant echo, shouting with joy along with the girls.

O Xiangxue! Xiangxue!

The Ancestor

祖　宗

Bi Feiyu

太祖母超越了生命意义静立在时间的远方。整整一个世纪的历史落差流荡在她生命的正面和背面。太祖母终年沉默。在太祖母绵软的沉默世纪里，我爷爷这一辈早已湮没，只剩下她老人家站在家族的断层带上遥远地俯视她的孙辈与重孙辈。太祖母的眼中布满白内障，白内障使她的俯视突破了人类的局限，弥散出宇宙的浩淼苍茫，展示了与物质完全等值的亘古与深邃。太祖母至今绵延清朝末年的习惯与心态。太祖母不洗澡。太祖母的身上终年回荡着棺材与铁钉的混杂气味。太祖母不刷牙。太祖母不相信飞机。太祖母不看电视。太祖母听不懂家园方言以外的任何语种，乃至电波传送的普通话。

太祖母的每个清晨都用于梳洗。百年以来一日不变的清代发式是她每天的开始仪式。然后太祖母就端坐在那里，一言不发，持续几个小时打量她第一眼所见的东西。她老人家的打量像哲学研究，却又视而不见、似是而非，历史结论一样有一种含混与空阔的笼罩。每年冬天太祖母总是盘在阳光下面，阳光似乎也弄不透她，就在她身体背后放了一块影子。——这是十多年前太祖母在我心中的木刻式构图。十年前我只身入京求学，离家的那个清晨我回眼看太祖母的小阁楼。太祖母早就起床，皱巴巴地站在小阁楼的窗口，岁月沧桑呈网状折皱盖在她的面颊上面。太祖母的静立姿态如一只古董瓷器，所有裂痕都昭示了考古意义。

Standing quietly at the far end of time, Great-grandmother has transcended the meaning of life. Her life encompasses an entire century of history. She is silent year round. During that weak and quiet century, my grandfather's generation all passed away, leaving only the old lady to look down from across the generation gap at her grandchildren and great-grandchildren. Her eyes are white with cataracts, which allow her to look down, beyond all human limits, shrinking the vastness and boundlessness of the universe while displaying the same immemorial and profound qualities of matter itself. To this day, Great-grandmother has maintained the customs and attitudes of the late-Qing dynasty. Great-grandmother does not bathe. All year round, the smells of a coffin and coffin nails hover over her. Great-grandmother does not brush her teeth. Great-grandmother does not believe in airplanes. Great-grandmother does not watch television. Great-grandmother understands nothing but her hometown dialect, not even the Mandarin radio broadcasts.

Great-grandmother spends every morning at her toilette. She has begun every morning for the last hundred years with the same ritual: fixing her hair in the Qing dynasty style. Afterward, she sits up straight without saying a word, spending hours measuring up whatever she first lays eyes on. The old woman's way of sizing up things is like philosophical speculation: she looks but does not see, what appears true is false, and any historical conclusion is always shrouded in the mists of ambiguity. Each winter, Great-grandmother sits in the sunshine, which seems incapable of penetrating her and instead merely casts a shadow behind her. That is the image, carved in wood, I had of my great-grandmother from ten years ago. Ten years ago, on the morning I left to study in Beijing, I looked back at Great-grandmother's garret. She was already up and standing at her window, time covering her cheeks with a network of wrinkles. She stood as tranquilly as a piece of antique porcelain, all the tiny cracks displaying archaeological significance.

我知道她老人家看不见，却对她招招手。我猜想这一去或许便是永诀，心中便无限酸楚。十年之后太祖母依旧古董瓷器一样安放在窗口，这时候我已是我儿的父亲了，处处可见十年风蚀。太祖母静然不动，十年的意义只是古瓷表层的另一层灰土。

我是收到父亲的加急电报携妻儿返回家园的，我的家园安放在灰褐色小镇的幽长巷底。走进我家要在小巷拐五个弯口同时跨越十一道门槛。这里头包括一个昏暗幽湿的过道，过道的上面便是一间木质阁楼，里头住着我的太祖母。

　　阁楼的空间因太祖母成了另一个宇宙，在家园的一角冥冥迷迷。太祖母不许人进去，很小的时候就听太祖母说："你们别想进去，除非我死了。"父亲这时总要说："好端端的说什么死，我们不进去，谁也别想进。"

　　这一回返回家园我目睹了极大变化，家园的四周因拆迁而衰败杂乱。拐过第三个弯口我就看见和我家共一堵西墙的邻居业已搬迁，只在我家的西墙留下砖头和木条的历史痕迹，那些痕迹过于古老，反而成了现代意味很浓的平面构成。太祖母的阁楼孤立在一方，显得苍凉无助，使人联想起峭壁上的悬葬木棺。

　　晚上太祖母被保姆搀下来吃饭，我走上去喊道，太奶奶。太祖母的眼镜杳远地盯住我，好半天说，下午我听到你的脚步了。我让妻子给太祖母请安，妻抱了儿紧张地甚至说恐怖地站立在太

I knew she couldn't see, but I waved to her anyway. I suspected I would never see her again, and I felt very sad. Ten years later, she was still there, as tranquil as an antique, standing at the window. This time, I was the father of a son, and I could see the ravages wrought by those ten years. Great-grandmother didn't move, as if the only thing that had happened in the last ten years was that the antique porcelain had acquired another layer of dust.

I returned home with my wife and son after receiving Father's urgent telegram. My home is situated at the far end of a long, dark alleyway in a dusty gray town. To get there, you must make five turns and pass by ten doorways. There is a dark, dank passageway, above which sits the wooden garret where my great-grandmother lives.

The space inside Great-grandmother's garret forms a separate universe, a dark, enigmatic corner of my home. No one is permitted to enter. I remember hearing Great-grandmother say when I was small, "Don't even think about coming in, not unless I'm dead." In those days, my father would say, "What's all this talk of death? We won't come in; nobody is thinking of entering."

Returning home this time, I noticed a number of major changes. The place was a mess and in decay; things had been torn down and removed from the house. After making only the third turn, I saw that the neighbor on the other side of our western wall had cleared out; the only remaining traces were some bricks and a few pieces of wood. And those ancient remains formed a very modern, flat composition. To one side, Great-grandmother's garret stood all alone, looking forlorn and helpless, making one think of a wooden coffin hanging on a precipice.

In the evening, when the maid was helping her down the stairs to dinner, I walked up and called loudly to her, "Great-grandmother."

Her eyes fixed on me, and after a long pause she said, "I heard your footsteps this afternoon."

I let my wife greet Great-grandmother. Clutching our son, she stood nervously, if not fearfully, before Great-

祖母面前。我一时想不起我儿子该怎么称我的太祖母，我只好替我不会说话的儿喊一声"老祖宗"。太祖母在我儿的面前站立良久，两只手在我儿的尿布里哆嗦抚摸。后来太祖母笑了，她笑时脸上如旱地开了不规则罅隙，我知道太祖母一定摸到了我儿的小东西。太祖母缩回手，在指头上蘸了些吐沫，摁在了我儿的眉心。我儿惊哭了一声，太祖母对我儿文不对题地喊：老祖宗。我以为这是个错误，但我无法破译这里的宇宙玄机。

太祖母说："他们到底还是走喽。"我知道她是说旧时的隔壁邻居。"祖上爷告诉我，我们做邻居有日子喽，"太祖母说，太祖母说话时一口完整无缺的牙发出古化石一样的光泽。"砌这房子时，崇祯皇帝还没有登基呢。"太祖母说完了就长叹一口气，这个晚上再也没有说一句话。她的长叹在我耳朵里穿越了太祖母的沉默，彗星的灵光一样一直倒曳到远古的明代。

我看见了家园在时间之液中波动，被弧状波浪拍打的岸一直是太祖母的牙。这真是匪夷所思。

父亲送走太祖母对我说："赶了一天的路，早点歇了，有事明天说，——你们就睡我和你妈的床。"父亲说完便打开了东厢房的木榉门，我记得那里头一直放着太祖母的棺材，父亲每年都要上一层漆，黑中透红。棺材几十年来安静地随地球绕太阳公转，与阁楼中的太祖母相互推委、相互盼望，期待赋予对方以意义、以

grandmother. For a moment, I didn't know what my son should call my great-grandmother. Since he could not speak yet, I could address her for him only as Old Ancestor. Great-grandmother stood in front of my son for a long time. She felt around inside his diaper, then smiled. When she smiled, it was like an irregular chink that had opened in parched ground. I knew she must have touched his little penis. She drew back her hands, spit on her fingers, and pressed them between my son's eyebrows. My son cried. Irrelevantly, Great-grandmother shouted, "Old Ancestor!" at him. I thought she had made a mistake, but I was incapable of deciphering the mystery and the profundity of her universe.

Great-grandmother said, "They've all left us." I knew she was referring to our neighbors of old. "Your great-grandfather told me that our days as neighbors were limited," she said. When Great-grandmother spoke, her perfect mouthful of teeth shone like fossils. "When this house was built, the Chong Zhen emperor had not yet ascended the throne." When she finished speaking, she heaved a long sigh and said nothing more for the rest of the night. Piercing my ears and her silence, that long sigh was like the light of a comet falling back across the ages to the Ming dynasty.

I saw our house moving in the fluid of time, and the shore upon which the arcing waves broke was Great-grandmother's teeth. That's really weird.

After seeing Great-grandmother back to her garret, Father said, "You've been on the road all day. Better go to bed early. If there is anything to do, it can wait till tomorrow. You two sleep in your mother's and my bed." When he finished speaking, Father opened the lattice door to the east wing. I remembered that Great-grandmother's coffin had always been stored there and that every year Father applied another coat of black lacquer tinged with red. For decades, the coffin had calmly followed the revolutions of the earth around the sun with Great-grandmother, both exchanging positions of responsibility, looking forward to each other. They had a mutual understanding that they would give each a significance

结局、以永恒的默契。

"你睡哪儿?"我问父亲。

"你太奶奶的棺材。"父亲说。

妻紧张地望我一眼,极不踏实,欲言又止的样。父亲安静地掩上门,随后东厢房就黑得如一只放大的瞳孔。

刚上床妻就说:"怎么睡在棺材里头?"我说:"这有什么,都是一家人,生生死死都在一起的。"妻说:"这有什么,都是一家人,生生死死都在一起的。"妻说:"再怎么活人也不能和私人住一起。"我安慰妻说:"这是我们的家风,睡棺材也是常事,有时还争着睡呢。早年我的一哥一姐夭折了,太祖母不许外葬,不就让爹埋在床下了。"

妻突然坐起来,——哪儿?

就床下,我用脚捣捣床板,发出空洞的回音,就在这块板的下面。

妻眼里渗出了绿光,她抓了我的小臂就说,你们家是怎么弄的?

也不是我们家弄的,我说,家家都一样。

妻抱紧了我的腰,我怕,妻说,我怕极了。

父亲说,叫你回来是为你太奶奶。我说,太奶奶快不行了?父亲很沉痛地摇头,说那样就好了,父亲说,不怕外人笑骂,我现在是巴不得她老人家死掉。我说你怎么这样,怎么说出这样的话来。父亲低了头就不语。父亲沉默的样子像太祖母的另一个

and eternal ending.

"Where are you going to sleep?" I asked Father.

"In your great-grandmother's coffin," he said.

My wife gave me a nervous look. Unsure, she refrained from talking. Father quietly closed the door, and the east wing quickly became as black as the giant pupil of an eye.

Once in bed, my wife said, "Why does he sleep in a coffin?"

"It doesn't matter, we're all one family. Dead or alive, we're all together."

"The living can't live with the dead, no matter what," said my wife.

To comfort her, I said, "That's the way our family does things. There's nothing unusual about sleeping in a coffin; sometimes we even fight over who gets to sleep in it. I had an older brother and an older sister who died young. Great-grandmother wouldn't permit them to be buried outside, so we buried them under the bed."

My wife sat up immediately. "Where?"

"Under the bed." I tapped on the wooden planks of the bed with my foot, making a hollow sound. "Right under this board."

My wife's eyes shone with fear. She clutched my arm and said, "Why did your family do that?"

"It's not just our family," I said. "Every family is the same."

My wife held me tightly by the waist. "I'm scared," she said. "I'm scared to death."

"I called you home for Great-grandmother's sake."

"Is she going to die soon?" I asked.

Silently, Father shook his head. "If only that were the case," he said. "I don't care what anyone says. All I wish is for the old lady to die."

I asked him what the matter was and how he could say such a thing.

Father lowered his head and said nothing. His silence reminded me of Great-grandmother

季节。

　　还有十来天你太奶奶就整一百岁了，父亲说。太奶奶看来已成了父亲沉重的木枷，父亲抬起头望着我。说，你看见她老人家的一口牙了？

　　我听不懂父亲的话。我弄不懂他的话里有什么意思。父亲拉拉我的媳妇袖口，悄声说，人过了一百岁长牙，死了会成精的。

　　怎么会呢？我说。

　　怎么不会呢？父亲说。

　　谁看见成精了？

　　谁看见不成精了？

　　怎么会呢？我这么自语，我的后背禁不住发麻排了凶猛的芒刺。我从父亲的眼里看到了妻子眼里毛茸茸的绿光。妻子怕的是死，父亲惧的却是生。

　　爆破声不停地在我家四周晃动。若干朝代在 TNT 的浓烈香味里化作齑粉与瓦砾。建筑与瓦砾之间的相对静止史书上称之为朝代。每一幢建筑的施工者总是近期可能使它坚固，而后人总是抱怨：你弄那么坚固又有什么意思？朝代就这样，如建筑与牙齿，长了又脱。TNT 的气味如佛国香烟，变更了体态呈现超度者的玄妙。

　　我的儿在天井里蹒跚。他扶着我儿时常扶的红木方机机子独自嬉戏在天井的一隅。他专注地玩一根竹筷子，玩了快两个小时了，流着口水哼着上帝才能听懂的礼乐。太祖母一定是因为我的

at another time.

"In another ten days or so, your great-grandmother will be one hundred years old," he said. It looked as though Great-grandmother had become a wooden cangue on him. Father lifted his head, looked at me, and asked, "Did you see her mouthful of teeth?"

I didn't understand him. I couldn't figure out what he was driving at.

Father tugged at the cuff of my Western-style suit and, lowering his voice, said, "If a person lives to a hundred and still has all her teeth, she'll become a demon after she dies."

"How can that be?" I asked.

"Why shouldn't it?" asked my father.

"Whoever saw anyone become a demon?"

How could that be possible? I asked myself. My back seemed to go numb and felt all prickly. I saw in Father's eyes the same look I had seen in my wife's. She was afraid of death, but my father was afraid of life.

Explosions were heard all around our house. Several dynasties were reduced to rubble and dust in the strong smell of dynamite. The state of relative rest between buildings and debris is what the history books call a dynasty. The workers had done their utmost to ensure that a building would last. Later, people would complain, "What's the point of making it so solid? Dynasties are like buildings and teeth: they grow, and they crumble." The smell of dynamite is like incense in a Buddhist country: it alters the mystery present in the redeemer's posture.

My son walked haltingly around the courtyard. Holding on to the same small redwood stool that I had held on to when I was a child, he played by himself in a corner of the courtyard. He was absorbed in playing with a bamboo chopstick. After two hours, he was drooling and humming a hymn only God could understand. Great-grandmother stood in another corner of the courtyard eyeing my son and listening to him sing. It must have been because of

儿才没有上楼去的，她站在天井的另一角落，打量我的儿，听我
儿的歌唱。太祖母走近了我的儿子，他们用非人类的语言心心相
印的交谈。他们的脸上回荡起大自然赋予人类最本质的契合，日
出日落一样呼应，依靠各自的心率传递春夏秋冬，使人类对应出
宇宙最美妙的精华。他们在谈。没有翻译。如同风听得懂树叶的
声音，水猜得透波浪的走向，光看得见镜子，瞳孔能包蕴瞳孔
一样。妻说，他们玩什么，怎么那么开心？太祖母回过头，对我
说："我死了，你从你儿身上撕块布下来，包上他的头发，缝在我
的袖口上。"我说太奶奶说什么死，您老还小呢。太祖母说："别
忘了。"我便说，好的。太祖母笑眯眯地说："活在世上，不论多
少年，就睁开眼、再闭上眼。要说到千年万年寿，还是在阴间里
头。一块布，你记好了，千万不要忘了。"

太祖母的百岁生日渐渐临近。我的整个家园被一层恐怖笼罩着，
仿佛拆迁的烟尘，无声无息飘落在我家的桌面、瓷器的四周。

　　父亲的十二个堂弟晚上聚集在我家。我坐在一边，太祖母的
牙齿在我的想象中发出冰块的撞击声。他们闷头抽烟。他们的心
不在焉里有一种历史关头的庄重气氛。没有人开口。在历史的沉

him that she hadn't gone upstairs. Great-grandmother approached my son, and they conversed with a natural affinity in a language not understood by other human beings. On their faces played an essential correspondence given to man by Nature, echoing each other like sunrise and sunset, relying on each other's heartbeats to transmit spring, summer, fall, and winter, making of humanity the most wonderful quintessence of the universe. They talked. There was no interpreter. It was the way the wind understood the sound of the leaves, or the way water guessed the direction of the waves, or the way light saw the mirror, or the way one pupil could contain another.

"They seem to be having fun. What are they playing?" my wife asked.

Great-grandmother turned and said to me, "When I die, take a piece of cloth from your son, wrap some of his hair in it, and sew it into the cuff of my sleeve."

"What is all this talk about death? You're still young."

"Don't forget," said Great-grandmother.

"All right," I replied.

"It doesn't matter how long you live; as soon as you open your eyes, it's time to close them," Great-grandmother said, smiling. "If you talk about long life, then it will be among the shadows. Remember: a piece of cloth. Don't forget."

Great-grandmother's hundredth birthday was slowly drawing nearer. My house was shrouded in fear like the dust that silently covered the table and porcelain.

That night, Father's twelve brothers gathered at our house. I sat to one side. In my imagination, Great-grandmother's teeth emitted a sound like breaking ice. The men smoked quietly. In their preoccupation was the solemn atmosphere of having arrived at a juncture in history. No one spoke. At a silent juncture in history,

默关头最初的结论往往直接等于历史的结果。这是我们的习惯性
做法。这时候门外轰隆又响了一声，这医生提醒我返家的道路已
把我送回了明代，这个想法增加了我内中的颤栗。

最终父亲从烟雾里抬起头，父亲坚定地说，拔。父亲说完拔
调头望了我一眼。这一眼使我感到我对历史不堪负重。我对他笑
了笑。我自己也弄不懂我笑什么。许多重要的场合我总挂这一脸
的蠢笑，内心空洞如风。我相信许多人都看到了我愚蠢的笑相。

一切全安稳下来妻抱怨说，怎么这么乱？你们家怎么这么
乱？孩子的手老师一惊一惊的，我说快好了，过两天就好了，马
上就会稳定下来。妻又说，孩儿的鞋怎么又不见了？我说怎么会
呢？谁要那么小的鞋。妻说是不见了，那双红色的，我找了很久
了。我有些不耐烦，说，丢了就丢了，明天再买不就得了。妻说
真见鬼了，昨天丢了你的耐克，今天又丢了孩子的，真是见鬼了。
我说你啰嗦什么？省两句，让母亲听到了又要生事。

给太祖母拔牙是我生命史上年最独特的一页。一大早飘起小雨，
那东西不完全是雨，只能说是像雾又像风。天空中分泌出很浓的
历史氛围。阴谋在我的家园猝然即发。只有被盘算的太祖母在
阴谋之外。我们全做好了准备，所有的人都默不作声，有一种

the first conclusion is the direct equivalent to the outcome of history. This is our accustomed way of doing things. At that moment, a rumble was heard outside. The sound reminded me that the road home had sent me back to the Ming dynasty, which caused me to tremble even more.

Finally, Father lifted his head in the smoke and said firmly, "Pull them." He turned to look at me. His look made me feel that I couldn't bear the weight of history. I smiled. But even I didn't know what I was smiling about. On many important occasions, I wore a foolish smile, my heart empty as the wind. I suspect that many of those present saw my foolish smile.

After things had quieted down, my wife complained, "Why are things such a mess? Why is your family such a mess? The boy's hands are always twitching."

"He'll be fine soon," I said. "He'll be fine in a couple of days. He'll calm down soon."

"I can't find the boy's shoes," my wife said.

"How could they disappear? Who'd want such little shoes?" I asked.

My wife said she couldn't find his red shoes. I looked everywhere. A little impatiently, I said, "If they're gone, they're gone. Just buy another pair tomorrow."

"That's ridiculous," said my wife. "Yesterday you lost a pair of Nikes, and today the boy's are gone. Ridiculous."

"Why make such a fuss over it?" I asked. "If Mother heard you, there'd really be trouble."

Pulling Great-grandmother's teeth constituted a unique page in the history of my life. A drizzle was blowing that morning. You really couldn't call it rain: it was like rain and like mist but also like wind. The sky secreted a viscous historical atmosphere. The plot in our house got quickly under way. Only Great-grandmother, who was the object of the plot, was left in the dark. We were prepared; nobody said a word. There was a sense

把握命运、参与历史的使命冲动与犯罪快感。这是人类对待历史
的常识性态度。太祖母坐在窗前，安闲如梦，像史书上的无事季
节。我们全埋伏在太祖母的四周，不动声色，在地上投下我们的
巨大阴影。

　　中午时分五叔来到我家。面色紧张，忧心忡忡。五叔喊出
父亲，站在屋檐下面对父亲说，麻药弄不到，医院控制很严。父
亲的脸色难看极了，像千年古砖长了青苔。拔不拔？五叔说。父
亲没开口，对太祖母的小阁楼低下头，父亲说，奶奶，让您老遭
罪了。

　　到处都潮湿湿的。久积的灰尘全膨胀了开来。很产风格时间
之后我都擦不干这段记忆中浅黑色的水迹。叔父们整个下午都在
我家堂屋里喝酒。这桌酒是为太祖母办的，她老人家爱下楼也就
格外地早。太祖母脸上是笑，能见度很低，隔了一层不详笼罩。
她的表情时常夹着相当弄不清的成份。太祖母一入座叔父们就忙
着敬酒。父亲说："奶奶，老寿星您就快一百岁了，奶奶您寿比南
山福如东海。"[1]太祖母笑笑："不能再活了，"太祖母端了酒杯很开
心地说，"再活不就成精了？"太祖母这么说着自个干了酒，叔父
们脸色就阴暗了下来，出现了惶恐神色，他们的酒杯在手里显

of taking fate in our hands and of participating in the excitement of a historical mission, and there was the exhilaration of committing a crime. This is the way humanity commonly approaches history. Great-grandmother was sitting at her window, easy as a dream, like an uneventful period in the written record. All around her, we were motionless and silent, waiting for the signal to stand up and cast the shadow of ambush onto the ground.

Around noon, Fifth Uncle came to the house. He looked nervous and worried. Fifth Uncle called for Father. Standing under the eaves and facing Father, he said, "We can't get any anesthetic; it's too tightly controlled by the hospital."

Father's face darkened, looking like the moss on an ancient brick.

"Are we going to pull them or not?" asked Fifth Uncle.

Father said nothing. Facing Great-grandmother's little garret, Father lowered his head and said, "Grandmother, you will just have to suffer."

It was damp everywhere. The accumulated dust swelled. For a long time I was unable to wipe away the gray streaks from this part of my memory. All afternoon, my uncles sat in the central room drinking. The table full of wine had been prepared for Great-grandmother, so the old lady came downstairs especially early. She was all smiles. She couldn't see well, her eyes hidden behind an inauspicious shroud. Normally her face wore a somewhat confused expression. As soon as Great-grandmother sat down, my uncles toasted her. My father said, "Grandmother, you will be one hundred soon. May you outlast South Mountain and be more prosperous than the Eastern Sea."

Great-grandmother laughed. "I can't live much longer," she said happily, holding her glass. "If I live much longer, I'll become a demon." Then she drank down the wine.

The faces of my uncles darkened, looking perplexed and alarmed. The wineglasses in their hands

得沉重而迟疑，幸好祖母看不见。

我对一下的沉默时间失去了概念。可能是几分钟，也可能是太祖母的肩头上了一层尘埃，我一直弄不清楚。在这个沉默的尽头父亲和他的十二个兄弟离开了坐席，齐刷刷地跪在了太祖母的面前。太祖母有些合不拢嘴，每一颗牙都在笑。太祖母母说，起来，小乖乖，都起来，早就不兴这个啦！小乖们在地上黑乎乎地站了起来，三叔拿了绳子，七叔手执老虎钳，九叔的手里托了一只红木托盘。过了一刻太祖母的牙齿全排在木盘里了，牙根布满血丝，我觉得这些带血的牙齿就是我的家族，歪歪斜斜排在红木托盘里头，后来我儿一声啼哭，那个念头便随风而去，不可追忆。我后来再也没能想起我当时的念头，只记得那种迅猛和生硬痛楚的心理感受，再后来我闻到了 TNT 的气味，我就像被冰块烫着了那样被 TNT 的气味狠咬了一口。

十叔说，大哥，这血是止不住了，要不要送医院。父亲说，不能去，医生一看会全明白的。太祖母倒在地砖上，两片嘴唇深深地凹陷下去，人的牙很怪，平时看不见，少了它人就面目全非。太祖母一百岁的血液在她的唇边蜿蜒，比时间流逝得更加无序。太祖母卧在地上气息喘喘，喉管里发出的吱吱声浆橹一样欸乃，她老人家的皮肤在慢慢褪色，与旧宣纸仿佛。九叔说，奶奶快不

appeared heavy; they hesitated. Fortunately, Great-grandmother couldn't see.

I have no recollection about the moment of silence that followed. Perhaps it was just a few minutes, or perhaps another layer of dust had settled on Great-grandmother's shoulders; it has never been clear to me. At the end of that moment of silence, Father and his twelve brothers got up from their seats and knelt before Great-grandmother. Her lips were slightly parted, and every tooth seemed to smile. Great-grandmother said, "Get up, get up, my darlings. We haven't observed that custom in ages." The dark shapes of her darlings stood up. Fifth Uncle held a rope, Ninth Uncle gripped a pair of pliers, and Seventh Uncle held a redwood tray. They pounced on her and held her fast. In a few minutes, Great-grandmother's teeth were all lying on the tray; the roots of her teeth were covered with bloody shreds of flesh. I stared at Great-grandmother's teeth; in them, I saw humanity's direct intuition of time. It is our fear of time that makes us draw a link between teeth and their loss. Seventh Uncle handed the redwood tray to me. The thought vanished, and I can't remember much. Later I was unable to recall what I was thinking at that time. All I remember is the swift, violent, harsh, and painful psychological experience. Later I smelled the dynamite; the odor of the dynamite burned like ice. I was bitten by the odor.

Tenth Uncle said, "Elder Brother, I can't stop the bleeding. Should we take her to the hospital?"

Father said, "We can't. The doctor will know what happened as soon as he sees her."

Great-grandmother had collapsed on the brick floor, her lips deeply sunken. Teeth are funny things. When they are there, they can't be seen, but as soon as they are gone, the face changes beyond recognition. Great-grandmother's hundred-year-old blood spread around her lips and flowed more disorderedly than time. Great-grandmother lay on the floor, breathing heavily. Her throat gurgled and creaked like oars. Her skin was slowly losing color and resembled traditional rice paper.

Ninth Uncle said, "She is fading

行了。五叔说，快灌水，你们都僵在这里做什么？七叔试了几回，抬了头只是晃，不行，灌不进。

这时候西厢房响起了我儿的啼哭，我冲进去对妻说，怎么弄的？你怎么孩子都带不好？妻说孩子要哭我有什么办法？你们吵吵闹闹都在干些什么？我说没你的事，你不要多嘴，我不叫你不要出来。妻一边哄着儿子一边说，走近你们家像进了十八层地狱，吸口气都不顺。我唬喜爱脸来，说，你说完了没有？

父亲说，卸块门板，地上太凉。几个老头七手八脚把太祖母抬上了门板。我走过去拨开太祖母的上眼睑，白内障的背后瞳孔如同夜色一样笼罩了太祖母生命的大地。我轻声呼唤：老祖宗，老祖宗！太祖母的脑袋就从我的肘弯滑向了手口。

十三个孙子们一同跪下去。他们的驼背使他们的跪显得虔诚。

太祖母的尸体平放在棺材盖上，这个棺材盖至少有三十岁年纪。许多相识和不相识的人一同前来吊唁，他们穿过那个湿暗的通道，提了纸钱来吃一口很长的寿面。我的十二个叔父连同我这辈的三十七个兄弟轮流为太祖母化钱，纸灰在我的家园四处飘拂，

fast."

Fifth Uncle said, "Get her some water. What are you doing standing around?"

Seventh Uncle tried several times; he lifted her head and shook it. It was no good, the water wouldn't go down.

At that moment, my son started crying in the west wing. I ran over and asked my wife, "What's going on? Can't you even take care of the child?"

My wife said, "If he wants to cry, what can I do? What's all that racket in there?"

I said, "It's none of your business. You are not to come out unless I call you."

While coaxing our son, my wife said, "Being in your house is like being in the eighteenth level of hell. One can barely breathe here."

I frowned and asked, "Are you finished?"

Father said, "Take down a door; the floor is too cold."

A bunch of old men scrambled to lay the very old lady on the door. I walked over and lifted her eyelids. The world of Great-grandmother's life lay shrouded in darkness behind her cataracts. Softly, I called, "Old Ancestor, Old Ancestor." Her head slid from my elbows to my hands.

Her thirteen grandchildren all knelt at the same time. Their bowed backs made their kneeling look pious.

Great-grandmother was laid out on the lid of her coffin. The coffin was at least thirty years old. Many familiar and unfamiliar people came to offer their condolences. They walked down the dark, dank passageway to bring funeral money and to eat a mouthful of the noodles prepared to celebrate Great-grandmother's birthday. My father and his twelve brothers as well as the thirty-seven male members of my generation took turns burning funeral money. The ashes floated all around the family house,

从我家经过的人身一律飘动起纸钱里栩栩如生的死亡气息。甚至连老鼠都出洞了，趁人不备时紧张地逃窜。

我跪在太祖母的面前心里积满麻木。作为太祖母的长房长孙长子，我捕捉到父辈们眼里宽松愉悦的神色。太祖母的牙被他们单独埋在了不同的地方，这使她死后成精的可能不复存在。我不停地设想太祖母成精时的样子，但我的想象力始终没有突破"人"的常规款式，这让我失望。好几次纸钱的火舌舔痛了我的指尖。我知道阴间的钱是烫手的，正如阳间的钱是冰冷的，总不易于让手接近。父亲在煮面条，他煮了一锅又一锅。全镇的人都来了，他们究竟要看什么谁也没有把握。不少人把太祖母脸上的纸掀开，太祖母的嘴巴很可怕。死亡总是把死者嘴部最难看的瞬间固定下来，使死亡变得狰狞可感。人们就 这样来了又出去，每个人都差不多。他们跨过我家明代就横卧在那里的门槛，临走时人们从明代跨出去，跨出的石巷又一直延续到明代。这个幻觉每个人从道义上说都应该有，TNT 的剧烈爆炸也无能为力。

叔父们提前给太祖母收殓说明了他们心中的慌乱。棺材收容了我的太祖母。棺材如一步经典著作记录了生死奥秘。父亲对我们说，你们给太奶奶守三天的灵。父亲说守灵时两手抚着棺材，我一听"守灵"心里就咯噔一下，"灵"是什么？在我的想象中"灵"比生命本身更加活蹦乱跳，这个想法叫我不踏实，但我不能说出来，说出来便是灭顶之灾。我儿子上衣上的那块黄布早已成了一面旗帜，飘扬在我太祖母的灵光之前，太祖母依靠这面生龙活虎的旗帜在阴间霸道纵横，大鬼小鬼于她奈何不得。父亲说，

and the smell of death from the money swirled around the people who walked through the house. The smell of death was so alive. Even the rats came out of their holes and skittered away, seeing that no one was paying attention.

Kneeling before Great-grandmother, I felt my heart go numb. Being the son of her eldest grandson, I caught a relieved look in the eyes of my father's generation. They buried Great-grandmother's teeth separately, eliminating the chances of her becoming a demon after death. I tried to imagine what Great-grandmother would look like as a demon, but my imagination could not break through conventional human patterns and styles, and that left me disappointed. Several times, the flames from the burning funeral money painfully licked my fingertips. I knew that money from the underworld could burn the fingers just as the money from this world was ice cold and thus not easily touched. Father cooked the noodles, one pot after another. Everyone from the village was there, not sure of what he or she wanted to see. Many of the people removed the paper from Great-grandmother's face. Her mouth was ghastly looking. Death always fixes the mouth of the dead at the worst moment, making death seem hideous. People came and went, each one about the same. They came, striding over the threshold into our Ming dynasty house; leaving, they strode over the threshold and down the ancient alleyway to leave the Ming dynasty. There was a moral imperative for everyone to participate in the hallucination against which the powerful explosions were powerless.

Putting Great-grandmother into the coffin a little early was a clear expression of how flustered my father and uncles were. The coffin housed my great-grandmother. A coffin is like a classic text that records the mysteries of life and death. My father said to us, "Hold a three-day wake for Grandmother's soul." When Father pronounced the word *wake* he touched the coffin. My heart jumped when I heard the word. What is a wake? In my imagination, a soul is more alive than life itself. This way of thinking left me worried, but I couldn't say it out loud, for that would spell disaster. The strip of yellow cloth from my son's clothes became a banner fluttering before my great-grandmother's soul. She relied on that vigorously waving banner to make her way with ease through the underworld, where ghosts, big and small, could do nothing.

Father said, "Great-grandmother's

太祖母可以逢凶化吉了。父亲对阴间的事比对阳世更具城府，我们的先辈大多如斯。

惊人的事发生在午夜。在这个飘满 TNT 气味的蓝色夜间，我的家园彻底陷入了生死困惑。遵照父亲的旨意我们在守灵。太祖母的棺材停在堂屋，被两只支架撑在半空。我睡在棺材的下面，豆油灯在棺材的前侧疲惫地摇晃。许多白蜡烛在畅想的缭绕中打着瞌睡。生面条、馒头以及正方体的豆腐、凉粉上布满铅色纸灰。外面有打桩机的声音，气壮如牛又粗喘吁吁，我的古老家园显得衰败、充满死气。零点过后守灵的人差不多全困了，几个叔还在四仙桌旁支撑，眼堂里闪着青色的光。他们在打麻将，每一张牌被他们放到桌面都棺材一样沉重。

二条.

八万。

跟。

我的耳朵里响着他们的叫牌声，梦如同傍晚的蝙蝠斜了身子神经质地飞窜。我不知道我睡着了没有。我没有把握。这些日子我睡下像醒着，醒时又像入眠，做的梦也大半真假参半难以界定。我听见七叔这么说，随后是洗牌的声音，像夏雨落在太湖石[2]的

bad luck can be turned to good." Father was better at dealing with the affairs of the underworld than with those of this one. All members of the older generation are like that.

The most shocking event occurred at midnight. On that blue night filled with the odor of dynamite, my house fell into an utter life-and-death confusion. We held a wake according to Father's orders. Great-grandmother's coffin was placed in the central hall on two supports. I slept under the coffin; a soy oil lamp flickered weakly in front of the coffin all night. A number of white candles dozed amid long coils of incense. Uncooked noodles, steamed bread, and cubes of tofu and bean jelly were covered with lead-colored ash. The sound of a pile driver could be heard outside, vigorous as a cow but a little breathless. My ancient home seemed in decline, filled with an atmosphere of death. Just after midnight, nearly everyone holding the wake fell asleep. A few of my uncles were sitting around a small square table, their eyes shining with a green light. They were playing mah-jongg. Each piece they placed on the table sounded as heavy as a coffin.

"Two."

"Eight ten thousands."

"Match."

My ears were filled with the shouting that followed as they played. Dreams like bats fluttered at dusk, their bodies flitting nervously. I don't know if I slept or not. I'm not sure. Those days when I slept, I seemed to be awake, and when I was awake, I seemed to be asleep. And the dreams I dreamed—half the time I couldn't tell what was real and what wasn't. I heard Seventh Uncle say, "Last game. After we finish this hand, let them take over." Then came the sound of shuffling mah-jongg tiles like a summer rain falling on Lake Taihu

背脊上。听这些声音我相当恍惚，但接下来的声音我听得真切。在神的预示下我听到了那种尖锐的声响，无限古怪从天的边缘而来。我撑起上身，我的头顶差点撞到棺材的底部。我闻着棺材板的古怪气味听到了指甲在木板上爬动的声音。我甩一甩脑袋，这时候屋里全静下来，他们显然也听到了什么。我们相互当量的眼神里有一种绿幽幽的惊恐。我们终于听清声音是棺材里发出来的，棺材如一只低音音响渲染了太祖母的指甲对棺材的批判与不适。我的两只手就松下去了。几个叔父一齐盯着我，他们的眼光过于炯炯接近了生物极限。棺材里指甲的抠动无力却又丧心病狂，如衔在猫嘴里的鼠，无望热烈的尖叫，充满死亡激情。太祖母在一片黑暗中一定睁开了她长满白内障的眼镜，同时长大了无牙的嘴巴。太祖母渴望光与空间。太祖母的三寸金莲憋足了力气，咚咚就是两下。这两句总结性的批判在我们的后背扯开了一道缝隙，八百里冷风直往里头飕。

五叔说，打开，快打开。其实五叔的表达没有这么完整，他的舌头咸肉一样硬。

三叔最初没有开口。三叔后来说，怎么指甲没有绞掉？我们就一同记起了太祖母的灰色剪指甲。这个危险的物质成了未来乡间传说中最惊心动魄的部分。

然后我们屏紧了呼吸，整个生命投入了谛听。声音越来越弱，间歇也越来越长。最后一切和棺材一样平静了。直到今天我仍然认为太祖母左手的食指一定翘着，她老人家当初不肯抠下来有她

stones. Hearing these sounds, I was as if in a trance, but I clearly heard the sounds that followed. Betokened by the gods, I heard a sharp sound coming strangely from the edge of heaven. I propped myself up and barely missed hitting my head on the bottom of the coffin. I smelled the strange odor of the coffin and heard the sound of fingernails on the wood. I shook my head. It was completely quiet. Apparently, they heard something. We exchanged a look of terror. We clearly heard the sounds coming from the coffin, which functioned like a bass drum, amplifying the criticism and dissatisfaction of Great-grandmother's fingernails against the coffin. My hands went slack, a number of my uncles looked at me, and their eyes shone to their biological limits. The scratching of her fingernails on the coffin was weak but frenzied, like the sharp, doomed cries of a rat in the mouth of a cat. Full of death's fervor, Great-grandmother must have opened her cataract-covered eyes in the darkness and, at the same time, opened her toothless mouth. Great-grandmother longed for light and space. Great-grandmother's tiny three-inch bound feet— her golden lotuses—must have burst with energy as they kicked out twice, decisively opening a crack behind us as a cold wind blew in from eight hundred miles around.

Fifth Uncle said, "Open it up. Hurry! Open it up." Actually, Fifth Uncle didn't express himself in such a clear manner; his tongue was as stiff as salted meat.

At first, Third Uncle didn't utter a word. Then he said, "Why weren't her fingernails clipped?"

We suddenly remembered Great-grandmother's pointed gray nails. This threatening material became the most frightening part of a future countryside legend. We all held our breath, all our energy focused on listening. The sounds grew weaker and weaker, the pauses longer and longer. Finally, dead silence. To this day, I still believe that Great-grandmother's left index finger was sticking up. We all knew

的道理。这实际上是常识，但我们一家等待了很久。

出殡后太祖母的后裔们跨完了火把。火把在旷野里筑成生死之间一道墙。不确切。跨过火把你就又一次逾越了生死屏障。火苗在每个人的胯下卖力工作，青紫色的烟飞上天去，变得多种图形，仿佛古人留给我们的谶语，难以辨别。我只知道那些话一半写在羊皮上，一半写在半空。

到家时走进过道我们情不自禁止步。我说，到小阁楼上看看去。父亲说，其他人站着，就我们俩上去。挪开门，上个世界的冷风披了长发长了长长的指甲就抓了过来。小楼圣桑空空荡荡。一张床一张梳妆台而已。父亲和我无限茫然，好奇心就向着现实做自由落体。

父亲说，鞋，你儿的小红鞋。我走上前，我儿的红色鞋口在床下正对了床板。我又看见了我的破"耐克"。在我的耐克后面，按时间顺序排列的是一双草绿色的解放鞋、松紧口单布鞋、两片瓦、面面相觑。自信而又揶揄。我的错觉就在这个时候产生的，我看见我的家族遗传神态向我招呼。像时间一样没有牙齿，长了厚厚的白内障。

父亲说，怎么回事，这是怎么回事？

我刚想向父亲问这样的话。听见父亲的声音我接下来又沉默了。

she had her reasons for not prying with her nails, but we still waited a long time.

After the funeral procession, Great-grandmother's descendants strode over the torches. In the field, the torches formed a wall between life and death. No, that's not accurate. After you've stepped past the torches, you've crossed over the screen between life and death. Flames blazed between each person's legs, and purplish smoke fled into the sky, where it formed a variety of hieroglyphs, like difficult-to-decipher prophecies left by the ancients. All I know is that half were written on sheepskin, the other half in the sky.

Entering the passageway at home, we just had to pause. I said, "Let's take a look at Great-grandmother's garret."

Father said, "Everyone else stay put. He and I will go up alone."

We opened the door, and a cold wind from the last century spread its long hair and long nails toward us. Her garret was devoid of furniture, save for a bed and a dressing table. Father and I were at a loss. Our curiosity was like a free-falling body in reality.

Father said, "Shoes. Your son's little red shoes." I stepped forward. My son's red shoes were under her bed, toes pointing toward the bed plank. I also saw my old, beat-up Nikes. Behind my Nikes, arranged in order of age, were a pair of green army shoes, a pair of cotton shoes, a pair of cotton slippers, and a pair of wooden clogs. I noticed that the shoes, which were laid out in a spiral, seemed to gaze at one another with a light-footed expression. Confident yet ridiculous. It was at that moment that the illusion occurred. I saw the arrival of the ranks of my clan in a long spiral procession. They greeted me in our local dialect and the inherited manner of our clan. Like time, they were toothless, their eyes clouded with cataracts.

Father said, "What's this? What's going on here?"

I was at the point of asking my father the same question. But hearing his voice, I held my tongue.

Dog

狗 子

Cao Naiqian

撞鬼呀，你。"

"爷咋了？"

"发灰呀，你。"

"爷咋了。"

人们尽都说狗子，可狗子就是闹不机明 [1] 撞上啥鬼和发上啥

灰了。

狗子虽说是老了，可狗子还受得动。谁叫他受他就给谁受。受得

实实在在不要奸。人们都说他担大粪不偷着吃，是个好牲口。

"狗子，下公社给买上五个铧。供销社的铧耐使。"队长说。

"行。"狗子说。

"狗子，给我捎上匹麻。纳大底没麻了。" [2]

"狗子，给我捎上包洋火。要白头的。" [3]

"狗子，给我捎上把夜壶。壶嘴碰跌了，尽割我。"

"狗子，给我捎上个顶针。顶针让猫娃要丢了。"

行行行。狗子都说行。就动身出了村，迎南朝公社走。

他妈的阳婆儿真毒，晒得爷一头一头出脚汗。狗子就走就骂

阳婆儿。

他妈的路真烫，想往熟烤爷脚板呀？狗子就走就骂路。

狗子冲两旁瞭望，想找草地走，草地不烫脚。可两旁没草地，

不是石头就是石头，不是沙子就是沙子。狗子只好还是走在土路

上。路上的干土面面就像是罗子罗过的山药粉面那么干那么细，

赤脚板踏踩上去噗噗地四下里喷溅。

Y ou've really gone and done it now."

"What did I do?"

"Are you nuts?"

"What did I do?"

Everyone was scolding Dog, but he couldn't figure out what was wrong or why they thought he was nuts.

Although he was old, he could still work. He worked for anybody who wanted him. He worked hard and was honest. Everyone said he was like a good beast of burden: he'd do the dirty jobs and never eat.

"Dog, go down to the commune and buy us five plowshares. The plowshares at the supply and marketing cooperative last," said the Brigade Leader.

"Okay," said Dog.

"Dog, get me a bolt of hemp. There isn't any hemp for shoe soles."

"Dog, get me a box of matches, the ones with white tips."

"Dog, get me a chamber pot. The mouth of this one is broken and I nearly cut myself on it."

"Dog, get me a thimble. The cat was playing with it, and now I can't find it."

Okay, okay, okay. Dog always said okay. He would set off from the village and head for Nanchao Commune.

The damn sun is scorching hot. I'm covered with sweat from head to toe. Dog cursed the sun as he walked.

The damn road is hot. Are you trying to roast my feet? Dog cursed the road as he walked.

Dog checked both sides of the road, looking for some grass to walk on because grass wouldn't be hot on his feet. But there was no grass on either side; there was nothing but rock or sand. Dog had no choice but to keep to the dirt road. The dirt of the road was so fine and dry that it resembled sifted potato flour. His bare feet threw up puffs of dust.

真要是山药粉面就好了。狗子想。

要真的是山药粉面能有这么多，就不往死饿人了。我的干妹妹也就不往内蒙嫁了。

> 对坝坝圪梁上那是谁
> 那就是要命鬼干妹妹
>
> 崖头上杨树不一般高
> 天底下就数干妹妹好
>
> 你在那圪梁上我在沟
> 亲不上嘴嘴就招招手

狗子一想起干妹妹就想唱这调子，多会儿想起多会儿唱。那次半夜他给想起干妹妹了，他就放开嗓子唱起来。也不怕聒吵了人们睡觉。唱呀唱，唱了一段又一段，唱得泪蛋蛋直往下流，可这次狗子唱了三段不往下唱了。倒不是嘴干得过，也不是舌燥得过。是他又给想起了他的狗女妹妹 [4] 了。老也不想狗女了，可这次不知咋的就给想起了狗女。一想起狗女，他就没气了。狗子赶快去想别的，好把狗女妹妹忘了。

该做点啥呢？总不能闲着。闲人出事故。人总得有点做的才对，狗子一下子给想起点做的，那就是想想三寡妇。一想起三寡妇狗子就高兴。不论是啥时候，狗子只要想起三寡妇，他就高兴了。

"叭!"

If only it were potato flour, thought Dog. *If it really were potato flour, no one would die from hunger and my adopted sister wouldn't have had to go away and marry in Inner Mongolia.*

Who is that on the ridge of the embankment?
It is my adopted sister whom I love to death

All the poplars on the cliff are of differing heights
My adopted sister is the best in all the world

You're on the embankment ridge, I'm in the ditch
Unable to exchange a kiss, we can only wave

Every time Dog thought of his adopted sister, he would sing this song. He would sing whenever he thought of her, regardless of the hour. Once, around midnight, she came to mind, and he began singing at the top of his lungs. He never worried about waking anyone. He'd sing and sing, verse after verse, until his tears fell. But this time Dog sang three verses and stopped. It wasn't because his mouth was parched or his tongue dry. It was because his sister, Dog Girl, came to mind. He hadn't thought about her in ages, but for some reason he did this time. Whenever he thought of Dog Girl, he was in no mood to sing. He would quickly try to think of something else in order to forget his sister.

What should I do? A man must always have something to do. Idlers get into trouble. Everyone must have something to do. Dog suddenly thought of something. He thought of Widow San. Thinking of Widow San made Dog happy. Dog was always happy whenever he thought of Widow San.

Plop!

狗子正要想三寡妇，天上给"叭"地跌下个大雨点。把路上的干粉面面给打了个坑儿。像是从天上给扔下个铜制钱。

"叭!"又扔下一个。

"叭!"又扔下一个。

"叭叭叭叭"，大雨点立马把土路给打成个麻麻脸。那闻了一辈子的泥土气的香味道，也就立马给扑上来。狗子狠狠地抽吸了几下鼻子。

真好闻。这味道为啥恁好闻。狗子就抽吸鼻子就想。

他妈的老天爷说变就变。这也倒好，凉荫荫的，头上也用不着出脚汗了。

狗子抬头瞭瞭飞来的一块镶着亮边儿的黑云。那云的屁股后头还紧迫着好大好大的一片灰云。

不好! 人灰撞乱子，天灰下蛋子。狗子的脚急急地加了劲儿。

狗子远远的瞭见前头有个场面，场面里有个窝头似的莜麦秸垛。狗子又在脚上加了些劲。

当狗子跑到了场面的时候，那冷蛋子也就"崩崩崩"地砸下来。

有的大豆大，也有的鸡蛋大。

狗子撅起屁股在莜麦秸垛三刨两刨就刨出个狗窝，把自个儿藏了进去。

完球了，又喝西北风[5]呀。狗子圪缩在窝里，就瞭外前的冷蛋在场面上跳高高就想。完球了，又喝西北风呀。

这时候，狗子又接住给想起了三寡妇。

As Dog was thinking about Widow San, a huge drop of rain fell from the sky, leaving a depression in the flourlike dust of the road, as if the sky had cast down a large bronze coin.

Plop! Fell another.

Plop! Fell another.

Plop, plop, plop, plop. The big raindrops immediately pocked the road's surface. The fragrant smell of damp earth he had smelled his whole life rose at once. Dog inhaled deeply through his nose several times.

It smelled good. As he inhaled several more times through his nose, Dog wondered why it smelled so good.

Damned Old Man in Heaven changes without a moment's notice, which is good 'cause it'll cool things off and I won't sweat so much.

Dog looked up and saw a bright-edged black cloud approaching. Close behind it spread a huge stretch of dark clouds.

Looks bad! When people get mad, they make trouble; when Heaven gets mad, it hurls hail. Dog stepped up his pace.

In the distance, Dog saw a threshing ground and on it a pile of oat straw shaped like steamed bread. Dog increased his pace again.

By the time he reached the threshing ground, the cold hail was falling.

Some of the hailstones were the size of beans, some the size of eggs.

Dog hoisted his ass and burrowed into his dog den of straw, hiding within.

Fuck it. He had to go hungry, too. Curled up inside his dog's den of straw, he could see the hailstones bouncing on the threshing ground. Fuck it. He had to go hungry, too.

It was then that Dog thought of Widow San again.

狗子想起的是那次。狗子老常老常能想起那次。那是多少年前的事狗子记不住了。可狗子记得，那次也像这样，冷蛋在"崩崩"地跳高高。那次不是在场面，那次是在野坟地。

狗子家的斋斋苗儿没有了。别的可以没有，可斋斋苗儿不能没有。山药咸稀粥、莜面煮鱼鱼、凉拌山药丝还有调苦菜，要想有味道就离不开斋斋苗儿，斋斋苗儿是穷人的调料。[6]

狗子听说野坟地的斋斋苗儿好，就乘着晌午花儿开得旺时去摘。起先，阳婆红耿耿的，热得狗子一头一头出脚汗。快进野坟地的时候，一股大风刮过来，紧跟着老天爷就往下跌铜钱大的雨点子。

狗子瞅中一棵大树就跑过去，避雨。狗子圪蹴在树下看雨点叭叭往下落。

从野坟地跑出两个人。狗子正要喊他们过这儿，他们却拐到了崖头底下。这时候狗子才看清那男的是锅扣那女的是三寡妇。也就是在这个时候，"崩崩崩"的冷蛋给从天上砸下来。

"你快看，冷蛋给跳高高呢。"狗子听出这是三寡妇在说话。

"管他。"这是锅扣的声音。

他俩咋就跑到一块儿了，他俩进野坟地干啥，也是摘斋斋苗儿？狗子想。

后来，冰雹停了。雨越下越大，都给从树叶叶上漏下来，把狗子给淋湿了。狗子也想下到崖底去。他看出雨扫不到那儿。

He recalled that time. He was always recalling that time.
He couldn't remember how many years ago it had been. But Dog
remembered that that time was like this time, with hailstones
bouncing all around. It wasn't on a threshing ground that time, but in
the wild, overgrown graveyard.

Dog had no wild garlic flowers at home. He could do without
many things, but not wild garlic flowers. Wild garlic flowers were a
must for thin, salty potato gruel, dough fish, cold potato strips, and
for seasoning bitter herbs. Wild garlic flowers were the poor man's
seasoning.

Dog had heard that the wild garlic flowers in the wild,
overgrown graveyard were good. So he set off to pick some in the
afternoon, when they were in full bloom. At first the sun was bright
red and hot and he was soon covered with sweat. By the time he
neared the wild, overgrown graveyard, the wind had picked up and
the Old Man in Heaven was casting down raindrops the size of
bronze coins.

Dog saw a big tree and ran over to take shelter beneath it.
Squatting under the tree, he watched the rain fall.

A couple of people came running through the wild, overgrown
graveyard. Dog was just about to shout for them to come over when
they turned to a place under the cliff. It was then that Dog saw that
the man was Uncle Pothook and the woman Widow San. It was then
that the hail started to fall.

"Look at how the hail is bouncing." Dog could make out the
voice of Widow San.

"Who cares?" That was Uncle Pothook's voice.

What were they doing together? What were they doing in
the graveyard? Were they also picking wild garlic flowers? Dog
wondered.

Later the hail stopped, but the rain fell harder and began
coming through the tree leaves, getting Dog wet. Dog also thought of
the place below the cliff and how the rain didn't reach there.

他两手抱住头冲出树下，一拐弯，他呆傻住了，他看见三寡妇和锅扣都是光溜着身子。锅扣正往地下铺展他们的衣裳。三寡妇站着看他铺，从她的手势能看出，她是让他重铺，再往崖壁靠靠。锅扣听了她的，就又重铺，三寡妇正是面朝着狗子站着。她没看见狗子，狗子可是把她全看见了。锅扣把几件衣裳全铺垫好后，三寡妇就面迎天躺下去。狗子看见她的两条大白腿像剪子似的给锅扣打开。正在这时候，有冷蛋又给"崩崩崩"的从天上砸下来。狗子赶快抱住头又往大树下返。

一阵云卷过去了。一阵雨浇过去了。一阵冷蛋砸过去了。狗子又出了树，想下去看西洋景。可是锅扣和三寡妇早走了。

这件事，狗子没和任何的别旁人说过。

自那以后，狗子老忘不了那天。老常老常能想起那天在树底下让雨水给洗了个灰。自那以后，狗子一看见三寡妇就想笑。

这阵子，他又是笑呀笑的，笑出了声才知道自己是在莜麦秸垛底。是在看场面的冷蛋在一蹦一蹦的跳高高。

"那是啥?"

狗子一下子瞭望见场面排排的排着的一溜一溜的土坯。

日你妈，那还不叫冷蛋全给砸成个稀巴巴烂?

狗子噌地从狗窝钻出来，忙忙的就是个往下揪莜麦秸。揪一抱就跑去苫土坯。再揪一抱就再跑去苫土坯。大豆大的鸡蛋大的冷蛋直往狗子的骨头上砸。

日你妈老天爷，你不把爷砸死你就不是个好牲口。日你妈狗

Covering his head with his arms, he ran from beneath the tree, turned, but stopped dead in his tracks. Uncle Pothook and Widow San were stark naked. Uncle Pothook was bent over, spreading their clothes on the ground. Widow San stood there watching him. From her gestures you could tell that she was having him spread them again, closer to the cliff wall. Uncle Pothook listened to her and spread them again. Widow San stood facing Dog. She didn't see Dog, but he saw every inch of her. After Uncle Pothook had spread the clothes on the ground, Widow San lay down on her back. Dog watched as she spread her white legs like a pair of shears for Uncle Pothook. It was at that moment that the hail started falling, *Beng, beng, beng.* Dog covered his head again and ran back beneath the big tree.

Black clouds rolled overhead. A cloudburst passed; a hailstorm passed. Dog came out from under the tree again to watch the hanky-panky, but Uncle Pothook and Widow San were already gone.

Dog never told anyone about what he had seen.

He could never forget that day. He always thought about how miserably he had been drenched under that tree. After that, whenever Dog saw Widow San, he wanted to smile.

This time, he smiled and smiled, and when he laughed, he realized he was inside his dog den of oat straw, watching the hailstones bouncing on the threshing ground.

What's that?

Dog looked out at the threshing ground and saw row after row of mud bricks being pounded into mush.

Fuck it! The hail would certainly ruin all the bricks.

Dog climbed out of his dog den of oat straw, hurriedly bent over, and grabbed some straw. He'd grab some straw and then run over and cover the bricks with it. He did this again and again as hailstones the size of beans and eggs fell around his head.

Fuck your mother, Old Man in Heaven. If you can't kill me with your hail, you aren't worth much. Fuck your mother, Dog.

子，你不把土坯苫好你就不是个好牲口。

狗子就骂老天爷就骂自个儿，就抱着麦秸去苫土坯。当鸡蛋大的冷蛋没有了，只剩下大豆大的时候，公社召集起的人顶着簸箕笸箩跑来了。远看，狗子觉得那些人一个个都像是长着手的蘑菇。当中的一个蘑菇给摔倒了，骨碌两个滚儿后想爬起来，可是紧接住又给摔倒了。狗子闹不机明得是，别的那些人一个个从他身边跑过去，可为啥都不管他。任他摔了一跤又一跤。当那些蘑菇们跑到场面，才知道土坯早已经给狗子苫盖好了。可狗子的脑袋瓜子叫冷蛋打得尽疙瘩。

公社把这件事告给到县里。县里把这件事告给到专署。专署派报社跟广播电台的人来到温家窑，来找狗子，要问问狗子为啥敢顶着碗大的冷蛋去抢救公家的财产。

"球。顶大的是鸡蛋大的。没有碗大的。碗大的还不得把我给楔死。"狗子说。

"球。我原根儿也不机明那是公家的还是母家的"。[7] 狗子说。

听了这话，报社的跟电台的都摇头，摇完头，他们又问狗子劳动的动机啦目的啦什么的。问了半天，解说了半天，狗子贵贱闹不机明这些城里头的人尽说的是啥。

最后，有个捉笔的人说："这样吧，就按你的说法。你说说，你为啥好受苦？"

"球。这会儿我是老了。年轻时候给皇军修炮楼，可比这能受呢。皇军每回都夸我要喜要喜[8] 大大的好。这是句日本话。"

报社的跟电台的人不摇头了。他们扭转身齐走了。

If you can't cover the bricks, you aren't worth much.

Dog cursed the Old Man in Heaven and himself as he ran to cover the bricks with oat straw. By the time the egg-size hail stopped and only bean-size hail was falling, the people summoned by the commune came running with bamboo scoops and baskets. From a distance, Dog thought they looked like mushrooms that had grown arms. One of them took a tumble and rolled a couple of times. He managed to stop, but fell again. Dog couldn't understand why the others all ran past the man without paying the least attention and why they kept letting him fall. When they reached the threshing ground, they discovered that Dog had already covered the bricks. But Dog's head was covered with bumps from the hail.

The commune reported the incident to the county. The county reported it to the prefectural commissioner's office. The prefectural commissioner's office dispatched newspaper and radio reporters to the Wen Clan Caves to locate Dog and ask him why he was willing to risk bowl-size hailstones to save public property from destruction.

"Fuck. The hailstones were the size of eggs, not bowls. If they had been the size of bowls, I'd be dead," said Dog.

"Fuck, I don't know anything about male or female property," said Dog.

Hearing this, the people from the newspaper and the radio shook their heads. When they finished shaking their heads, they asked him about his motives and his goals. They spent a lot of time asking him questions and trying to explain their questions, but Dog couldn't figure out what the city people were talking about.

Finally, one reporter said, "Okay, in your own words, just tell us why you were willing to suffer."

"Fuck. I'm an old man. When I was young, the Japanese Imperial Army had me build a gun turret, which was a lot harder. The Imperial Army praised me, saying, '*Yoshi, yoshi*,' that's Japanese for 'good, good.'"

The newspaper and radio people didn't shake their heads. They turned and left together.

"撞鬼呀，你。"

"爷咋了？"

"发灰呀，你。"

"爷咋了？"

人们尽说狗子。可狗子就是闹不机明撞上啥鬼和发上啥灰了。

"You've really gone and done it now."

"What did I do?"

"Are you nuts?"

"What did I do?"

Everyone was scolding Dog, but he couldn't figure out what was wrong or why they thought he was nuts.

Plow Ox

耕 牛

Li Rui

牛、耕牛也。《易系》、黄帝尧舜服牛乘马，引重致远，以利天下；盖取诸随，未有用之耕者。《山海经》曰，后稷之孙叔均始作牛耕；世以为起于三代，愚谓不然。牛若常在畎（quan，犬）亩，武王平定天下，胡不归之三农，而放之桃林之野乎？故《周礼》、祭牛之外，以享宾、驾车、犒师而已，未及耕也。不然，牵牛以蹊（xi，音西，小路。）田，正使藉稻，何足为异，乃设"夺而罪之"之喻耶？在《诗》有云，"载芟（shan，音删）载柞，其耕泽泽，千耦其耘，徂（cu，二声，往、到。）隰（xi，音习，低湿的地方。）徂畛（zhen，音枕，田间小路。）"；又曰，"有略其耜（si，四），俶载南亩"；以明竭作于春，皆人力也。至于"获之""积之""如墉""如栉"，然后"杀时（牛）犉（run，二声，黄毛黑唇的牛。）牡，有捄其角"，以为社稷之报。若果使之耕，曾不如迎猫、迎虎、列于蜡祭乎？盖牛之耕，起于

牛 pronounced niu, plow ox. The Appended State-
ments to the *I Ching* states that the Yellow
Emperor, Yao, and Shun made oxen and hitched horses
available to pull heavy loads over great distances in order
to benefit all under heaven; they probably took this from
Sui before they were used for plowing. According to *The
Classic of Mountains and Seas*, using oxen to plow was
started by Shujun, the grandson of Houji, the minister
of agriculture under the Emperor Shun (2255–2205 BC).
Everyone thinks it began with the Xia, Shang, and Zhou
dynasties, but I disagree. If oxen were often used in the
fields, why did Emperor Wu of Zhou, after quelling the
land, free them in the wildness of peach groves instead
of returning them to the three agricultural lands: the
flatlands, the mountains, and the wetlands? Therefore, in
The Rites of Zhou, oxen are used as a sacrifice in addition
to entertaining guests, pulling carts, and as rewards for
troops, but never used to plow. Otherwise why make a law
to "confiscate the oxen" of the owner who, when leading
his ox down a path, lets the ox trample a rice field? In *The
Book of Songs*, "They clear away the grass and the trees,
their plowing lays open the ground. In thousands of pairs
are the cultivators, they go to the wet lands, they go to the
field dikes," and again "Sharp are the ploughs, they start
work on the southern acres" indicates that the hard work
starts in spring and that it is all manual labor. So far as
to "They reap, they heap, the stacks are high like a wall
they are closely arrayed like a comb," then "They slay this
black-lipped bull whose long horns are curved" in this
way to repay the state. If the ox was used to plow, why
weren't they present in the ancient practice of sacrifices
to the gods in the twelfth month of the lunar year as were
the cat and tiger? Because the use of ox to plow started

春秋之间，故孔子有"犁牛"之言，而弟子冉耕字伯牛。《礼记》、《吕氏月令》、季冬出土牛，示农耕早晚。前汉赵过又增其制度，三犁一牛，后世因之，生民粒食，皆其力也。……

——图、文引自《王祯农书》"农器图谱集"之二

我国古书中记载，夏初后稷（ji，记）之孙叔均开始使用牛耕，这是古代传说。近人据甲骨文推断，商代后期，殷人有用牛耕田的。不过必须指出，直到春秋前期，用牛拉犁耕田的并不多，一般都用耒耜耕田。当时牛所以不能推广，原因之一是，在奴隶社会中，奴隶被看作是能说话的牲口，使用奴隶比使用牲口更合算。在这样的社会中，拥有奴隶的人，根本没有使用畜力的必要。

大致春秋中叶，牛耕才渐渐多起来。孔子是春秋后期人。记载孔子言行的《论语》一书中有"犁牛之子

in the Spring and Autumn Period, hence Confucius's reference to plow oxen and hence his student Rangeng, whose style name was Boniu. In the chapter "Proceedings of Government in the Different Months" in *The Book of Rites*, "In the third month of Winter, [the Son of Heaven issues the order] "to send forth the oxen of earth. . . . The husbandmen to reckon up the pairs which they can furnish for the plowing." Zhao Guo of the Former Han dynasty increased its system to one ox with three plows, which was followed by later generations. The food of the people comes from the ox's labor.

—from Wang Zhen's *Book of Agriculture*, 2

The ancient Chinese classics record that it was Houji's grandson Shujun, of the early Xia dynasty, who started to use oxen for plowing. This is an ancient legend. Based on inferences from the oracle bone inscriptions, people these days believe that farmers used oxen to plow during the Yin dynasty. However, it is important to point out that using oxen to pull plows to till the land wasn't popular until the early part of the Spring and Autumn Period. Plows and plowshares were used to till land in general. One of the reasons that the use of oxen wasn't popularized at the time is that the slaves were mute beasts in the slave society. In such a society, it didn't pay the slave owners to use the labor of the beast.

It wasn't until the middle of the Spring and Autumn Period that the use of the plow ox gradually spread. Confucius was born in the late Spring and Autumn Period. In *The Analects*, which record the words and deeds of Confucius, is found the words: ". . . a bull born of plow cattle

骍（xing，星）且角"一句话。另外，孔子有一个弟子姓冉（ran，染）名耕，字伯牛；他又有一个弟子姓司马，名耕，字子牛。孔子称牛为"耕牛"，……和孔子差不多同时代的左丘明，在他所著的《国语》一书中就明白地说：原来杀了用于祭祀的牛，现在驱使到田里干活了。这也表明春秋后期牛耕已比较普遍。用牛耕田是耕作上的一大进步，由耒耜发展到犁，是农具上的一大进步。

——引自《中国古代农机具》第二讲[1]

红宝拍拍黄宝的头，红宝说："黄宝，你放心。咱俩人藏在这儿哪个龟孙也寻不着！狗日的们梦梦也梦不到这儿来！狗日的们派来多少警察也寻不着！"

黄宝不说话，黄宝用大眼睛看看红宝。

红宝的眼圈就红了。红宝指着地上摊开的那一堆东西安慰说："你看你害怕得你。我说他们寻不着，就是寻不着。你怕啥呀你？我把吃的、用的都带来了，米，面，锅，勺子，水桶，镰刀，被子，马灯，我连咸盐都带上了，够咱们在这儿藏一夏天的。

has a [sorrel coat] and well-formed horns. . . ."
Additionally, Confucius had a disciple surnamed Ran
and named Geng who had the style name Boniu; he had
another disciple surnamed Sima, named Geng, who had
the style name Niuzi. Zuo Qiuming, who lived about the
same time as Confucius, states clearly in his work *The
Discourses of the States* that the ox, which was originally
killed and used in sacrifices, is now driven to work in the
fields. This would indicate that the use of plow oxen was
fairly widespread by the late Spring and Autumn Period.
The use of plow oxen was a great advance in the tilling of
the soil, as the plow evolved from the spade was a great
advance in agricultural implements.

—from *Ancient Chinese Agricultural Implements*

Hongbao patted Huangbao on the head and said, "Don't worry,
Huangbao. We'll hide ourselves so that no bastard can find us. The
fuckers will never find us even in their wildest dreams. They won't
find us no matter how many police they send looking for us."

Huangbao said nothing. Huangbao looked at Hongbao with her
big eyes.

Hongbao was on the verge of tears. Pointing at the things
spread out on the ground, he said to Huangbao to comfort her,
"Look, I know you're afraid, but I tell you that they will never find
us, never. What are you afraid of? I've brought everything we need:
rice, flour, a pot, ladle, bucket, sickle, blanket, and a lantern. I even
brought salt. Fuck, this stuff will last us the entire summer.

窑² 也收拾了，也用蒿草熏了，能顶上招待所啦，你还有啥不放心的呀你？你要实在不放心，咱就垒了洞口在这儿过秋，过冬！咱就住在这儿不回家了!"

黄宝还是不说话，还是用大眼睛伤心地看着红宝。红宝终于忍不住，抹着脸大声哭起来，

"黄宝，我日他妈的呢！我那天就不该叫你看见那个坑，我也不知道他们那是埋牛呢。这都是哪个龟孙定的规矩，他们凭啥要扑杀咱呀，咱又没得那五号病（注：口蹄疫），我日他妈的呢，凭啥别的牛得了五号病，就得把村里的牛都杀了呀？挖恁深的坑埋进去，还得撒恁多的石灰，比日本鬼子还狠心！我爷爷说，只有日本鬼子才烧光杀光抢光，只有日本鬼子才这么狠心，这么没人味儿，他还没见过有谁这么狠心的呢。凭啥人得了病就花钱给治，凭啥人得了'杀死'病（注：SARS）就不扑杀呀？凭啥牛得了病就得扑杀呀？咱肚子里还有个牛犊呢，两条命呢，凭啥母子俩就叫他们白白杀了呀？再说咱好好的，咱根本就没得病……"

看见红宝哭，黄宝就把自己的脸拱到红宝怀里。一股温暖熟悉的味道扑面而来。这么一来，红宝哭得更痛了，红宝伸手抱住黄宝的头，红宝发誓说，

"黄宝，黄宝，你放心，要活咱俩一块儿活，要死咱俩一块儿死，除非他们把我也挖坑埋了，除非他们也给我撒上石灰……乱流河这一道川里都成了他们的屠宰场啦，咱俩永辈子也不回家了，就住在这儿，就把咱的牛娃生在这儿，在这儿开荒种地，咱俩一块儿老死在这儿吧……"

The cave is ready—I've even fumigated it with burning wormwood. It is as good as any guesthouse. So what are you worried about? If you're really worried, we'll cover the cave entrance and spend the autumn here; the winter, too! We'll stay here and not go home!"

Huangbao remained silent. She just looked at Hongbao with a pained expression. Hongbao couldn't restrain himself any longer and broke into tears as he wiped his face.

"Fuck them, Huangbao! I shouldn't have let you see that pit, but I didn't know that they were burying oxen there. What bastard ordered that? Why do they want to stamp out all oxen? We don't have hoof and mouth disease. Fuck their mothers! Why on earth do they want to wipe out all the oxen in the village, just because some other oxen got hoof and mouth disease? They dug out a pit deep enough to bury them and also spread so much lime. They're crueler than the Japs. My grandpa said that only the Japs burned, slaughtered, and pillaged until nothing was left; only the Japs were that cruel and inhuman. He never saw today's cruelty. If someone gets sick, you spend money and cure them. If someone comes down with SARS, do you kill them? If an ox gets sick, do you destroy it? And we have a little calf in your belly; there're two lives. So you'd exterminate mother and child for no reason? Besides, we're fine, there's absolutely nothing wrong with us. . . ."

Seeing Hongbao weep, Huangbao thrust her face into his breast. A warm, familiar scent wafted over him. Hongbao wept all the more. He held Huangbao's face in his hands and swore:

"Huangbao, Huangbao, don't you worry. We will live together and we will die together. Only if they also bury me in the pit and only if they also scatter lime over me . . . Luanliu Stream has become their slaughterhouse; we'll never go home. We'll stay here. You can calve here. We can open this wasteland to cultivation. The two of us will grow old and die here. . . ."

被熏过的窑洞里，弥漫着一股蒿草烧过的烟香。土窑洞坍塌的洞口上，静静地镶嵌着一块碧蓝碧蓝的天，是那种看一眼就会让你头晕的透蓝。塌下来的黄土把洞口堵了一多半，人只能低下头钻进来。窑洞前的空地上长满了一搂粗的橡树、杨树、山核桃树，大树底下满是密密麻麻的灌木和蒿草，把洞口严严实实地挡在后边。如果不留意，谁也看不出这曾经是原来的农家小院。茂密的蒿草被红宝和黄宝踩出一道沟来，草们倒伏在沟底，草叶的背面翻过来，在太阳底下白亮白亮地闪着银光。漫山遍野的寂静中，有一只蝉在枝头上独唱，纤细的声音很快就断绝在正午灼人的阳光下面。

红宝的爷爷说这个荒村子原来叫七里[3]半，住过五六户人家。红宝的爷爷当年就和红宝的太爷爷住在这个院子里。从五人坪往北二十里，翻过老林沟，往南背的大坡上一股劲爬七里半，再过一条沟就到了。这村子就是当年叫来扫荡的日本鬼子给烧毁了的，从那以后六七十年就再没有人来住过。前两年满金爷在七里半村口的老核桃树上吊死了，这个地方就更没有人敢来了。埋满金爷的时候，红宝来抬过人，他就是从那时候才看见了爷爷当年住过的这个院子，院子里的三孔窑洞塌得只剩下这一孔了。

黄宝终于说话了，它扎在红宝怀里轻轻地哞了一声，一道口涎从嘴角上长长地拖下来。它晃晃头，两只黑黑的大眼睛轻轻地一眨一闭。可惜，脖子上的牛铃铛没有了，要不然就能听见悠长

The scent of wormwood lingered in the fumigated cave. A patch of brilliant blue sky mounted quietly through the cave's excavated opening. It was so blue that the sight of it made you dizzy. The yellow earth had collapsed and covered more than half the entrance to the cave. To enter, you had to stoop and squeeze your way in. In front of the cave grew a bunch of large oaks, poplars, and hickory trees, under which was a dense growth of brush and grass, solidly screening the cave from sight. The inattentive eye would never recognize that it was once the small courtyard of a farmhouse. Hongbao and Huangbao had cut a path through the dense vegetation. The grass had been trampled into a rut, exposing the pale underside of the leaves, which shone whitely in the sunlight. A single cicada cried on a branch, breaking the silence hanging over the hill and dale. Soon the tenuous sound would break off under the scorching noon sun.

Hongbao's grandpa said that this deserted village was called Qiliban (seven and a half *li*) and had been home to five or six families. In those days, Hongbao's grandpa and his great-grandpa had lived in this very courtyard. To get here from Wurenping, you had to walk twenty *li* north, crossing Laolin Ditch, toward the southern ridge of the big slope, then climb seven and half *li*, and then across a ditch. The place had been destroyed by the Japs during their mopping-up operations. In the sixty or seventy years since then, no one had moved there. Since Old Manjin had hanged himself from a hickory tree at the entrance to Qiliban village two years ago, even fewer people dared come here. When they buried Old Manjin, Hongbao had come to carry the body. It was at that time that Hongbao had seen the courtyard where his grandpa once lived. Two of the three openings in the cave dwelling had collapsed, leaving this one.

Huangbao finally replied. She mooed softly against Hongbao's breast as a long dribble of saliva dropped to the ground from the corner of her mouth. She shook her head and blinked her two large, deep black eyes. Unfortunately, she no longer wore a bell around her neck; otherwise the gentle and relaxing sound of cowbell could have

舒缓的牛铃声。

听见黄宝叫，红宝止住了哭声。他抹抹眼泪，从怀里掏出牛铃来，

"黄宝，你不待见我哭呀？行，我听你的，我日他妈的我不哭啦，哭得没意思。黄宝，你饿了吧，你得再等等，现在天太毒，日头把草都晒蔫了、晒热了，这会儿割下的草不好吃，等傍黑的时候我给你割草去，傍黑的时候草们就都醒了，都缓过来了，那时候的草好吃，明天清早的挂上露水就更好吃。"说着，他摇摇牛铃，"你看，我把你的铃铛也带来了，咱先把铃铛挂在窑里，等以后没事了再戴上回家。"

黄宝懂事地又哞了一声。红宝的眼圈立刻就又红了，

"黄宝，咱俩真（竖心旁）西惶呀，连吃口草都得偷偷摸摸的……我不能让你到坡上吃草去，我实在是担心万一叫什么人看见你。你放心，等天黑了，我跟你一块出去到坡上透透气。"

黄宝又眨巴眨巴眼睛，黄宝什么都明白。

火红的晚霞漫天烧起来的时候，红宝拿着镰刀来到窑洞外面。站在山坡上，红宝眯着眼睛笑起来，他看见晚霞映红了满山坡的嫩草，火条烧，白蒿苗，喇叭花，都被晚霞镀了一层金光，在晚风中漫山遍野地涌动。红宝和他的镰刀也被镀了一层金光。红宝满脸堆笑地挥起了镰刀，红宝说，

"黄宝，黄宝，你瞧瞧，你瞧瞧这草！都是你爱吃的！别说你一个人，就是赶来一群牛大家伙儿一块吃，一夏天也吃不完。

been heard.

Hearing Huangbao moo, Hongbao stopped crying. He wiped his tears away and took out the cowbell.

"You don't want to see me cry, do you, Huangbao? Okay. I won't. Fuck it. There's no point in crying. Are you hungry, Huangbao? You'll have to wait. It's too hot out—the sun has withered and softened the grass. If I cut it now, it won't taste very good. Wait till it gets dark and then I'll cut you some grass, because the grass revives just before dark. That's when the grass tastes good. It'll be even better early tomorrow morning, when it's covered with dew. As he spoke he rang the cowbell. "See, I even brought your cowbell. We'll hang it in the cave. Later, when everything is all right, you can wear it home."

Huangbao mooed sensibly. Hongbao was on the verge of tears again.

"Huangbao, how pitiful we are! We even have to sneak around for a mouthful of grass. . . . I can't let you graze on the slope, because I'm afraid someone might see you. Don't worry. As soon as it gets dark, I'll go to the slope with you for a breath of fresh air."

Huangbao blinked several times. Huangbao understood everything.

As the flames of sunset burned, Hongbao took his sickle and left the cave. Standing on the slope, Hongbao's eyes narrowed as he smiled. He saw the whole hillside, which was covered with tender grass, paintbrush, artemisia, and trumpet flowers, reddened and shining in the glow of sunset and surging in the evening breeze. Likewise, Hongbao and his sickle were plated in gold by the light. Hongbao was all smiles as he brandished his sickle. He said, "Look, Huangbao, look at this grass! It's what you like best! You're not the only one—a whole herd would eat together here and not finish in an entire summer.

你还发啥愁呀你，我日他妈的呢，能在这儿开个养牛场！"

红宝右手握定镰刀，有力地弯下腰去，镰刀把密集的草丛分开，整个镰刀向左一压，把草挡在左手上，锋利的刀刃紧贴地皮唰地一声，茂密的草地上就留下一道泛着浆水的新茬子。割上两刀，红宝就要转过身来把手上的青草放在空地上。随着身体有力地起伏，和唰唰的割草声，在红宝身后渐渐留下一片泛着青草味儿的空地，在空地崭新的草茬子上面，排列起一摊一摊的青草。霞光满天，群山无语。远远看去，寂静高远的霞光中，红宝起伏的身影就好像在操演一个什么古老的仪式。

一转眼的工夫，红宝兴冲冲地扛着一捆青草回到土窑里。闻见新鲜的青草味儿，黄宝立刻兴奋地伸过鼻子来，红宝故意挡住它，

"看你急的，看你急的，连绳子也不叫解啦你？"

黄宝不理他，黄宝咬住垂下来的青草一甩头，把一绺青草拽下来叼在嘴里，有滋有味儿地吃起来，窑洞里立刻响起一阵咯嘣咯嘣的咀嚼声。

红宝拉开草捆的绳扣，鲜嫩的青草摊在地上。红宝专门把喇叭花秧子挑出来，堆到黄宝嘴跟前，

"我说黄宝，你缺心眼儿呀，要吃就先吃最爱吃的呀！我又不和你抢！"

拖着个怀孕的身子走了二十多里山路，黄宝早就饿了。黄宝不抬头，伸出长长的舌头把鲜嫩的青草一绺一绺卷进嘴里，窑洞里一片酣畅的咀嚼声，咯嘣咯嘣，咯嘣咯嘣……

Why do you worry? Fuck it, I could start a cattle ranch here!"

Grasping the sickle in his right hand, Hongbao stooped down with force. With the sickle, he parted the thick growth of grass and then pushed it down into his left hand. As he pressed the sharp blade close to the ground, he gave a swift cut, leaving only a juicy stubble. Every two cuts, Hongbao turned around and placed the green grass down on the empty ground. Accompanying the rise and fall of his body and the swish of cutting, the aroma of fresh grass floated in the air and the grass was lined up in pile after pile on the fresh stubble behind him. The sky was filled with sunglow, and the hills were silent. In the silent and remote evening sunlight, Hongbao, bending and stooping, looked as if he were performing some ancient ritual.

In the twinkle of an eye, Hongbao excitedly lifted a bunch of grass with both hands and returned to the cave. Smelling the scent of fresh-cut grass, Huangbao excitedly stretched forth her nose, but Hongbao blocked her on purpose.

"You're in such a hurry, in such a hurry! Won't you even let me untie the cord first?"

Huangbao ignored him. She latched on to the grass hanging there with a swing of her head, pulled out a tuft, and consumed it with relish. The cave was immediately filled with the sound of her munching grass.

Hongbao undid the knot in the cord and spread the tender grass on the ground. With great deliberation, he plucked out the trumpet flower buds and pushed them toward Huangbao.

"I say you are not smart enough, Huangbao! Why don't you eat your favorite first! I'd never grab it before you."

After walking more than twenty *li* of mountain road, Huangbao, heavy with calf, was famished. She lowered her head, stretching out her tongue to roll bunch after bunch of green grass into her mouth. The merry sound of her munching filled the cave.

看着黄宝吃草，红宝觉得比自己吃饭还香。红宝舔舔嘴唇，咽下一口唾沫，也揪了一棵白蒿苗放进嘴里咬了一口，然后拍拍黄宝的脖子，

"黄宝，你好好吃吧你，我刚才就着凉水吃过窝窝了，我不饿。黄宝，我想明天再去给咱弄张饭桌来，咱们来的时候我在水沟边上看见一块青石板，洗干净搬回来正好顶个桌子用，等弄好了，你在上头舔盐，我在上头吃饭，咱俩就把光景正儿八经地过起来。一家人过光景，咱啥物件儿也不能短了，啥营养也不能缺了，黄宝，你说是不是？"

黄宝不抬头。黄宝忘情在酣畅的咀嚼之中。残破的窑洞里充满了野草的清香和黄宝身上那股熟悉温暖的味道。红宝又拍拍黄宝的脖子，心里充满了说不出的温暖和宽慰，他觉得这孔爷爷当年住过的窑洞，简直就是专门留给他和黄宝用的，简直就是一个活神仙住的福地洞天。他揉揉黄宝的耳朵，

"黄宝，不着急，你吃吧你，慢慢吃，等你吃饱了咱就睡，你放心，明天早上太阳保管还是从东边儿升起来！"

睡到半夜时分，忽然响起了雷声。紧接着，大雨在震天动地的电闪雷鸣中倾盆而下。一道一道的闪电直劈山顶，撕天裂地的炸雷震得窑洞四壁落下一缕一缕的烟尘。红宝被雷声震醒了，借着闪电他看见卧在地上睡觉的黄宝已经吓得站起来了。红宝赶紧点燃了马灯，看见黄宝焦躁不安的眼睛，红宝笑起来，

"黄宝，不用怕，有我在这儿呢，你怕啥呀你？"

看见灯光，黄宝果然安静了许多。红宝把灯捻捻大，窑洞里

Watching Huangbao eat the grass, Hongbao felt it seemed more savory than eating rice. Hongbao licked his lips and swallowed his saliva. He then picked up a stalk of wormwood and chewed on it as he patted Huangbao on the neck.

"Eat up, Huangbao. I had some steamed bread with water just a while ago, so I'm not hungry. I think I'll get a dinner table for us tomorrow. I saw a large flagstone by the ditch on our way here; it'll make a good table. All I have to do is wash it and bring it here. When it's ready, you can lick your salt off it and I can set my food on it. We'll live our lives like a family. We cannot be short of anything; we cannot be short of food. Isn't that right, Huangbao?"

Huangbao didn't look up. She was selfishly chewing to her heart's content. The dilapidated cave was filled with the scent of fresh grass and Huangbao's familiar warmth. Hongbao patted Huangbao on the neck again, his heart filled with an inexpressible warmth and comfort. He felt that this cave in which his grandpa had once resided had been left especially for him and Huangbao and that it was a paradise fit for an immortal. He rubbed Huangbao's ear.

"Don't worry, Huangbao. Take your time and eat up. After you're done, we'll go to bed. Have no fear. The sun will come up in the east as it always does."

At midnight, thunder cracked, followed by a huge downpour with thunder and lightning. Streaks of lightning struck the peak, shaking the ground and making dust fall from the walls of the cave. Hongbao was awakened by the thunder. He could see in the flashes of the lightning that Huangbao, who had been asleep on the floor, was frightened and now on her feet. Hongbao quickly lit the barn lantern and saw Huangbao's anxious look. Hongbao laughed.

"Don't be afraid, Huangbao. I'm here. What are you afraid of?"

Seeing the lamplight, Huangbao was much calmer. Hongbao turned up the wick, and the cave grew

顿时明亮起来，红宝又笑笑，

"黄宝，你要是害怕，咱就亮着灯，过来吧黄宝，就卧在我身边。"

黄宝走过来，安安静静地卧在红宝身边。

两个人躺了一会儿，红宝还是有点舍不得灯油，就和黄宝商量，

"黄宝，你一闭上眼，天就成了黑的，就啥也不用看了，你说是不是呀？灯油咱得省着点用，往后的日子长呢。你要是害怕，你先睡，我灭了灯再给咱守一阵儿。"

红宝熄灭了马灯，在黑暗中静静地守着。大雨和雷鸣不知什么时候忽然停了下来，山野里立刻又恢复了原来的寂静。整个世界都被洗干净了，湿漉漉的树林和野草，在天地间弥漫出让人消魂的清新。远处，被雨水壮大了的溪流，在清新的寂静中淙淙流进深不见底的黑夜。满天荧荧闪光的星星，好像刚刚哭泣过的伤感温柔的眼睛。柔和的夜色中，红宝和黄宝一起进入了梦乡……

黎明前的黑暗当中，那个荒废多年的农家小院里发出一声闷响，被雨水浸泡过的残窑忽然整个塌了下来。

两天以后，县里畜牧局和公安局的人到五人坪来强制执行的时候，到处找，也没能找到红宝和他的牛。村里有人说，红宝带着他的牛下山找他姐夫去了。也有人说，你们就不用费那个事啦，寻着也是白搭。红宝光棍一条，那头牛红宝养了十年了，又给他耕地又给他下犊子，黄宝就是红宝的命，红宝亲黄宝比亲亲骨肉

bright at once. Hongbao laughed once again:

"If you're afraid, I'll keep the lamp lighted. Come on over here and lie down next to me."

Huangbao walked over and lay down quietly by Hongbao.

Having bedded down with Huangbao for a short while, Hongbao was reluctant to waste any more lamp oil, so he consulted with Huangbao:

"Huangbao, close your eyes and everything will be dark. You don't need to see anything, right? We have to try to save some lamp oil, because there are a lot of days to come. If you're afraid, you go to sleep first, and I'll keep watch for a while."

Hongbao put out the barn lantern and quietly kept watch in the dark. At some point the rain and lightning suddenly stopped and the mountain recovered its silence again. The whole world had been washed clean. The dripping trees and grass between heaven and earth left one spellbound and refreshed. Far off, the swollen stream flowed off into the night amid the refreshing silence. The twinkling stars in the sky above looked like warm and sentimental eyes that had just shed tears. In the tender night, Hongbao and Huangbao entered the world of dream. . . .

In the predawn darkness, a muffled sound was heard from the small, long-deserted courtyard of the farmhouse as the rain-soaked cave suddenly collapsed.

Two days later, when the people from the Livestock Bureau and the Public Security Bureau arrived in Wurenping to carry out their orders, they looked everywhere but could not find Hongbao and his ox. Some of the villagers said that Hongbao had gone to see his brother-in-law below and had taken his ox with him; others told them not to bother looking, because it was a waste of time. Hongbao was a poor unmarried man, and he had cared for that ox for ten years. It had plowed the fields for him and borne him calves.

还要亲呢，寻着，也别想带走，除非你们把红宝也埋了，除非你们把红宝抓起来，给他判刑，叫他蹲监狱！

其实，连五人坪的人自己也纳闷：全村的牛都叫公家给杀了埋了，你说这红宝和黄宝到底是逃到哪儿去了他们？一个月过去了，不见人。半年过去了，还是不见人。整整一年过去了，还是没有半点消息。

这个世界上没有人知道，也没有人看见，七里半的那孔土窑洞塌了，夏天的杂草和野藤早已经盖满了新塌的黄土。

Huangbao was Hongbao's life. Hongbao loved Huangbao more than his own flesh and blood. Even if they did find them, they might as well not think of taking the ox away unless they were prepared to bury Hongbao as well, or unless they were prepared to arrest Hongbao, convict him, and throw him in jail!

Actually the Wurenping villagers were themselves mystified. All the oxen of the village had been destroyed and buried by the authorities. Where had Hongbao and Huangbao gone? A month went by and there was no sign of them. Six months went by and still there was no sign of them. After a whole year had gone by, still there was no news of them.

No one in the whole wide world knew or had seen the cave at Qiliban collapse. The summer grass and wild creepers had long since covered the fresh yellow earth.

The Mistake

错　误

Ma Yuan

玻璃弹子有许多种玩法，最简单又最不容易的一种，是
使弹子途中毫不担搁，下洞。

——题记

一

这两个孩子一个有妈没爸，一个没妈没爸。有妈的那个不是爸死
了，是他妈不说谁是他爸——他爸自己又缺乏自觉站出来的勇气。
三十多个男人谁都是可遗分子，除了我。我知道不是我才这么说
的。我翻动这些旧事无非是想写一篇小说什么的，这些事情已经
过了十几年，所谓恍若隔世。俩孩子是同一个夜里出现的。

我实在不想用倒叙的方法，我干吗非得在我的小说的开始先
来一句——那时侯？

我不知道那件事的因由结果，我甚至不知道这俩男孩是不是
活下来了。他们要是活着已经到了搞女人跳迪士高的年龄。十七
岁吧。

那个夜里还发生了另外一件事。我的军帽不见了，丢了！丢
得真是又迅速又蹊跷。

我想罗里罗嗦地讲一下我们住的地方。

我们十六个人住一个两间通堂的大屋子，是我们东北农村特
有的土火炕，[1]中间过道走人。南炕北炕各住八个人，中间被几个
简易衣箱分割成小块领地。我和赵老屁住最里面炕梢儿，我们行
李挨着，我们的两个衣箱摆放在我行李外侧。这个地方没电，晚
上谁有事自己出钱买蜡烛。有人就是钻了这个空子。[2]

There are many ways to play marbles. The simplest way, which is also the most difficult, is to shoot a marble so that it hits its mark directly without hesitation.

1

There were two kids. One had a mother but no father, the other, no mother or father. It's not that the father of the one who had a mother was dead, but that his mother refused to say who his father was—and the father lacked the courage to step forward. Any one of thirty men was suspect, except me. I wouldn't say so if I didn't know for sure. I'm stirring up all these old events because I want to write a story. Everything took place more than a decade ago, events, one might say, from a different world. The two kids appeared on the same night.

I really don't like using flashbacks, but I'll do anything to avoid beginning a story with "Once upon a time." I don't know how the story begins or ends. I don't even know if the two kids are still alive. If they are, they must be chasing skirts and disco dancing—seventeen or thereabouts.

Something else happened that night: my army hat disappeared.

I may as well take the trouble to describe the place where we lived. There were sixteen of us living in one of these houses with heated *kangs* so characteristic of rural Manchuria. The *kangs* faced each other across a hallway. Eight people lived on both the south and north *kangs*. In turn, each *kang* was further divided into smaller areas by the placement of several suitcases. I shared the innermost corner with Old Fart Zhao. Our belongings were piled there, surrounded by our bags. There was no electricity in the place. If you had something to do at night, you needed to go out and buy a candle. Someone took advantage of this.

先有十三个躺下睡了，也就是说有三个人没睡。我是一个，还有赵老屁，另外一个叫二狗的偷鸡摸狗什么都干，他出去了。赵老屁和我最铁，[3] 我俩每晚总要在睡前玩上个把小时的跤。他拜过师，是方圆四十华里没有敌手的大名鼎鼎的跤王。我跟他学了一年了。按理说应没人敢动我的帽子了，帽子就放在我箱子上。我们也不过在房子前面百多步远的碱滩上玩了个把钟头，回来帽子就不见了。

就这么简单。

当时正时兴军帽，大该是七〇年吧，也许是六九年我记不清了。我们所在的锦州市黑市卖军帽至少要五元钱一顶，五元钱当时是五斤肥膘新鲜猪肉的价钱。主要它还是一个小伙子可否在社会上站得住脚的象征。那时候抢军帽成风，你经常可以听到诸如为了抢军帽而杀人的传闻。不是马路消息。我军帽就这么丢了。

丢得轻轻巧巧。而且那天晚上有了那两个孩子，人们因为这两个新奇的尤物马上把我的悲痛淡忘了。

那个有妈孩子的妈是江梅，江梅和我和我们许多人是同一个车来的，江梅也是我私下里最关注的女人。她肚子大了这事实也许我才认真看待，她是把孩子生在知青农场[4]的第一个女人，她没有去医院。这以后我也曾不只一次地猜度那个把江梅肚子搞大的人是谁，当然没有结果，她甚至对我不理不睬，她是突然冷淡我的，她是女人，她不会感不到一个男人对她的关注。我是个高大健壮的男子汉呵，虽然我也只有十九岁。我们从小学到中学一直是同班同学。就是这个不寻常的夜里，江梅生了一个儿子。

Thirteen people went to bed first, which is to say that three people didn't sleep. I was one of them, Old Fart Zhao was another, and Second Dog, who was capable of anything from petty theft to robbery, was the third. He went out. Zhao and I were best buddies, so we killed some time every night by wrestling before we turned in. Zhao had trained under a master and was the undisputed king of wrestling within a twenty-mile radius. I'd been studying with him for a year. Normally no one dared touch my hat, which I kept on top of my suitcase. That night, we wrestled for an hour on the alkali flats a hundred yards from the house. When we got back, my hat was gone.

It was that simple.

At that time army hats were all the rage. It must have been 1970, or maybe it was 1969, I can't recall for sure. On the black market in Jinzhou, where we lived, the hats sold for five yuan, which in those days was enough to buy ten pounds of fresh pork, so I wasn't going to let someone get away with taking mine. With army hats being the order of the day, we often heard rumors of people being killed over them. Anyway, my hat disappeared, and that's no lie. It was gone just like that. Those two kids were born the same night, and that exciting news made everybody forget my grief.

Jiang Mei was the name of the mother of the kid who had a mother. Jiang Mei and I, and many other people, had arrived on the same truck. She was also the woman I secretly liked the most. I was perhaps the only one who treated her pregnancy seriously. She was the first woman to have a baby at the relocation farm for educated youth; she didn't go to the hospital. I always tried to guess who the guy was who got her pregnant. Of course I never did figure it out. She began to ignore me, then suddenly treated me coldly. She was a woman, and it was impossible for her to not know that I was interested in her. I was a big strong guy, even though only nineteen. We'd been classmates from grade school through middle school. It was on that unusual night that Jiang Mei gave birth to a son.

二

赵老屁好象看见二狗曾经回屋子一次,问睡下的十三个人都说睡了什么也不知道,这种时候没人愿意作证,二狗说他绝对没有回来过——可他不说在什么地方,什么人可以为他作证。后来我才知道他为什么不说,本来他说了就会从嫌疑中解脱出来。不过换了我,我也不回说,绝对不会。问题就是那顶帽子。

关于帽子我还想再罗嗦几句。我的帽子一年前是崭新的,我拿到帽子的当时就下决心与他共存亡,我咬破右手食指用血在帽里写上我的名字。这一年时间我几乎帽不离头,谁都知道这顶帽子是我的命,相信整个农场都知道我为这顶帽子会毫不犹豫地跟人玩刀子玩命。戴了一年可以想见它已经不那么崭新了。

结果问题就出在血写的名字上。后话。

我和赵老屁在仔细寻找失败后决定打扰一下同屋的伙伴。我挨个儿搬动十三个已经远在睡乡的脑袋。

"哎,起来一下。"

"哎,起来一下。"

"哎,起来一下。"

"哎,起来一下。"

"哎,起来一下。"

"哎,起来一下。"

"哎,起来一下。"

"哎,起来一下。"

"哎,起来一下。"

2

Old Fart Zhao thought he saw Second Dog walk back inside once, but all thirteen of the others said they'd been asleep and didn't know anything. At times like that no one wanted to be a witness. Second Dog said he hadn't been back, but he wouldn't say where he'd been or whom he'd been with. Only later did I find out why he'd refused to say. If he had said something then, he wouldn't have been a suspect. But if I'd been in his shoes, I'd have done just the same; I never would have spoken, never. But my hat was at stake here.

I guess I should say a little more about the hat. The year before, my hat was brand-spanking new. When I first got it, I decided I'd live and die with it. I bit my right forefinger and wrote my name on the inside in blood. I hardly took it off the whole year. Everybody knew it was my life. I believed that everyone on the farm knew that I wouldn't hesitate to use a knife on anyone who messed with my hat. After my wearing it for a year, it's easy to imagine that it wasn't exactly new anymore. The name I wrote in blood became the key point. On that, more later.

Old Fart Zhao and I, after failing to locate the hat by a thorough search, decided to wake up our roommates. I woke up all thirteen of them.

"Hey, get up for a minute."

"Hey, get up for a minute."

"Hey, get up for a minute."

"Hey, get up for a minute."

"Hey, get up for a minute."

"Hey, get up for a minute."

"Hey, get up for a minute."

"Hey, get up for a minute."

"哎，起来一下。"

"哎，起来一下。"

"哎，起来一下。"

"哎，起来一下。"

大约七分钟时间大家都起来了。

我站在门口，大块头把门堵得严严实实。赵老屁黑着脸坐在门边炕沿上。我说话了。

"哥们，对不起了。我帽子丢了，就刚才的事儿。我和老屁在房前场子上呆了一阵，也看得见咱们这房子的门。我想先问一下，是不是有人拿错了？拿错了没关系，现在拿回来还不晚。谁拿错了？有人拿错了吗？"

我是先礼后兵，我决定等上一分钟。可是赵老屁不等。他说："别他妈罗嗦，谁拿了痛快点拿出来，别找不痛快。"

一分钟以后我说："那么就对不起了。我请哥们把箱子打开……"

黑枣插断我的话。"你要翻可以，翻不出来怎么办？"

"在谁那儿翻出来大家找谁说话。翻不出来谁要怎么办就怎么办，我没说的。"

黑枣说："这话是你说的，大家听好。"

大家肯定都听好了，可是没人有所表示。多数人都不想找麻烦。于是很快就开了全部十三个破木箱，全是破的，破得藏不下任何值得藏的秘密，军帽自然没有。

我也是这时才注意到这个残酷的事实的，我们这些人都是一

"Hey, get up for a minute."

"Hey, get up for a minute."

"Hey, get up for a minute."

"Hey, get up for a minute."

"Hey, get up for a minute."

It took seven minutes to get everyone up.

I stood blocking the doorway while Old Fart Zhao, his face darkening, sat on the edge of the *kang*. I spoke.

"Brothers, I'm sorry about this, but my hat disappeared a short time ago. Old Fart Zhao and I were down on the alkali flats in front of the house for a little while. From there we could see the door of the house. But first I want to know if anyone took something by mistake? If it was taken by mistake, that's okay; it's still not too late to return it. Did anyone take something by mistake, anyone?"

I decided to be polite first, then get tough; I'd give them sixty seconds. But Old Fart Zhao interrupted: "You talk too damned much. Whoever took the hat had better return it soon—if they don't want any trouble."

After sixty seconds, I said, "Well, sorry, but I'll have to ask each of you to open your trunk. . . ."

Black Date cut in before I finished speaking. "You can search, but what happens if you don't find it?"

"We'll talk with whomever we find it on. If we don't find it, well, we'll just have to see. I've got nothing more to say."

"Whatever you say," Black Date replied. "Everybody remember that."

They all heard, but no one said a word; they didn't want any trouble. So all thirteen beat-up suitcases were hastily opened—they were so battered they couldn't conceal any secret worth hiding. Of course the hat wasn't found.

It was only then that I came to a cruel realization: there wasn't one of us who

无所有的穷光蛋，我没看到任何人有一件可以值五元钱的或者衣服或者其他什么物件。这个发现更使我坚定了找回军帽的想法。虽然我同时也在暗自担忧黑枣可能会找麻烦。当然我不怕他。

我清楚知道他不是可以容人的角色。

事情已经闹得很僵，我决定错就一错到底——我开始不客气地翻动所有人的行李。我在得罪大家了。而且我有种预感，我感到我不可能找出帽子，我甚至想不出我该怎样向大家交待。事情总归有个结束，看怎么结束吧。

多数人都不作表示，愤懑的或是厌烦的都不作。我看他们都抱了解脱干系的想法。只有黑枣和找老屁例外。赵老屁不动生色地坐在老地方等待结果，黑枣则用手勾住门框做单杠动作中的引体向上。黑枣干瘦且力大胆大，平时他话不多，可是他什么事都干得出。

我心里有点打鼓。

我盼望出现奇迹。我大概是我们这些人中最不信奇迹的了。我还是盼望。没有奇迹。都翻完了。不，还有二狗。二狗不在。

就在我犹豫着是不是也翻二狗行李时她们女宿舍有人跑来说江梅生孩子了。

三

我想江梅生孩子这件事也许没人比我更沮丧了。我和大家都眼看着她肚子慢慢鼓起来，日复一日，但我没有充分的精神准备面对怀孕可能导致的结果。我只是想，她被人干了，肚子干大了，

wasn't dirt poor. No one owned a piece of clothing, or anything else for that matter, that was worth five yuan. This discovery fixed my determination to recover the hat. Though I worried that Black Date might give me trouble, I wasn't afraid of him. It was widely known that he couldn't tolerate other people.

The matter had reached an impasse. Though I may have been wrong, I decided to push on anyway. Rudely I began to go through their things, offending everyone. I already knew I wouldn't find my hat, so I couldn't justify my actions. Every event has its conclusion, and so would the affair of my hat.

Most of them had no reaction, expressing neither anger nor disgust. I knew that none of them wanted to get involved, with the exception of Old Fart Zhao and Black Date. Old Fart Zhao sat silently without moving, awaiting the outcome. Black Date was doing pull-ups in the doorway. He was strong, wiry, and had guts. Normally he didn't say much, but he was capable of anything. My heart was pounding.

I hoped for a miracle. Now I probably believed less in miracles than anyone else among us, but I hoped for one nonetheless. There was no miracle. I looked through everyone's things—no, there was still Second Dog's things, but he wasn't there. Just as I was considering whether to go through his stuff, a girl from the women's quarters came running over to announce that Jiang Mei had just had a baby.

3

I don't think there was anyone more depressed about Jiang Mei having a baby than I was. Like everybody else, I'd watched her belly grow day by day, but I didn't have enough nerve to think ahead to the outcome. I could think only of how she'd been fucked, knocked up by

她不是叫我干的。如此而已。

现在她生孩子了。我这时才隐约觉到有什么东西没了，完全彻底地没了。我当时也忘了我的不幸，我记不得我是怎样被人流裹挟到女宿舍门前去的。我们一百二十多个人都在门前，人们甚至不再悄声细语。

孩子已经生下来，我前面说了是个男孩。这样我们这些男人外人就没有避嫌的必要了。江梅围着被子躺在烧着柴草的火炕上，头上缠着一条花枕巾。那个问世还不到一袋烟工夫的小杂种也裹着毛巾被蜷缩在江梅旁边。我格外注意那个燃着烈火的灶炕口，我想不出是谁在这么短的时间就拾了这么多干柴。我们这里最缺的就是烧柴，碱滩无烧柴呵。

假如我没记错，那是在六月。

那以后这个小东西成了整个农场的儿子，他非常讨人喜欢，我得说我喜欢他，这个小杂种。每个男人都对他说："让爸抱抱。"他就让每个想当爸的人抱。每个男人都说过，"叫爸爸。"他就痛痛快快满足每个想听别人叫自己爸爸的人。后话不提。

这个江梅后来死了，我也是听说。我先回锦州了，她留在农场，听说她终于自杀了。又是后话，后话不提。

这天夜里她收到很多很多礼物。估计全农场一百二十几个人人人都送了礼物。

主要是食品罐头，还有些新毛巾新香皂什么的，是女友们的心思。当时农场职工平均年龄二十岁，主要是那个贫农出身的田会计和那个下中农出身的李保管员两个人[5]都已经五十开外，把

someone, but it wasn't me who'd done it, that's all I knew.

Now she had a baby. I had the strange feeling of having lost something forever. At the time, I forgot even my own misfortune. I don't remember how I was swept up in that crowd of people and carried over to the women's quarters. There were more than a hundred twenty of us there in front of the women's quarters, and not one so much as whispered.

As I said previously, the child was a boy. That being the case, there was no need for a man to try to avoid being suspected. Jiang Mei lay wrapped in a quilt on the heated *kang*; she had a flowery towel tied around her head. The bastard child, who hadn't been around for the time it takes to smoke a pipe, was wrapped in a towel and curled up beside her. The flaming mouth of the *kang* caught and held my attention. I wondered who could have gathered so much dry firewood in such a short time. Good firewood was in short supply, and there was absolutely none to be found on the alkali flats.

If I'm not mistaken, that was June. Later the little guy became the son of the whole village. That little bastard was adored by everyone, me included. Every man would say to him, "Come, let Daddy hold you." He'd let anyone who wanted to be his daddy hold him. Every man would say, "Say 'Daddy.'" He'd gladly satisfy anyone who liked to hear himself called Daddy by someone else. But that's enough about that.

Later Jiang Mei died—that's what I heard. I'd gone back to Jinzhou while she remained on the farm. I heard it was suicide, but more on that later.

That night she received lots of gifts. All one hundred and twenty people on the farm gave her something—mostly canned goods, but her girlfriends gave her things such as towels and soap to show their kindness. At that time the average age on the farm was twenty. Tian the accountant, who was from a poor peasant family, and Li the clerk, who was from a middle peasant family, were both over fifty,

平均年龄几乎抬上了一岁。我没送东西是因为我恨那个小杂种进而恨她。

我没送东西的另外一个原因是我独自回到我们的宿舍时，失掉军帽的不幸再次抓住我。我在期待另一桩事的到来。大家过一阵就要回来啦，黑枣也在其中。

"你要翻可以，翻不出来怎么办？"

这句话跟了我十几年了。我不是那种怕威胁的胆小鬼，这句话似乎也没有很大威慑力。

黑枣谁也不怕。可我怕谁？我也一样。况且我有赵老屁。我相信黑枣没有什么人。事实（我说的是后来的事实）也证实了这一点。

大家逐渐回来了，最后一个是黑枣。赵老屁没有回来。赵老屁永远没回来，我不信他死了，他一定有什么事要干，他反正不见了。

黑枣进屋的时候手里挂着直柄锹。他进门时显得懒洋洋，一副漠不关心的样子。

他头也不抬，谁也不看，自己蹲在门内地上很有耐心地拽住固定锹头的铁钉来回摇动。别人都以为没事了，自己关上自己的衣箱，铺好自己的行李重新躺下去，我坐在自己的位置上，用眼角的余光注意着黑枣。

他看来心平气和，一点着急的样子都看不出来。他慢慢摇动钉头，钉子被他拔出来了。接着他利用门槛退下了锹头。

我知道好戏就要开场了。我记不住细节，因为时间已经过去

so they added at least a year to the village average. I didn't give her anything because I hated that little bastard and I hated her.

Another reason I didn't give her anything was because when I was returning by myself to the men's quarters, I was again seized by the misfortune of having lost my hat. I expected something else rotten to happen. Everybody would be back soon, including Black Date.

"You can search, but what if you don't find it?"

These words have haunted me for more than ten years now. I was no coward to be pushed around, and Black Date's words weren't much of a threat at the time.

Black Date wasn't afraid of anyone. I was the same. Besides, I had Old Fart Zhao to back me up. Black Date, on the other hand, had no one. This fact (I'm speaking of what later became fact) was confirmed.

Slowly everybody returned; Black Date was the last. Old Fart Zhao didn't come back. He never came back. I didn't think he died; he must have had something to do. Anyway, he disappeared.

Black Date returned with a spade in his hands. He came in sort of listlessly, as if he had nothing on his mind. He kept his head down, looking at no one. Squatting on the floor, he patiently took hold of the nail that held the blade to the spade's handle and wiggled it back and forth. Nobody suspected a thing. They all closed their suitcases, rearranged their things, and went back to bed. I sat in my place, watching Black Date out of the corner of my eye.

He seemed calm enough, not the least bit nervous. Having removed the nail, he wiggled the blade of the spade back and forth. He placed the spade against the wooden threshold and pulled the blade from the handle.

I knew something was bound to happen. I don't remember the details, because it all happened so long ago.

太久。结果我的脚踝被木锹把扫成粉碎性骨折，我成了终生跛脚。

我记得我极认真地对黑枣说我要挑他两根大筋。我记得黑枣完全不在乎地笑了一下。黑枣没下暗的，他是个男人。他是打过招呼以后才动手的，他把那条齐头高的硬木杆抡圆了。我想过用手臂挡一下，结果他没让我来得及挡，他的硬木杆在接近我腰部时突然变了方向直扫下三路，而且扫得极低。

我没去医院，太远了。是他们请了一位民间巫医为我治了伤腿。据说他的药里面有一味是乌骨鸡的骨灰，他的药方秘不外传。他死时据说一百零七岁。也是他治的黑枣。

四

这个故事比较更残酷的一面我留在后边，我首先想的是这样可以吊吊读者的胃口；其次我也在犹豫，我不只道我讲了是否不太合适。我说了它比较更残酷一些，我无法从原罪或道德的角度对这个事件作出恰如其分的评价。

讲不讲？怎样讲？

这都是我在后面要遇到的难题。我相信船到桥头自然直。我暂且不去过多地伤脑筋。

我说要挑黑枣大筋是以后的事，当时我瘫在门前地上，这天夜里的故事似乎完结了。

细心的读者马上会说没完。说我在开篇时讲过有两个男孩。是的，没完。那个男孩还没出现。他就要出现了。

但是首先出现的是我这个故事中另外一个没出现的角色，

Anyway, my ankle ended up getting fractured by the handle of the spade. I became a cripple for life.

I remember telling Black Date in all seriousness that I was going to tear him to pieces. Black Date merely laughed. He hadn't done anything underhanded; he was a man. He let me know it was coming before he moved. He swung that long, hard wooden handle in a firm arc. I had thoughts of warding it off with my hand, but he didn't give me the chance. He feinted for my waist, but brought it down sharply, all the way down.

I didn't go to the hospital; it was too far away. They asked a local witch doctor to take care of my injured leg. It was said that among his medicines was the ash of black-boned chicken; his prescriptions were closely guarded secrets. It was also said that he died when he was 107. He treated Black Date, too.

4

I'll save the crueler side of this story till later—that way I can lead my readers on, but I wonder if that's proper. By referring to it as "crueler," perhaps I've precluded a just appraisal of the events from the standpoints of original sin and morality. Should I say it that way, and if not, how should I put it? These are difficulties I'll have to confront later on. I'm sure there's an answer, but I'm not going to worry about it now.

Telling Black Date that I'd tear him to pieces was something that occurred later. At that time I was on the ground in front of the door, unable to move. The story of that night seems finished. The careful reader might well say that it isn't finished, that at the beginning of this story I mentioned two boys. Yes, that's true, and I'm not finished yet. One of the boys still hasn't appeared, but he will presently.

But first another character who has to make an appearance:

二狗。

二狗进来时显得神神鬼鬼，他先绕过黑枣进而绕过我，我特别沮丧因为刚挨了恶棍，我没用正眼看他。他进去了先到了自己的位置，大约有三分钟时间没一点声音。我是完了，没人理睬我，别人都睡了（也许有的在装睡）。

三分钟后的第一个声音叫我（当然还有黑枣）大吃一惊。婴儿的啼哭！而且居然是从二狗的方位传过来的。

我第一个念头，他拿来的江梅的男孩。第一个念头确定以后接着我就明白了是他二狗和江梅生的小杂种。我想也没想就开口了。

"刚生的就抱出来，能活吗?"

"不知道。养养看吧。"二狗头也没抬。

"江梅舍得吗?"

"江梅? 她舍得舍不得跟我有什么关系?"

"这就怪了。跟你没关系? 她就让你抱出来了?"

说话时黑枣已经凑到婴儿旁边，他也象二狗一样仔细看那孩子。可是黑枣突然说话了，他问二狗帽子是谁的? 二狗支吾了一阵，没说出是谁的。黑枣转向我。

"你看看是不是这个?"又转向二狗，"你把孩子挪到被上去!"见二狗发愣，黑枣的口气越发狠了。"你挪不挪?"

二狗犹犹豫豫。"被上太凉，你俩能不能帮忙找点柴禾，把炕烧一下?"

黑枣二话没说，动手把孩子挪到被上，孩子哇哇大哭起来。

Second Dog.

When Second Dog came back, he looked a little odd. First he circled Black Date; then he circled me. I was very upset—what with just having taken a sound beating—so I really didn't take a good look at him. The first thing he did upon entering was go straight to his place, where he remained silent for about three minutes. I was finished; nobody paid me the least bit of attention. They'd all gone to sleep, though some of them may have been pretending.

Three minutes went by before a sound was heard, and, when it came, it really surprised me (not to mention Black Date). It was the sound of a baby crying, and, surprisingly, it came from Second Dog's place.

My first thought was that he'd taken Jiang Mei's baby; once that thought had taken hold, my next thought was that the little bastard must have been fathered by Second Dog. I blurted out, "Will he live if you take him out this soon?"

"I don't know; we'll see," said Second Dog without looking up.

"Didn't Jiang Mei object?"

"Jiang Mei? What does she or her objections have to do with me?"

"That's strange. She'd let you take the kid out even if it has nothing to do with you?"

While we were talking, Black Date approached the baby and, like Second Dog, scrutinized it. Suddenly Black Date asked Second Dog whom the hat belonged to. Second Dog murmured something, but didn't say whose it was. Black Date turned to me. "Look, is this yours?" Then, turning to Second Dog, he said, "Put the baby on the quilt." Seeing Second Dog standing there with a blank stare, Black Date turned vicious: "Well, are you going to move or not?"

Second Dog hesitated. "The quilt's too cold. Can you two help me find some firewood to heat the *kang*?"

Without a word, Black Date placed the baby on the quilt. The baby bawled.

黑枣把二狗用来包裹孩子的军帽扔到我眼前。"你看看，是不是这个？"

我说："听你的口气，二狗，这个不是江梅生的那个？"

黑枣说："哎，你看看是不是你的。"

二狗说："你是说江梅也生了？"

我说："江梅生儿子你不知道？"

黑枣说："你他妈不看老子可不管了。"

二狗说："什么时候？"

我说："这真怪了，全农场都翻个儿了，你不知道？那这个又是谁的？"

二狗说："我刚才出去了……"

我说："这个呢？这个是谁的？"

二狗顿了一下，坚决地说："捡的。"

"捡的？哪捡的？"

二狗不再说话。我这时才转过神来，看到黑枣扔过来的那个血已经浸透的军帽。

我想我的脸立刻白了。

二狗也是这时才发现我受了伤，他走过来低声问我怎么啦？同时蹲下身撩起我左裤脚，他接着不由自主地大叫了一声。

看到紫黑色的肿胀到惊人程度的脚踝已经比小腿还粗，恐怕很少有人能叫得不那么尖利刺耳。这声惊呼唤醒了大家，已经睡倒的十二个人都一下坐了起来。马上有人光腚就跳到地下，我被人群围住了。

Black Date took the army hat that Second Dog had used to wrap the baby in and brought it over to me. "Look, is this yours?"

I said, "Let's hear what you have to say, Second Dog. Is that Jiang Mei's baby?"

Black Date said, "Hey, take a look and see if it's yours."

Second Dog said, "Are you saying that Jiang Mei had a baby, too?"

I said, "You didn't know Jiang Mei had a baby?"

Black Date said, "Damn it, if you're not going to look at it, then I'm not going to either!"

Second Dog said, "When?"

I said, "Now, that is strange. The whole farm was in an uproar about the baby, and you didn't know? Then whose baby is that?"

Second Dog said, "I just went out. . . ."

I said, "The baby, whose is it?"

Second Dog paused, then said firmly, "I found it."

"Found it. Where did you find it?"

Second Dog didn't say anything more. Then I turned my attention to the bloodstained hat that Black Date had tossed to me.

My face must have gone white instantly.

Only then did Second Dog discover that I'd been injured. He walked over and, lowering his voice, asked me what had happened. He squatted down to have a look, lifting my left pant leg, then screamed in alarm.

He saw my ankle, black and blue and swollen up larger than my calf. I don't think anyone could have screamed more shrilly than he had. He woke everybody up. All twelve people, who had been sleeping soundly, sat bolt upright. Some were already out of bed in their bare feet. Soon I was surrounded by a crowd.

现在想起来我仍然说不清道理，我为什么突然来了气恼，气不打一处来，我恶恶狠狠地叫大家"都他妈的滚开"。马上又都滚开了，好象同伴的好心真的成了一场自找的没趣。

只有二狗仍然蹲在我跟前。这正好。

五

帽子不新也不算旧。一股腥臭味借着粘滑的血泊直冲到我鼻腔里面。它完全给血浸染透了，但我仍然可以断定这就是我的那顶。我又仔细查看了帽里，我的血写的名字已经被新血覆盖得不露一点痕迹。

我同样不露一点声色，一把抓住他衣领，接着用那条没受伤的右腿直捣二狗胯下，他当时就倒下了，倒在地上疯狂般地打滚嚎叫。

人们重新跳到地上，我记得有人不停地进去，好象过不多久全农场的人又都集合到我们宿舍门前。我记不清了是因为我马上进入谵妄状态，神志不清，但我敢肯定还没有休克。

后来我知道农场派了马车，连夜把二狗送回锦州，同时有很多人护送，与二狗同行。

这件事的重提还是因为二狗。二狗在家里养了三个多月，他反正残废了。这不能怪我，是他自找的。起码他丧失了找老婆生儿育女的能力，这也是他手脚不干净的报应。相信不是我也会有别人，反正他没别的结果。我由此想到一句老话：不孝有三，无后为大。

Thinking back on it now, I don't know why I was so pissed off or why I shouted, "Damn you all, get the hell away from me!" And that's what they did, but not without feeling they had wasted their sympathy.

Only Second Dog remained squatting there in front of me. And that was perfect.

5

The hat was not new, but neither could it be considered old. The stench of the sticky blood assailed my nose. The hat was completely soaked in blood, but still I was certain it was mine. I carefully examined the inside of the hat. My name, which I'd written in blood, was completely obliterated by the fresh blood. Without warning, I grabbed Second Dog by the collar, then went for his hip with my uninjured right leg. He went down and rolled around on the ground, screaming like a crazy man.

Everybody jumped out of bed again. I remember that the people just kept coming, and within a short time it seemed that the entire farm had turned out in front of our quarters. I really can't remember, because I must have been in a daze or unconscious, but I'm sure I hadn't gone into shock. Later I learned that the farm had gotten a horse and wagon and sent Second Dog to Jinzhou that very night. He was escorted by a large contingent of people.

I bring this up on account of Second Dog. He lay in bed for three months. He became an invalid. It's not my fault; he asked for it. It was also retribution for his bad ways: he couldn't even marry a woman and bring up his own kid. I believe that if it hadn't been me, it would have been someone else. He would have come to a bad end no matter what. Thinking back on this, I recall an old saying: "There are three unfilial acts, the worst being not to leave any descendants."

后来我去看他，我们都绝口不提这回事。他没有再回农场，户口关系调回到市里，在一家街道小工厂搞金属网编织。

后来他又患了癌，直肠癌。他命不好，他只活了二十三年。到现在，他死也是十几年的事了。他死前的那段时间，我们成朋友了。有保留的朋友，不能无话不谈。

有障碍。

那一年（出事的那一年），他十八岁。

六

我刚才忘了叙述一个比较关键的细节，就是二狗被大家抬上车以前，大声喊着对我说："赵老屁让我告诉你，他走了，不回来了。"

我同样大声喊道："为什么？他说没说为什么？"

"没说！他就说告诉你。他还说让你管管江梅，管管那孩子。"

"哪个？哪个孩子？"

他被抬上大车。他没回答我，也许是没听到我的话。我们再见面是半年以后了。

七

有两个孩子。都是江梅在喂养。好在孩子的爸爸比较多。三十多个爸爸养活两个儿子就比较不那么费劲了。

我后来想出了头绪。江梅生孩子，赵老屁走了，走时又让我管管江梅管管孩子，当然是管管江梅生的孩子，也就是说赵老屁

Later, when I paid him a visit, neither one of us wanted to bring up the incident. Second Dog never went back to the farm. He was transferred to the city, where he worked in a small factory weaving steel mesh.

Sometime after that, he came down with cancer—colon cancer. He had a lousy fate; he was only twenty-three when he died. His death occurred more than ten years ago. Before he died, we became friends. With some friends you can't talk about everything; certain things get in the way.

That year (the year all this happened) he was eighteen.

6

A moment ago, I left out one crucial detail. Just before Second Dog was placed on the wagon, he shouted to me, "Old Fart Zhao asked me to tell you that he's left and won't be back."

"Why? Did he say why?" I shouted back.

"He didn't say! He just told me to tell you. He also asked that you look after Jiang Mei and the kid."

"Which one, which kid?"

Second Dog was placed on the wagon. He didn't answer me—maybe he hadn't heard me. It was six months before we met again.

7

There were two kids. Jiang Mei cared for both of them. It was a good thing there were plenty of fathers for the kids; with thirty fathers, their upbringing was made much easier.

Later I figured things out—why Jiang Mei had a baby, why Old Fart Zhao left, and why he asked me to look after Jiang Mei and the kid. Naturally he meant Jiang Mei's baby, because he was the father.

和江梅生的孩子。这个赵老屁，平时一声不吭，见了女的更没话，怎么就使江梅怀孕了？况且他知道我喜欢江梅，他还要插一杠，他也叫男人？他白长了男人的家什。

我反正不能给他擦屁股。他拉屎就该自己擦屁股，亏他还是跤王。我从此没再理江梅，我和江梅都一直在农场，我们很少回锦州去。我后来考到沈阳的一所中等专业学校，那以后就再没回去过。江梅死是听说。没听说那两个男孩子怎么样了。

就是现在我仍然想不好，为什么二狗的那些话留到他的最后的时间，他本来可以早说，早说早就有个结果。早有结果有什么不好？

我于是努力回忆那个夜里的种种细节，然后我明知道是白费劲，我知道有什么东西挡住了我的回忆。我说不好那是什么。

有一点我记得还是清楚，二狗一直不在屋里，他回到屋里到被抬出去总共不过是十分钟里面的事。我闹不懂的是他怎么就碰到了赵老屁；赵老屁为什么不打招呼就走了呢；还有他走时为什么自己不留下话，单单选中二狗传话。

我是在一年多以后离开的。离开的时候大家都来送我，先出村，以后过了那座随时可能坍塌的小木桥。我看到江梅也夹在人群里，她一次也没正眼看我，显得心不在焉。我跟许多人握过手道再见，她是例外。我想不好她怎么好意思来送我。女人的事谁也说不清楚。

我也记得那两个已经会走路的孩子没来。

Normally Old Fart Zhao was quiet, and he was even more so in the presence of a woman. Then how did he get Jiang Mei pregnant? He knew I liked her, and still he cut in. Can someone like that be called a man? His family wasted their time raising him to manhood.

In any case, I wasn't going to wipe his ass. He was the one who shit all over, so he could just clean up his own mess. What a shame—he was the king of wrestling. From that point on, I had nothing to do with Jiang Mei. We both remained on the farm, rarely going to Jinzhou. Later I tested into a mediocre vocational training school at Shenyang. I never went back after that. I heard that Jiang Mei died, but I never heard what happened to the two kids.

Today I still can't understand why Second Dog never spoke up until the very end. He could have said something earlier. He could have cleared things up earlier. What would have been the harm in that?

I've tried very hard to recall the details of that night, but I've realized it's pointless. I know something has been blocking my memory, but I can't say what.

One thing I do remember quite clearly is that Second Dog was away from our quarters for a long time, and it was about ten minutes from the time he entered the room until he was carried away. Several things really bothered me. How did he happen to meet Old Fart Zhao? Why didn't Old Fart Zhao say anything before leaving? And why ask Second Dog to tell me to look after Jiang Mei and the kid, instead of telling me himself?

I left the farm a year later. When I left, everybody came out to see me off. They saw me out of the village and across the rickety old wooden bridge. I saw Jiang Mei in the crowd, but she never once looked at me—as though she had something else on her mind. I shook hands with several people and said good-bye, but not to her. I don't understand why she wanted to see me off; it's hard to say with women.

I also remember that those two kids, who were already walking, didn't show up.

八

我没想到二狗竟有那么高的威信。那十二个同屋的伙伴全都跟在大车后面把二狗一路送到锦州。那里离锦州四十多里，徒步估计至少要四、五个小时。

也就是说这个住了十六个人的宿舍只剩下了我们两个，我，和黑枣。我站不起来，我不能出门送这一行人，黑枣去了，人走了他回来了。

他先是回到自己铺位上一个劲儿地抽烟，我估计至少是抽了五袋烟已上。也就是说大约一个多小时他一直不停地抽烟。天快亮了。

我依然半卧在地上，没人管我，我自己也管不了自己。我疼得厉害，也就没一点睡意。我嗅着好闻的青烟，心里宁静得象一泊死水。

远处有公鸡叫了。黑枣随着公鸡的第一声啼鸣突然跳到地上，他经过我身边时也留一点迹象，他是跨过我两步以后弯身捡起锹头的。我没来得及想他可能干什么，他已经动手了，他看来用力很大又很猛，他的左腿后脚跟上面给剁开了，血汩汩地流了一地，他当时就倒了，倒下的时候神志还清，他朝我笑了一下，那是多么满足多么灿烂的一笑呵。

"我们两清了。"

8

I never realized that Second Dog was so well liked until I saw the twelve people in our room fall in behind the wagon taking him to Jinzhou. Jinzhou is more than twenty miles away, and it takes four or five hours to get there on foot.

What I'm saying is that of the sixteen people in our quarters, only two of us stayed behind: Black Date and I. Not being able to stand up, I couldn't go along. Black Date saw them out the door, but came back after everyone else had left. The first thing he did was go over to his place and smoke a pipe. In all, I counted five pouches that he smoked, which is to say he smoked continuously for over an hour. It was going to be light soon.

I was still on the ground. Nobody looked after me, and I couldn't look after myself. I was in terrible pain and couldn't sleep. Smelling the tobacco made my heart as calm as a pool of stagnant water.

A rooster crowed in the distance. With the first call of the rooster, Black Date was on his feet. I didn't notice him walk past me, but two steps beyond me he bent over to pick up the blade of the spade. I didn't have time to consider what he might do. Exerting considerable strength, he viciously slashed at his left leg. Blood gushed, and he fell. When he fell, his mind was still quite clear. A smile of satisfaction flashed across his face.

"We're even."

九

我得说有一段时间我并不是很明白。他当时挑了自己左腿大筋就蜷成了一团。

他和我同样没叫一声，同样在同一个夜里跛了左脚。我原来听说挑了大筋就永远站不起来了，看来听说总归不大可靠。那位老巫医先为他接上了已经短了一截的大筋，那是个很可怖的手术，剁断的时候也没叫一声的黑枣自始至终大叫不止。后来老巫医说他没问题，说搞女人当铁匠都没问题，大筋短了走路难免脚高脚低，他说"远看春风摇柳，近看骏马歇蹄，起身站桩射箭，躺下长短不齐"，说得黑枣也笑了。

我的手术就比较简单一些，而且看来遗留问题也不多。我只是微跛而已，不仔细看还看不出来。要是机缘好我也许能当上宇航员呢，我身体棒极了。

黑枣是大跛，走路左右晃动幅度极大。不过让老巫医说着了，他果然很快就在农场附近村子里找了个女人，很快就生了两个孩子，都是女儿，他日子过得蛮好，成了能干且富庶的农民。以后我们见面都很愉快。用他的话说，我们两清了。

江梅的死讯就是他告诉我的，江梅对我来说早就不存在了。

9

I must confess that there was a time when things were not very clear to me. When Black Date severed one of the tendons in his left leg, he curled up and, like me, didn't cry out. We were both crippled in our left legs on the very same night. Originally I heard that if a tendon is severed, a person will never be able to stand up again, but that's just a rumor. The operation performed by the witch doctor to connect Black Date's severed tendon was frightening. When Black Date slashed his leg, he didn't make a sound, but all through the operation he never stopped screaming. Later the witch doctor told him he wouldn't have any problems; he could still have a woman, and he could still be a smith. However, since he'd severed an important tendon, one leg would be shorter than the other for the rest of his life; or as the witch doctor put it: "Seen from afar, you'll move like a spring breeze through willows; from nearby, like a fine nag at rest on hoof. Standing, you'll look like an archer; lying down there'll be one long, one short." This made Black Date laugh.

By comparison, my surgery was much simpler, and there were no serious complications. I'm only slightly crippled, and you can't even tell unless you look closely. If my fate is good, maybe I can even become an astronaut, since I'm in fine health.

Black Date was badly crippled. He rocks back and forth when he walks. However, what the witch doctor said was true: not long after that, he found a woman near the farm and bang! bang! He had two kids, both girls. He's pretty comfortable now since he's become a rich and competent farmer. We're always happy to see each other. As he said, we're even.

He was the one who told me about Jiang Mei's death. Very early on, Jiang Mei had ceased to exist for me.

我后来象许多正常人一样恋爱，结婚，生孩子，江梅已经过分遥远了。那是前不久他来市里卖活鸡，碰上我就一定要拉我喝啤酒，酒到半酣他讲起了江梅，讲江梅一直不嫁人可是肚子又大了，后来就投井死了，死得很惨，身子泡得象水缸一样粗。

"我说，你，你为什么不跟她，她好？"黑枣的舌头发硬了。"就因为，因为他怀了田会计，田会计的孩子？那有什么关系？"

我闹糊涂了，"怎么是田会计的？不是赵老屁的吗？"

"老屁？笑话！老屁看，看都不看江梅，他知道，江梅心里，心里对你好。是田会，会计，没错。"

"你怎么知道的？"

"后来，江梅，说的。她说你肯定，肯定不会爱她，她了。她后来怀的，还是田会，会计的，她没法半，就，死啦。"

我说不出话。我的头一下大了。

十

这时二狗死时的情形才象蛇一样重新爬回到我的心里。

直到这时我开始知道全都错了。

二狗死的当天上午还是清醒的，我到时他说他本来昨天前天就应该死了，但他说他死不了，死了也闭不上眼睛，因为我没有来。

Later, like so many other normal people, I fell in love, married, and had children. By then Jiang Mei was far away. Not long ago Black Date came to town to sell chickens. When we ran into each other, he insisted that we go have a beer together. With a little drink in him, he brought up Jiang Mei—how she never married, how she got pregnant again, and how she threw herself down a well. She died a miserable death: her whole body was filled with water just like a big water jug.

"Hey, why, why didn't you and, uh, Jiang Mei ever get together?" Black Date stammered. "Was it because, because she had a kid by Tian, Tian the accountant? What does that matter?"

I was confused. "What do you mean Tian? Wasn't it Old Fart Zhao's?"

"Old Fart's? You must be joking. Look, Old Fart Zhao never, he never paid any attention to Jiang Mei. He knew, in her heart, in her heart, she liked you. It was Tian the accountant's. No mistake."

"How do you know?"

"Jiang Mei, she told me. She said you'd never, you'd never love her, not her. Then she got pregnant again by Tian the accountant. She had no choice, she, uh, killed herself."

I was dumbfounded.

10

Now the circumstance of Second Dog's death crawled back into my heart like a snake. A cruel event is not by itself the cruelest, the absolute cruelest thing; rather it's only after everything has returned to normal, when you realize the truth behind the event, that the enormity of the cruelty then asserts itself.

It was then that I began to suspect I'd been completely mistaken.

Second Dog was still coherent when he died that afternoon. When I arrived, he told me that he should have died a day or two earlier, but he couldn't die, he couldn't close his eyes because I hadn't yet shown up. He knew I'd come. He had to wait till I came so he could tell me something; then he could die in peace.

　　我怨他不早说，他苦笑着说没有时间，说他进门马上就发生了那件事，他没时间也来不及，说他也知道已经如此了再说也没什么意思了。"我反正废了，说又能怎么样呢？"

　　"说了就不会象今天这样！"我说。

　　"你认定江梅的孩子是赵老屁的，其实你听错了，另外的那个，我捡的那个才是他的。他和前村的小寡妇张兰生的，这事谁都不知道——我也是那天夜里才知道的。我到前村去偷——偷什么我也记不得了，我碰巧听到张寡妇房间里声音不对。

　　我进去才知道她要生了，你知道她一个人住得又偏僻，没人知道她要生孩子。我于是问她要我干点什么，她带着哭腔叫我去喊赵老屁。我刚出门她突然大叫起来，我知道不好急忙折身回到屋里，她疼得发疯了，从炕上滚到地下，我不知道该怎么办，我不敢去解女人的裤子，我没碰过女人。

　　"他后来不出声音了，我就一直傻站在旁边看着她死。我吓坏了直到她咽气我才想到孩子。我这时不在乎去解她裤子了，反正她死了。那孩子的屁股已经挤出来，头和手脚还都在娘肚子里。现在说就是难产吧。

　　"我很费力地把孩子拽出来，用刀子割断连着肚脐的那条带子，在脸盆的脏水里马马虎虎给孩子洗了一下就往回抱。

　　"路上我碰到了老屁，我把他儿子还他，可他不要，他说要去跟张兰告个别，说他以后不出来了，说让你把孩子交给江梅管，

I complained that he should have told me sooner. He smiled sadly and said there hadn't been time. That night when he returned, everything had happened so quickly that he'd had no time to speak, and even if he had, it still would have been too late. "I'd still be an invalid, so what good would it have done if I had said anything?"

"If you'd said something, you wouldn't be in the state you're in now," I said.

"You were certain that Jiang Mei's baby was Old Fart Zhao's. Actually, you were mistaken. The one I found was his. It was his and Zhang Lan's, the widow from the next village. Nobody knows this; I learned about it only that night. I went to lift a few things from the next village—I don't even remember now what it was that I went to steal. Anyway, I happened to hear a voice from Zhang Lan's place that didn't sound quite right. Only after I went in did I realize she was going to have a baby. You know she lived in that out-of-the-way place, so nobody knew she was going to have a baby. I asked her if she needed my help. In tears, she asked me to go get Old Fart Zhao. Just as I got out the door, I heard her scream. I hurried back in, only to find her rolling on the ground, crazy with pain. I didn't know what to do. I didn't dare take off her pants because I'd never touched a woman before.

"Later she grew silent, and I just stood by and watched her die. I was scared to death, and I didn't even think about the baby until she stopped breathing. By that time it didn't bother me to take off her pants, because she was already dead. The kid's butt was already out, but his head, arms, and feet were still inside his mother. Nowadays that's what's called breech birth.

"I had a difficult time getting the baby out. I cut the umbilical cord with a knife, then washed him off a little with some dirty water from the washbasin. Then I ran back.

"On the way, I ran into Old Fart Zhao. I handed him his son, but he wouldn't take it. He said he wanted to go and say good-bye to Zhang Lan. He said he wouldn't be returning and that I was to give

我那时还不知江梅也生了。"

"可是你当时说让我管管江梅管管孩子，我敢肯定你是这么说的。"

"我怕得要死，我糊里糊涂地往回走，这时赵老屁又喊我了，他匆匆忙忙塞给我那个军帽说是叫我交给你，让我告诉你是你自己带到摔跤地方忘在地上了。这事我回去忘了说了。我顺手把孩子放到帽子里，孩子身上还带着血。我要死了才把这些话告诉你，我怕你心里不好受，可我不说我心里也憋得难受。也许我不该对你说这些话，我是不是不该说?"

"二狗，你早该说。早就该说了。"

"你别哭。男人掉眼泪让人受不了。我求求你了，别哭。别哭吧。"

他死的时候我一直守在旁边。癌症真是不得了，他本来个子矮小，现在只剩下一把干枯的骨头了。他火化，他妈留了骨灰。

十一

我想找老屁那个夜里一定是因为听说江梅生孩子想到了他的小寡妇张兰，张兰死了他又到什么地方去了呢?

the baby to you to hand over to Jiang Mei to look after. I didn't know that she was having a baby of her own."

"But you said I was to take care of Jiang Mei and her baby. I'm sure of that."

"I was scared to death. I started out in a daze, but Old Fart Zhao called me back. He hurriedly handed me your hat and told me to return it to you and tell you that you'd left it where you two had wrestled. I forgot to tell you when I got back. I just wrapped the baby in it; he was still covered with blood. I wanted to wait until I was on my deathbed before telling you all this because I was afraid you wouldn't be able to take it. But at the same time, if I didn't tell you, I'd feel bad, too. Maybe I shouldn't have told you at all. What do you think?'

"Second Dog, you should have told me earlier. Don't cry. It's hard to watch a man cry. I beg you, please don't cry, don't cry."

When he died, I was by his side. Cancer is terrible. He had always been small, but by then he was nothing but skin and bones. He was cremated, and his mother kept his ashes.

11

I'm sure that when Old Fart Zhao heard that Jiang Mei had a baby that night, he thought about Zhang Lan, his little widow. But after Zhang Lan died, where did he go?

Lanterns for the Dead

冥 灯[1]

Jiang Yun

一

范西林来这座小城，是为了看黄河。

这城紧靠黄河边上，有些寂寥，大河上游的小城通常总给人一种寂寥的感觉。范西林这一伙人，热热闹闹来了，来开一个可开可不开的萧条的会。不想，萧条的会却开得挺红火，城中最阔气的宾馆楼上，扯起巨幅横标，欢迎某某会议在我县隆重召开，范西林初见了，竟有些受宠若惊的感觉。

城却照旧是苍茫寂寥的。

晚饭后，有人喊范西林，说，看黄河去。范西林就去了。几步远的地方，有一条土路，大家在土路上橐橐地走，就有人唱起《一无所有》[2]这一首歌来。很快地，窜出三条稀脏的狗，一黑，一黄，还有一条不黑也不黄的，挡在这一群人中间，汪汪地叫。范西林尖叫一声，朝人身后直躲。狗很得意。人群中有人就笑，说道，"范西林，做小姐状!"一边大声地斥狗。大多的人，却是不怕狗的，昂扬地过去了，范西林也跟着溜过去，回头看，狗在土路上落寞地摇着尾巴。

范西林再次转过头的时候，一道旧城门，静寂地，画一样画在有着夕阳余辉的苍老的天上。人群向画中走去，人的背影看上去有些荒凉。范西林知道，城门那边，就是黄河了，范西林在这时候闻到了这条大河的气息。

范西林不是第一次见到一条大河。

1

Fan Xilin came to this small town to see the Yellow River. The town sat right on the Yellow River and was filled with a somewhat desolate air, like so many small towns on the upper reaches of the big river. She was part of a group that had come, lively and full of excitement, to hold a dull and unessential meeting there. However, the dull meeting wasn't so dull. Fan Xilin was overwhelmed when she first saw the huge horizontal banner proclaiming, "Welcome, Conference Participants," which was hanging high on the plushest guesthouse in town.

But still the town was pretty desolate.

After dinner, someone called to Fan Xilin to go see the Yellow River. She went. Not far away was a dirt road. As they walked, their leather shoes clacking on the road, someone started singing "I Walk This Road Alone." Then three dirty dogs—one black, one yellow, and one in between—suddenly appeared and blocked their way, barking at them. Fan Xilin screamed and tried to hide behind someone else. Seeing that the dogs meant no harm, someone laughed and said, "Fan Xilin is acting like a little girl!" as they drove the dogs away. Most of the group were not afraid of the dogs, and walked by them in high spirits. Fan Xilin followed, slipping by. She looked back and saw the dogs dismally wagging their tails on the dirt road.

When Fan Xilin looked ahead again, she saw an ancient city gate, silent as a painting done on the aged sky, where the afterglow of sunset lingered. The group entered the painting; from behind, they looked somewhat bleak and desolate. The Yellow River was on the other side of the city gate. It was then that Fan Xilin smelled the breath of the big river.

This wasn't the first time that Fan Xilin had seen a big river.

第一次见到一条大河，是在很久以前。那河叫长江。范西林在江边等轮渡。和范西林同行的会议上的人们远远看着范西林走到江边去。江水打湿了她的鞋袜，她的脚丫被卷上来的温暖的江水淹没。这是长江，范西林想，范西林仅仅这样想着眼睛便潮湿了。

范西林是个北方人。

范西林后来常常想起看到长江的这个早晨。汽车在薄雾中爬一道长长的斜坡时范西林就感到了激动。没人暗示什么，但范西林知道坡的尽头就是长江，范西林闻到了长江的气息。长江辽远成熟的江面在刚一出现的瞬间便感动了这个北方姑娘。

她在江边站了很久。她远远看见江对岸有洗衣服的女孩儿。她还看见了轮渡和一座城市。后来有人叫范西林去吃东西，范西林就去了，是江边一所极小的茅屋，门扉两边贴着被江风和雨洗旧的对联，上面写着吉祥如意的话，"生意兴隆通四海，财源茂盛达三江"。范西林在这小店里吃了热的油炸臭豆腐。

小店是座无名的小店，渡口却有名字，叫做裕溪口。

那时，范西林想，"裕溪"是一个很好听的名字，"裕溪"就是一条大水。

一座戏台，搭在高高的河岸，脚下是河水，对面是河神庙。那庙，早已破败到荒芜的程度。这个夏天多雨，雨水使野草们长得丰肥。夕阳将落未落，对岸内蒙古的山峦上，天血红血红，红得极凄伤，叫人想起许多伤感的事情。

The first time she saw a big river was a long time ago. The big river then was the Yangtze, and Fan Xilin was on the riverbank, waiting for a steam ferry. The people traveling with her watched her from afar as she walk toward the riverbank. The warm water soaked her socks and shoes as it rolled toward her, covering her feet. *This is the Yangtze River,* thought Fan Xilin, and her eyes grew moist at once.

Fan Xilin was a northerner.

Later, Fan Xilin often recalled that morning she saw the Yangtze River. She was excited as the car drove up a long slope in the mist. No one said anything, but Fan Xilin knew that at the end of the slope was the Yangtze River. She could smell its breath. She, a girl from the north, was moved the moment she saw the vast old surface of the Yangtze River.

She stood on the banks for a long time, looking toward the distant shore. She could see girls washing clothes, the steam ferry, and a city. Later, she was called to go eat in a restaurant with a thatched roof beside the river. An auspicious couplet, weathered by wind and rain, was pasted on either side of the restaurant door. It read: "A thriving business extends to the four seas / the source of income runs in three rivers." Fan Xilin had hot deep-fried stinky tofu in that small restaurant.

The small restaurant had no name, but the ferry did; it was called Yuxi Kou.

At the time, Fan Xilin thought that Yuxi was a good name—it means big stream.

A stage was erected on the high riverbank; at its foot, the river. The stage faced the Temple of the River God, which was dilapidated, having gone to waste. There had been a lot of rain that summer, and the grass grew lush. The sun was on the verge of setting and the sky above the mountains of Inner Mongolia across the river was blood red. It was a tragic color that made people think of all sorts of sad things.

黄河流着。

人们默不作声，嗅着腥的水汽。黄河在这里拐了一个大大的弯。斜对岸那个远的小村，叫马栅，马栅再朝西，就是陕北了，这是一个鸡鸣三省的地方。

大家拣一条深的草径，爬上戏台，临风眺望，做沉思状。水声很近，又很遥远，空冥地流到一个人所不知的地方。湿的水汽，人粪和狗粪的臭气，在岸上苍茫地飘散。范西林想，河很孤独。

有人蹲在岸边，也不抽烟，也不说话，只是看着河水。那人是本地人，本地的汉子。不是本地人的范西林们，觉得那汉子蹲在那里，又诗意又突兀。还有一首流行歌曲，从他们身后不知哪所民居里，抑或是别的什么地方，断断续续飘扬出来，迟志强[3]在那里忧伤地唱着关于窝窝头和监狱的歌。

范西林又想，河很孤独。

对岸天的颜色，淡了下来，渐渐变成一派苍青。蚊子忽然间变得猖獗。大家开始拍臀打腿，再也不能保持凝神肃穆的那份深沉。坚持了一会儿，就有人说，回吧回吧。大家就说，回吧回吧。于是，就沿了旧路，择草径橐橐地走回去，一边谈些感受之类。他们经过一条狭巷时，这巷里有一家人家，正在打夜工做一口白茬的棺材。

范西林想，明天，还来看河。范西林这么想着的时候，黄河在他们身后，依旧空冥地流向前去。

巷里的那家人家，点一盏马灯，打夜工在做一口白茬的柳木

The Yellow River was flowing.

In silence, they breathed in the fishy smell of the water. Here there was a big bend in the Yellow River. Diagonally across the river, on the opposite shore, was the small village of Mashan; farther west lay the northern part of Shanxi Province. From here, a cock's crow could be heard in three provinces.

They chose a deep grassy path up to the stage. Facing the wind, they stood lost in thought. The flowing water sounded close by but also distant, flowing empty and darkly into the unknown. Dampness and the smell of human excrement and dog shit wafted boundlessly over the riverside. *The river is very lonely,* thought Fan Xilin.

Someone squatted by the river. He wasn't smoking or talking; he was just looking at the water. He was a local man. To someone like Fan Xilin, who was from elsewhere, the man squatting there was both poetic and lofty. A popular song floated on the air from a house behind them, or from some other place. It was a sad song about steamed corn bread and jail, as sung sadly by Chi Zhiqiang.

The river is very lonely, thought Fan Xilin again.

The sky opposite grew paler, gradually turning an ashen blue. As hordes of mosquitoes appeared, the people there started patting their arms and legs to drive them away and were unable to maintain their solemn reserve and focused concentration. They persisted in staying there for some time, until someone suggested they return. So they slowly returned along the same grassy path while talking about what they felt. Passing a narrow alley, they saw a house where the whole family was working at night to build a coffin of white, unfinished willow wood.

Tomorrow, I'll come to see the river again, thought Fan Xilin. Behind them, the Yellow River flowed on, empty and dark.

The family in the alley lit a lantern by which to work on the white, unfinished willow-wood coffin. All night long the neighbors could hear the sound of wood being planed. The following morning,

棺材。左邻右舍，彻夜听见了"嚓嚓嚓"刨木头的响动。到早晨，出来倒尿盆的女人和挑了空桶去担水的汉子，均闻到了被一夜水声打湿的那一股刨花的清香。

二

一条十字路，北向，出城，就上了公路。公路颠簸不平，两边是树。再一拐，缓缓岔出一条土路来，两边也有树。树是杨树，硕大的杨树叶在阳光里明晃晃闪动出一片白炽。又有一蓬蓬的灌木，紫穗槐一类，密匝匝封起一堵荆墙。小孩儿们从不到这里割草、放羊。大人总是说，"不敢到坡上去。"大人们把这里叫做坡上。

春天，坡上死了一个女人，是被枪毙的。女人是杀人犯，毒死了自己男人，坡上就做了法场。死前，女人想不通，哭了一夜，到早晨，不再哭了，说，"我想通了。"还梳了头。

女人只有十八岁。

总之，坡上总有事情。

三

会议开始不久，范西林和琼，就溜出了会场。

琼到过这里。琼曾经独自从这里过黄河到内蒙去。琼是一个有经历的女人，江湖上的女人，琼穿一件绿色时尚的上衣，那绿很漂亮。

琼说，河的气味很重。

the women who took out the chamber pots to empty them of urine and the men who took empty buckets to fetch water could smell the fragrance of the wood shavings dampened by a night of moisture.

2

They drove north from the crossroad to the edge of town and onto the highway. The bumpy highway was lined with trees on both sides. Turning off, they went down a dirt road, which was also lined with trees, poplar trees. In the sunlight, the large poplar leaves shimmered, forming a burning white patch, and there were clumps of bushes, probably false indigo, whose tightly interwoven branches formed a wall. The children never came here to cut grass or herd sheep. The adults called the place Upper Slope. They were always going on about how they "don't dare go to Upper Slope."

A woman had been shot at Upper Slope last spring. She was a murderer who had poisoned her husband, and Upper Slope was used as the execution ground. Before she died, she was irrational and cried all night long. In the morning she stopped crying and said, "I understand." She even brushed her hair.

The woman was only eighteen years old.

In short, things were always happening at Upper Slope.

3

Fan Xilin and Qiong sneaked out of the meeting shortly after it began.

Qiong had been here before. She had once crossed the Yellow River alone to Inner Mongolia. She had been all over the country. Qiong was wearing a fashionable green top; it was a very attractive green.

The river smells, said Qiong.

琼从这里渡黄河的时候，还很年轻。琼是一个人过河去的。琼压根儿不知道渡河去干什么。她在河边小旅馆里过夜，就想，河的气味很重，像男人的身体。

琼很健康，看上去，绿色的身体就像一棵漂亮的青菜。范西林走在琼的身边，就感到了一种从里向外的枯槁。琼这样的女人就像高原，无论什么人，只要一登上高原，就总是缺氧。

这时，她们刚好站在一个类似十字街口的地方，琼说，我们沿这条街走。琼说这句话的时候有一点意味深长。

就沿这条街走了。范西林不知道琼在拉她走进一个故事。这是一条商业街，一家一家门面，冷冷清清，生意做得萧条，却又分明觉出，人很不安。所有的人，都在等待着一桩事情发生。门市里没有生意可做，大家都在等待着一桩事情发生。孩子们沿着马路朝前跑，马路上有新鲜的牲畜的粪便。人人都很不安，又都很兴奋。

孩子们喊着，来了，来了。

这时就听到了远处高音喇叭的声音。这声音很突兀，没有一点准备和酝酿，就响了起来。整个小城就像一口钟，嗡地一声变得生动。人们开始朝前跑，前边是十字街，人们朝那里跑去，不光是小孩，连同大人和老人。大家气喘吁吁跑着，说，来了，来了。

来了摩托车，横穿十字街。又来了吉普车，不止一辆，也横穿十字街。人们开始拥挤。喇叭声从最前面的吉普车中传出，人们说，来了，来了。这时就看到了他。

他站在军用卡车上，双手反剪，插长长的亡命牌。

Qiong was very young when she crossed the river here by herself. She didn't have any idea what she was going to do after making the crossing. She stayed overnight in a small riverside hotel and thought the river was very smelly, like a man's body.

Qiong glowed with health. All in green, she looked like a beautiful green vegetable. Fan Xilin, who walked next to her, felt a withering from the inside out. As a woman, Qiong was like a high-altitude plain; anyone who climbed up felt short of breath.

Standing on the corner of something like an intersection, Qiong said, let's walk down this street. Her words seemed to imply something.

They walked down the street. Fan Xilin didn't realize that Qiong was leading her into a story. It was a commercial street, with shop after cheerless shop. Business was bad, and a feeling of uneasiness prevailed. The people were obviously restless, and seemed to be waiting for something to occur. Children ran on the street, where piles of fresh dog shit could be seen. Everyone was restless, but excited, too.

"He's coming, he's coming," shouted the children.

At once a high-pitched horn was heard from far off. There wasn't a moment to prepare or think. Like clockwork, the whole city became alive with a buzz. People ran toward the intersection; children, adults, and the old people ran, saying, "He's coming, he's coming."

Motorcycles passed through the intersection. Then the jeeps passed through the intersection without stopping. A crowd formed. The horn blared from the first jeep, and the people kept saying, He's coming, he's coming. At that moment they saw him.

He stood on the military truck. Both hands were tied behind his back where a placard bearing the word *criminal* was inserted.

若干年前，在浩劫的年代，发生过一起暴乱事件。暴乱者是一伙村民。村民们在一天深夜里，手执火把，聚集在村头崖边那一座灰砖到顶的天主堂前，十里八村的乡民们，在同一时刻翻沟越涧，举了火把聚集在这里，几千乡民望着弥撒。几千张沟壑纵横的乡民的脸，映了火光，高喊着"阿门"，几千个乡民高喊着"阿门"忽喇喇跪倒一片。那真是一个迷狂壮观的弥撒，穿破旧法衣的神父，在几千乡民的头上，挥舞着十字架。几千只火把照出了一个更深邃的黑夜。

神父说，"阿门!"

多年来范西林逃不出这个有火把的神秘的夜晚。这事有点奇怪。范西林一向不是个想象力丰富的人，范西林总是在逃出故事，却终究没有逃出这个有火把的望弥撒的黑夜。发生那事的时候，范西林还很小，小孩子范西林始终不知道那天夜里发生了什么，就是现在，早已长大成人的范西林也仍然不知道那天夜晚发生了什么，那本来是一个完全于她无关的黑夜，但是有一天，范西林无所事事地走在街上，遇到了示众的死囚，她就无可选择地落入到了那个黑夜中来。

那是她第一次看到一个死囚。那时她还是一个爱清洁的小姑娘，忘了是什么原因使她混在了人群里，囚车浩浩荡荡开过来，很缓慢，很冷。刮着风。她被看热闹的人群挤在了最前面，她年轻的小身子滑腻腻就像一条鱼。马路很窄，囚车几乎是擦着她的鼻尖开过，五花大绑的死囚，就屹立在她乌黑的头顶。死囚是一个男人，看不出年岁，胸前的牌子上，写出了他同那次暴乱那个

Some years ago, during the time of the great catastrophe, a riot occurred. The rioters were a group of villagers from eight villages in a ten-*li* area. They tramped over ravines and gullies, torches in hand, to assemble at midnight in front of the gray brick Catholic church at the head of the village by the cliff. Several thousand villagers attended Mass, their furrowed faces shining in the firelight; several thousand villagers shouted, "Amen," and fell to their knees in unison. The Mass was a fantastic and magnificent sight. The priest, who was dressed in old and shabby vestments, wielded a cross high above the heads of the several thousand villagers. Several thousand torches illumined a deeper night.

"Amen," intoned the priest.

For many years, Fan Xilin had been unable to escape from that mysterious night of torches. It was a bit strange, because she was not the imaginative type. Fan Xilin always fled from stories; however, she could never escape from that torch-lit Mass that dark night. It had happened when she was little, and she never knew what was going on that night; even now, as an adult, she still didn't know what had happened that night. It was a night that had nothing to do with her, but one day, when she was idling away her time in the street and saw a convict who had been sentenced being paraded in public, she fell back into that night without choice.

That was the first time she saw a convict who had been sentenced to death. At the time, she was still a little girl with a morbid preoccupation with cleanliness, and for some reason she couldn't remember, she was part of the crowd. The prison van drove by in a formidable array, slowly and coldly. The wind was blowing. She was squeezed, like a slippery fish, to the very front by the crowd watching the excitement. The road was very narrow; the passing prison van almost brushed her nose, and the convict, who was trussed up tightly, stood right above her dark-haired head. The convict who had been sentenced to death was male, but she was unable to tell his age. At his chest hung a placard on which was written his part in the riot on that night.

黑夜的关系，一根细的铁丝紧紧勒在死囚张开的嘴里。她看着，她生平第一次看到了她永远无法洞悉的东西，那东西从本来极遥远的地方向她逼近。她知道完了。这时有一团污秽的血水，从死囚洞开的嘴里，滴落下来，落在她脚边，如同一个祈祷。

人们说，来了，来了。

车上站满了兵，枪口对外，荷枪实弹，押解着一个他。他很矮小，头发的样式很可笑。他站在车上，左顾右盼。前边的人说，来了，来了，他忽然扭头朝人群中一个谁点头打了个招呼。他扭过头来，那可笑的头发就像一蓬草似地刷地一摆。

人群跑起来，范西林也跟着跑，琼也跑。范西林跑起来很可笑，踉踉跄跄就像一只刚落窝的母鸡。琼跑得很快，琼身体极其敏捷。琼和范西林追赶着那束飘扬的头发，好像那是命中注定的一个什么召唤。她们看到了他的头发草似的刷地一摆，这总有些古怪，有些不合情理，有些神秘。太阳那么好，太阳照耀着城外的黄河，太阳也照耀着成百上千看热闹的人群和这个有着草似的头发的小个子男子汉。

兵的电警棍，几乎捅到了范西林身上，范西林面色灰白。兵用电警棍向两边驱赶着看热闹的人群。琼叫道，"范西林！"琼不知什么时候停在了一辆绿色老式吉普车旁，琼说，"上来上来！"范西林就懵懵懂懂一头钻到了车里。

前排车座上的男人，扭头和琼说话，男人说，"昨晚上说了，

His mouth was tightly bridled with a thin metal wire. She watched. The first time in her life she saw something that came from very far and that she would never understand clearly. She knew it was over. A dirty clot of blood fell from the prisoner's mouth and landed at her feet, like a prayer.

"He's coming, he's coming," said the people.

The truck was filled with standing soldiers, their guns loaded with live ammunition and muzzles facing outward while they escorted a solitary individual. He was very short, and his hair looked funny; he stood in the truck and glanced right and left. "He's coming, he's coming," said the crowd in front. He suddenly turned his head to one of the people in the crowd and nodded a sign of greeting. Then he turned back, his funny hair blowing like a clump of grass.

The crowd started running. Fan Xilin followed at a run, as did Qiong. Fan Xilin looked funny when she ran, stumbling like a hen that had just fallen out of the nest. Qiong was light on her feet and ran very fast. They chased that shock of hair fluttering in the air as if it were fate calling. Both of them saw his hair, like a clump of grass, sweeping in the wind. It was a bit odd, unreasonable, and mysterious. The wonderful sun shone on the Yellow River just outside of town; it also shone on the thousands of people who watched the excitement, and on the short guy whose hair was like a clump of grass.

The soldiers' electric batons almost touched Fan Xilin. Her face turned pale. The soldiers used electronic batons to drive away the crowd on both sides. "Fan Xilin!" Having stopped beside a green jeep at some point, Qiong called out to her, "Get in! Get in!" Fan Xilin got into the jeep without thinking.

The man in the front seat turned his head and spoke to Qiong, "Last night I told you to come, but you didn't." "Last night was last

叫你来，你不来。"琼回答，"昨晚是昨晚，今天是今天，昨晚怎么知道今天的事?"琼看上去泰然自若又理直气壮。琼无论走到什么地方都能够碰到熟人，哪怕走到非洲，走到纽约，或者是火星上都一样。琼的理想是做一个江湖上的女侠客。

琼说，"这是范西林。"又说，"这是老某。"范西林便向老某点点头，却没听清老某到底姓什么。老某很客气，问，"怕不怕?"范西林没回答。老某笑了，老某说，"搞艺术的嘛，啥都该体验体验嘛。"老某这么说的时候实在是很洒脱。

琼说，"不错。"

老某就讲了关于那个女人的故事。

女人有个好听的名字，女人叫杏花。女人说生她的时候坡上的杏花已经落了，娘却说，就叫杏花吧。杏花家对面的山坡上，有五六棵细瘦的山杏树。

枪毙杏花那天，全城的人都跑来看热闹。杏花仔细梳好了头。杏花梳好了头，竟还真有几分姿色。杏花说，我想通了。

其实杏花哭了一夜。据同住的两名犯人说，杏花一夜不停地哭，不停地说，孩子气地絮絮叨叨。杏花说她本来不想杀人，只想自杀，投河上吊吞洋钉，却总也死不成。杏花自己死不成，就毒死了买她来却又总是做践她的男人。

杏花孩子气地絮絮叨叨说道，"早也是死，晚也是死，为啥不让我早死?"

但是到早晨，天亮的时候，法警来带她，她说，"我想通了。"

night, today is today. How could anyone foresee last night what was going to happen today?" she replied with calm assurance. No matter where she went she ran into people she knew, even in Africa or New York, and most likely even on Mars. Qiong's ideal was to be a woman knight-errant traveling to all corners of the world.

Qiong said, "This is Fan Xilin," and continued, "This is Old Mou." Fan Xilin nodded to Old Mou, but didn't catch his last name. Old Mou politely asked her, "Are you scared?" Fan Xilin didn't answer. "You're an artist; you should experience everything." Old Mou laughed and spoke in a carefree manner.

"That's right," said Qiong.

Old Mou then told them the woman's story.

The woman was called Apricot Blossom, a pleasant-sounding name. She said that when she was born the blossoms on the apricot trees on the mountain slope had already fallen, but her mother said, So let's call her Apricot Blossom. There were five or six apricot trees on the mountain opposite Apricot Blossom's house.

The day Apricot Blossom was executed, everyone from the town came to watch. Apricot Blossom carefully brushed her hair. After having brushed her hair, she actually looked pretty. She said, I understand now.

According to her two cellmates, Apricot Blossom actually cried the whole night, she cried and cried and at the same time babbled endlessly like a child. She said she didn't mean to kill him; she only wanted to commit suicide. She tried to jump into the river, hang herself, and swallow iron nails, but never succeeded in doing herself in. Since she couldn't kill herself, she decided to poison the man who bought her but often disparaged her.

She kept repeating, "We all die sooner or later. Why can't I die sooner?"

However, at daybreak the next morning, when the bailiff came to get her, she said, "I understand now."

谁也不知道她想通了什么。她压根儿没时间去想。她却说，"我想通了。"她说完这句话后忽然变得很沉静。她几乎是在瞬间完成了一个蜕变。所有将要继续活下去的人，永远无从知道杏花在早晨清澈的阳光中想通了什么。

那次也是老某监法场，老某说，那次活儿干的不漂亮，三枪才完事。

汽车拐弯的时候，范西林忽然失落了方向感。她不知汽车是朝北还是朝南开。公路很温暖，玉米叶子上顶着极饱满的阳光。车猛然加速了，先是摩托，后是吉普，再后来是军用卡车。车猛一加速的瞬间，他泰然自若的脸刷地一白。他的脸终于白到了不再像一个真人。许多的车轮，碾起了灰尘，灰尘裹住了那一束可笑的脆弱的头发。太阳很亮，亮得有些神经质。

听不见河水声。

这时范西林忽然觉出，他很像她的一个熟人。

琼说，"所有要死的人看上去都很面熟。"

小城的人，骑自行车，涌向法场。所有的门市，这一上午都没有什么生意可做。

老某说，到了。车就嘎地停下。眼前一暗。杨树和灌木和草，绿成极繁茂幽深的一片，毫无鬼气和凶气，不空旷，也不荒凉。琼以为车停错了地方。早有人侯在了这里，等着看热闹。兵们整肃

Nobody understood what she had come to understand. She had no time to think about it, but she blurted out, "I understand now." After saying this, she sank into silence, completely transformed in the blink of an eye. Not one of those who went on living ever understood what Apricot Blossom had come to understand in the limpid morning sunshine.

It was Old Mou who was in charge of the execution ground that time. He said it was a bad job and took three shots to finish.

When the jeep turned, Fan Xilin suddenly lost her sense of direction. She couldn't tell if the jeep was heading north or south. The highway was very warm; the corn leaves were full of sunlight. They suddenly sped up, first the motorcycles, then the jeeps, and last the military trucks. The moment they sped up, the condemned man's face turned white, so white that he didn't look like a real person. The dust raised by the wheels enwrapped his funny shock of hair. The sunshine shone with a quickening brightness.

The sound of the river couldn't be heard.

At that moment, Fan Xilin suddenly felt that he looked like an acquaintance of hers.

"All of those who are about to die look familiar," said Qiong.

Riding bicycles, the people of the small town poured onto the execution ground. Not one shop had any business to do that morning.

"Here we are," said Old Mou, as the car stopped. For a moment they found themselves in the dark, in a place of luxuriant poplar trees, bushes, and overgrown grass. The place was completely devoid of any gloomy or clammy feeling; it wasn't exactly an open space, nor was it desolate. Qiong thought they had stopped in the wrong place, but people were already there waiting to see the excitement. The soldiers

地跳下车，刷地散开来，拉起警戒线，将人群拦在路的一边。路
极窄，宽不多三米，三米之外草窝中就是行刑的地方。范西林和
琼，竟被允许站在警戒线的里侧，人群里就有人极羡慕地瞅着这
两个女人。兵用电警棍维持着秩序，却仍是嗡嗡挤挤地乱。押下
来了他。范西林睁大了眼睛，却没看清他是怎样跳下抑或是被拖
下那具卡车。兵整肃地迅疾地推他走向那一块草窝中去。紫穗槐
开着花，也许不是紫穗槐，蓬乱的一丛一丛，似乎早已过了植物
开花的节令。他白着脸自己走向草窝，太阳很好地照着，人群中
一阵骚乱。又一队兵，刷刷从范西林身边迅疾地跑过，持着枪。
他在草窝中跪下，背影挺小，像舞台上一个演戏的做作的小孩儿。
这时范西林猛然背转身去，就有差不多一万片金晃晃的树叶，翻
卷着，金晃晃向她扑来。

　　琼很冷静。琼青葱的身体看上去像一棵青菜。

　　枪响了。很突兀，很平淡，闷头闷脑，谈不上清脆，更谈不
上响亮，极短促的一声，听上去远不如婚礼或者是"开业大吉"
之类的庆典上，那一声二踢脚来得漂亮。枪声落地，突然间就有
了瞬间的静寂。静寂从一切地方，从阳光、天空，从树、草、灌
木丛和地心的深处，悄悄漫出来，仁慈地淹没了活着和不再活着
的生命。

　　只一会儿，兵们就又刷刷地迅疾地跑回去，跑向军用卡车。
行刑的兵，戴上了一副遮光墨镜，刷刷跑着，突然脚底像被石子
一绊似的，打个趔趄，后面的人扶住他，托他爬上卡车。

　　警戒撤了，人群从公路那边呼啦拥过来，包围了草里的
死人。

jumped stiffly out of the vehicles and formed a security line to hold back the crowd to one side. The road was narrow, less than nine meters wide, and beyond it, in a nest of grass, was the place where the death sentence was to be carried out. Fan Xilin and Qiong stood inside the security line, which made those outside stare at them with envy. The soldiers used electric batons to keep the order, but even so, it was still all chaos. The prisoner was escorted down. Her eyes wide open, Fan Xilin didn't see if he jumped down or was dragged down from the truck. The soldiers quickly and stiffly pushed him toward the grassy ground. Clumps of false indigo—or perhaps they weren't false indigo—were blooming, seemingly long after the flowering season had passed. Face pale, the man walked toward the grassy ground, the sun shining brightly. The crowd created a disturbance. A group of soldiers holding guns hastily ran past Fan Xilin. The man knelt down on the grass. Viewed from behind, he looked small, like a boy performing onstage. At that moment, Fan Xilin turned around and felt ten thousand shining golden leaves flutter, rush at her.

Qiong was calm. All in green, she looked like a beautiful green vegetable.

The gun fired. The sudden, short, and muffled sound was nothing special, not even as clear and sharp as double-exploding firecrackers set off at weddings or grand-opening ceremonies. Following right after the gunshot was a moment of silence. The silence slowly seeped out from everywhere, from the sunshine, the sky, the trees, the grass, and bushes, and from deep in the earth, kindly drowning the lives of the living and the dead.

Shortly, the soldiers hastily ran back toward the truck. The soldier who had carried out the sentence ran hastily but suddenly stumbled as if he had tripped over a stone. The person behind him caught him and helped him climb into the truck.

The guards dispersed. From the other side of the road, the crowd swarmed over in a flap and surrounded the dead man lying in the grass.

老某说:"今天的活儿干得利索。"

狗冲着人群狂吠,狗很兴奋,摇着一根孤独的尾巴,狗是一条野狗。灌木被人群踩倒一大片,都是一些叫不出名字的植物。只有割草的孩子认识它们,割草的孩子会说,"这是苍耳","这是紫荆"。但是割草的孩子却不上这儿来。大人总是说,"不敢到坡上去。"大人总是用"坡上"来吓唬他们,所以,坡上的植物长得极肥美丰茂。

太阳升高了,老式的北京吉普就跑得有些慵懒。路面很白,路上,有一个汉子,拉一辆平车,弓腰驼背,马一样朝坡上去。车上有一具新鲜的柳木棺材,白茬,没有上漆,于是就存有夜风和马灯的气味。一路上,人们都闻到了这一股清香又凄苦的棺材的味道。

四

晚上,县里的剧团,来给会议上的人们演"二人台"。

晚饭有酒,菜也丰盛,当中一盆气锅鸡冒出罐头的气味。酒是白的,北方烧,还有地方上的特产,海红泡制的一种饮料,颜色浓郁美丽。

琼喝酒。琼和男人们一次一次碰杯。琼有一股杀气。琼掩藏着她内心的巨大的困扰,琼说,"干!"琼想说的其实不是这个,

"The job was done neatly today," said Old Mou.

A stray dog kept barking at the crowd, its tail wagging in excitement. The crowd trampled flat a great patch of the plants, the names of which were unknown. Only the kids who cut the grass knew what they were called. The kids would point and say, "This one is Siberian cocklebur, and this one is Chinese redbud." But the kids never came here. "The kids don't dare come to Upper Slope," said the adults. The adults often used "Upper Slope" to scare the kids. Therefore the plants at Upper Slope were beautiful and luxuriant.

The sun was high overhead and the old Beijing jeep went slow. The surface of the road was white, and a man was bent pulling a flatbed cart toward Upper Slope. A new unfinished willow-wood coffin sat in the cart. It gave off nothing but the night breeze and the barn lantern. Along the road, people smelled the delicate and dreary fragrance of the coffin.

4

The county theatrical company came to perform a popular Inner Mongolian song-and-dance duet for the conference participants that evening.

There was wine with dinner and many good dishes, among them a pot of steamed chicken that smelled canned. The wine was from the north and strong. There was also some local produce, a kind of beverage made from mussels, thick and beautiful.

Qiong drank wine. She clinked glasses with the men many times. Qiong was furious, but she kept her trouble pent up inside. "Bottoms up!" she said. But that wasn't what she really wanted to say.

琼只是看见枪响的那一瞬间，他的头发竟那样奇怪地四散飘扬，像蒲公英。琼斜视着范西林。

范西林喝着果汁，很渴的样子，范西林像个老人一样将那浓郁的东西吞咽下去。有人一生下来就老了，范西林就是这样。琼深知范西林将永远逃不出对于枯槁的恐惧。

晚饭后，他们又看河去了。他们甚至还坐了船。木船载着他们，逆水而上，马达突突突地嘶吼。这时他们看见了落日。落日如血，河变得悲壮。大家寂然无语。船靠近一座小岛，岛叫娘娘滩，有人在滩边下钩打鱼。琼第一个跳到滩上去，惊起了草丛中大约一万只蚊子。他们在滩上草丛中呆站一会儿，落日忽然没有了颜色。

就又顺流而下。

回来的时候，"二人台"正演到高潮。这晚演出的是一折叫做《捏软糕》的旧戏。戏中男女，一式短打扮，男人脸搽得很白，唱到高亢处就用假声。台上男女，极欢快地做挑水、淘米、磨面状，男的唱道：

"二妹妹你把那，你把那米来淘呀。"

女的就唱：

"三哥哥我给你，捏呀么捏软糕呀。"

非常的小康，叫人觉得，活着是那样单纯，那样有滋有味，那样地久天长。但是那曲调，却是高亢、悲壮、荒凉到无可奈何的地步，荒凉到无以诉说，荒凉到像是从空无中流来的那一条大河。

When the gun fired, Qiong had seen nothing but the man's hair flying strangely in all directions like dandelion fluff. She cast a sidelong glance at Fan Xilin.

Fan Xilin drank fruit juice and looked very thirsty the way she quaffed the thick stuff like an old man. Some people were born old; that was the case with Fan Xilin. Qiong knew very well that Fan Xilin would never escape the fear of withering up.

After dinner they went once again to see the river. They even took a boat, its motor roaring as it traveled upstream against the current. They watched the sun set. The sunset looked like blood, and the river turned solemn and stirring. Nobody spoke until the boat neared a small island named Niangniang Shoal. Someone was fishing by the shoal with a fishing pole. Qiong was the first to jump to the shoal and disturbed thousands of mosquitoes in the brush. They stood blank there for a while. The setting sun soon faded.

Then they took the boat back downstream with the current.

When they got back, the "Inner Mongolian song-and-dance duet" was reaching its climax. They performed *Kneading a Soft Cake* that night. It was an old play in which the man and woman were dressed in Chinese-style jackets and trousers. The man's face was very white and he sang falsetto at the resounding places. The man and woman onstage joyfully carried water, washed rice, ground flour.

"Sister Er, would you go wash the rice," sang the man.

"Brother San, I'm going to knead a soft cake for you," sang the woman.

The life depicted in the drama was good, and gave the impression of being pure and simple, everlasting and enjoyable. But the tunes were high-pitched, moving, tragic, and dreary to the extent that it made one feel helpless and unable to say anything, just like that huge river flowing out of nowhere.

五

翌日，农历七月十五，鬼节，依照古俗，地方上放了河灯。河灯，是放来祭河神、祭亡灵的。人们吵吵嚷嚷、红红火火，却又极庄重地做着这桩事情。人们喊道："放——灯——啰——"，于是，纸的灯，顺黄河一路而下，黑的河面上，起伏出一星一点的温暖和眩惑，极美丽地，在永远无法穿越的黑暗中，灭亡。

杏花说，我想通了。杏花说完这句话，沉静地看着自己的头发如蒲公英般四散飘飞。

5

The next day was the Ghost Festival, the fifteenth day of the seventh month on the Chinese lunar calendar. According to ancient custom, the local people put water lanterns in the river as offerings to the River God and the dead souls. The show was raucous, but it was performed very seriously. They shouted, "Put the lanterns in ah . . . " Then the paper lanterns sailed downstream on the current of Yellow River. On the black surface of the water the lanterns rose and fell, starlike points of warmth and confusion, and with great beauty, vanished in that eternally impenetrable darkness.

I understand now, said Apricot Blossom. As soon as she uttered these words, she calmly watched her hair fly in all directions like dandelion fluff.

Greasy Moon

油 月 亮

Jia Pingwa

尤佚人一出审讯室便大觉后悔话不该那么说。七月的天气已经炎热，湿漉漉的手一按在椅子上就出现五个指印。三年前的公园条椅上起身走去了一对极厌恶他的男女，女人做过的地方就有一个湿漉漉的圈。他以为发现了一种秘密。"尤佚人!"审讯员猛地叫了他的名字。"嗯。"他应着，立即就又说："有!""你杀了人吗?""杀了。""杀了几个人?""这怎么记得，谁还记数吗?"一个，两个……有位是胖妇人，腰碌碡般粗搂不住，两颗大奶头耷拉下来一直到了腰裤带的。下雨天来的一男一女，不是父女，也绝不会是夫妻……臭男人本该早死去却去上了茅房了。女子就先死。男人回来一下没有死，还一脚踹在他的交裆处……但最后也是死了。女子白脸子，真好。尤佚人扳着指头搜寻起记忆，便发现审讯员脸色全白，立即被又一种记忆打断，将湿漉漉的手垂下来懊丧起说过的话。虽然那系一派真诚。"八个。"他懦懦地说。

河水构成一条银带，款款地在前面伸展；贴着已经裂脱而去了生命的知了壳的白杨，绿柳，急速地向后倒去。炎炎的红日真是有油的，汗全然变成珠子顺鼻尖滑，腻腻的。浴在这灼灼的烈日，看着不知何时从山梁的那边出现的寺院山门，以古柏古松浮云般的叶浸沉在袅袅的钟声，就这样，尤佚人和两名武装的刑警坐了三轮摩托，溯着汉江往瘪家沟去。

对于女人的生殖器，乡下人有着乡土叫法，简单到一个音，×，名字很不中听。所以又以另一个音代替，但这音没有文字写

You Yiren regretted what he had said as soon as he came out of the courtroom. The weather of July was already hot. The moment his clammy hand touched the chair, he left five fingerprints. Three years before, in a park, a man and a woman who were disgusted with him got up from the bench. A moist ring was left where the woman had been sitting. He thought he had discovered a secret. "You Yiren!" The judge suddenly called out his name. "Yeah," he replied, and immediately responded with, "Present!" "Did you kill anyone?" "Yes." "How many people did you kill?" "How should I know? Who can keep count?" One, two . . . there was a fat woman who was as big around as a stone roller, impossible to hold, and whose huge tits hung down to her waist. And there was that man and woman who came in on a rainy day. They weren't father and daughter, nor were they husband and wife by any means . . . that goddamned man should have died first, but he went to the toilet, so the woman died first. He came back, but he didn't die right away, my foot still on his crotch . . . he finally died. The woman's face was white, very nice. You Yiren counted on his fingers trying hard to recollect, but seeing how the judge's face had gone white, his memory failed him. He hung his clammy hands and felt dejected about what he had said. But it was all true. "Eight people," he said weakly.

The river formed a silver belt, slowly stretching out ahead; white poplars, on which were stuck the dead skins of cicadas, and green willows receded rapidly. The scorching red sun was indeed greasy; beads of sweat like pearls slipped to the end of the nose, oily. Bathed in the burning sun, they were unaware of when the temple gate appeared on the other side of mountain ridge, the leaves of the ancient cypresses and old pines like floating clouds and immersed in the lingering toll of the bell. In this way You Yiren and two armed criminal police rode a three-wheeled motorcycle upstream along the Han River toward Biejia Gully.

The country folks had their own name for female genitalia, just a single syllable, X, but it wasn't pleasant to the ear, so they used

169

出来就只好别替为"瘪"了。有学着说中国的文化主要表现在两个方面，一个是关于吃上，一个是关于瘪上。尤佚人和他的乡亲如果要做学问，必定会同意这观点的。

尤佚人知道自己生命的来源，虽然小时候问过娘，娘回答是从水中捞来的。"怎么捞的呢？""用笊篱一捞就捞着了。""人都是这般捞到的吗？""是的。"母亲的表情极其严肃。这严肃的表情给尤佚人印象颇深，以致后来逐渐长大，成熟了某一块肌肉，就对母亲给予他的欺骗甚为愤慨。

夏日的夜晚，低矮的四堵墙小屋闷如蒸笼，有跳蚤，有蚊子，有臭虫，光棍们就集中到村口水田边的一座破旧不堪的古戏楼上。风东西往，男人们可以数着天上的星星，一遍于一遍数目不同。又可以谈神秘的东西如女人和之所以是女人的标志。尤佚人的清楚大学就从这里开始。

如果从汉江边的公路遥遥往北山看，这尤佚人已经习惯了。就看到那里一处方位的绝妙。一个椭圆形的沟壑。土是暗红，长满杂树。大椭圆里又套一个小椭圆。其中又是一堵墙的土峰，尖尖的，红如霜叶，风风雨雨终未损耗。大的椭圆的外边，沟壑的边沿，两条人足踏出的白色的路十分显眼，路的教会处生一古槐，槐荫宁静，如一朵云。而椭圆形的下方就是细而长的小沟生满芦

another sound instead. But that sound didn't have a written character to represent it, so they substituted the character *bie*. Some scholars held that Chinese culture found expression mainly in two areas: one was food and the other was *bie*. If they had engaged in scholarship, You Yiren and his fellow villagers certainly would have approved of this view.

You Yiren knew his origins. When he was little he asked his mother where he came from. His mother told him that he had been dredged up out of the river. "How was I dredged up?" "With just one scoop of a bamboo strainer." "Does everyone come by being dredged up?" "Yes." His mother looked very serious. It was her serious expression that most impressed You Yiren. That is, until he gradually grew up and a certain "muscle" matured. He was angry with his mother for lying to him.

Summer nights and the small four-walled houses were as hot and stuffy as food steamers; they stank and were filled with fleas and mosquitoes, too, so the unmarried men would go to a shabby, old opera house by the paddy field at the entrance to the village. The wind would blow here and there, the men would count the stars in the sky, and every time they would come up with a different number. They'd also talk about mysterious things such as what made a woman a woman. You Yiren's adolescent education began there.

If you stood by the highway beside the Han River and looked toward the distant mountains to the north—as You Yiren was accustomed to doing—you could see a marvelous place, an oval-shaped gully with dark red soil and filled with a variety of trees. Within the oval was a smaller oval with a heaped-up wall running through the middle and as red as an autumn maple leaf, which no trials or hardships ever seemed to diminish. At the edge of the larger oval, around the gully, were two conspicuous white trails trod out by human feet. The two trails intersected at an ancient pagoda tree. The peaceful shadow of the pagoda tree was like a patch of cloud. At the foot of the oval was a small ditch, long and thin, filled with reeds,

苇，杂乱无章，浸一道似有似无的稀汪汪的暗水四季不干。

这就是天造地设的一个"瘊"。村子的穴位就是"瘊"的穴位。但生活在"瘊"的世界里的光棍们却享受不到那一种文化，活人就觉得十分没劲。一次躲在芦苇丛里的尤佚人偷听了一对夫妻在沟里烧香焚纸说："儿呀你就出来吧，我们是三间房一院子，长大了能给你娶个媳妇的，你就出来吧!"他就想，母亲和父亲，一定没有按风俗曾在这里祈祷过，否则他是绝不会到这个人世间来了，来了也绝对不会就做了父亲和母亲的儿子。对于没征求他的一间就随便生下又以"捞来"之说欺骗他的母亲，尤佚人几乎是恼怒不已了。

从瘊家沟到县城是五十里。从县城到瘊家沟是五十里。五十里顺着汉江横过来的却是深涧似的漆水河。河上一座桥，十八个石磙子碌磆堆起的墩，交通了山区与城市，也把野蛮和文明接连一起，河水七年八年就要暴溢。一年里，水满河满沿，结果将桥冲垮了一半，十八个石磙子碌磆丢失了五个，瘊家沟的人都去下游泥沙里探寻，尤佚人踩了三天沙，退肚子上患了连疮，夜里睡着烂肉和袜子被老鼠啃去了几处。最后石磙子碌磆却在上游找到，尤佚人莫名其妙，遂愤愤不平到这一个夏天，"文革"的运动就来了。村里人便跑贼似地往南山石洞跑。爹不跑，武斗的人扇了爹一个耳光。"扇得好，扇了我一颗铁耳屎!"爹就随着走了，背上

that ran with scant dark water all year round.

It was a perfect *bie*. The village was situated on a *bie* acupuncture point. But the unmarried men who lived in this *bie* world were unable to enjoy that type of culture, and all lacked energy. One time You Yiren hid in the reeds and eavesdropped on a couple who came to burn joss sticks and spirit money and pray. "My son, come out. We have a house with three bedrooms and one courtyard. When you grow up, we'll let you marry. Come out!" Then, You Yiren thought, his father and mother certainly hadn't followed the tradition to come here to pray; otherwise he'd never have come into this world, and even if he had, he'd never have been born the son of his parents. He was angry with his mother because she gave birth to him without seeking his permission, and the worst was that she had lied to him by saying he had been dredged out of the river.

It was fifty *li* from Biejia Gully to the county town and fifty *li* from the county town to Biejia Gully. Fifty *li* up the Han River was the confluence of the Qishui River, which was deep like a gully. Over the river was a bridge with a pier composed of eighteen stone rollers that connected the mountainous area and the city as well as the savage and the civilized. Every seven or eight years, the river would flood suddenly and violently. One year, the water rose in a flood, shattered half of the bridge, and washed away five of the eighteen stone rollers. The villagers of Biejia Gully went downstream to look for them in the mud and sand. After stepping around in the sand for three days, You Yiren ended up with ulcers on his calves, and while he was sleeping at night, the mice bit off several pieces of rotten flesh along with bits of his socks. The stone rollers were finally found later upstream, which was inexplicable to You Yiren and left him feeling indignant until the movement known as the Great Proletarian Cultural Revolution began that summer. The villagers ran like thieves to a cave in the southern mountains. His dad didn't want to run, and one person who resorted to violence slapped him in the face. "Good slap! You've slapped a hard ball of wax out of my ear!" Then his dad followed him, carrying

一杆自制的长筒土枪。

石洞开凿于民国初年,在光溜溜的半石崖,从下边不能上去从上边不能下来,崖壁上凿着石窝载着石椽架上木板,可以走,走过一页板抽掉一页板。尤佚人捉住了十只蝙蝠,还有一头猫头鹰,就眺望起远远的在烟里雾里笼罩的家。家里守着半死的老爷,一咳嗽就咯出鸡屎般的一口痰,他突然听到了娘的声音。

一条粗如镰把的长蛇正在洞外的石砭上吸将起一只金毛松鼠了。

"啊? 啊?!"

娘慌乱得叫着。那松鼠怎么不逃掉还盯着蛇一步步挪进去?"松鼠是吓昏了吗?"

他抱起一块石头抛过去,蛇跑了,他几乎在石头抛过去的时候连自己也抛过去。夜里娘就偷偷夏冬回家了,正式一派攻克了一派的胜利之后,十二个人,一派的带枪者将奶奶个压倒在炕上轮奸。赤条条的儿媳昏死在堂屋,老爷从厦房的病床上爬过来,用红布蒙住娘的眼睛,开始用烤热的鞋底敷那肿地像面团一样的穴位竟敷出半碗罪恶来。老爷就撞在捶布石上死了。

这是一个相当清幽的院落。东边是一片竹篁,太阳愈是照,叶片

a long-barreled homemade rifle on his back.

The cave had been cut out of the rock in the early years of the Republic and was located halfway up a slippery cliff. No one could get up to it from the bottom or down to it from the top. Niches had been cut in the cliff to hold pins on which boards were placed to walk. After walking over one board, it could be taken up and moved forward to provide another step. After catching ten bats and an owl, You Yiren gazed at his distant home, shrouded in fog. His grandpa, who was half dead, had stayed at home. When he coughed he coughed up globs of phlegm as big as chicken shit. He suddenly heard his mom's voice.

A long snake as thick as the handle on a big hoe was about to seize a golden squirrel on the stone point outside the cave.

"Ah? Ah?!"

His mom cried in alarm. Why did the golden squirrel just stare at the snake and not even try to run away? "The golden squirrel was struck dumb?"

He picked up a stone and threw it to scare away the snake, and when doing so he almost threw himself away, too. The snake slithered off. At night, his mom stole out of the cave, descended, and went home. It was right after one faction had victoriously overcome another faction. Twelve people with guns held his mom down on the *kang* and gang-raped her. His old grandpa climbed out of his sickbed upstairs and crawled down to the central hall and covered the eyes of his daughter-in-law, who had died stark naked, with a red cloth. He heated the cotton sole of his shoe and laid it on that acupoint of hers that was as swollen as raised dough, and he was unexpectedly led to commit a sin. Later, Grandpa smashed his head against the stone used for beating clothes and died.

It was a very quiet and secluded courtyard. There was a bamboo grove on the east side. The bamboo leaves would shine all

愈是青，没有风你却感到腋下津津生凉。一支竹鞭从院墙的水眼
道孔中爬过来，只有五天的时间，已经爬到了台阶下如黄蛇一般
僵卧在砖缝繁衍的菌草里。一只麻雀湿脚从瓦楞上踏过，将双爪
与扑撒的竹叶织就了一片"个"字。尤佚人半呆地立着，陡然生
喜的心情悠忽如死灰如槁木。暑热底下一种空洞，惟一能听见的，
粗糙的，愤怒的，是掘土的声，掏石块的声，镢头哐地掷下。西
边院角的石磨被推翻了，墙角的土墙上，一根木楔，空吊着一幅
牛的"暗眼"。牛是戴着"暗眼"在磨道里走完了一生，于前三年
就倒下死了的。而院墙的每一个打墙留下的椽眼塞满了头发窝子
……尤佚人保持不动的姿势立在院中，默看着雇佣来的人挥汗如
雨地挖掘着，像是在觅寻什么金窖，紧张，又是湿漉漉的手。

"能让我说话吗?"他终于忍受不了炸弹之前的静寂。

"说!"刑警看着他。

"挖的都不是地方。"他指着台阶下的那个捶布石说，"都在下
边，曾经是个渗井的。后来倒污水就到院外去。"

于是，挖出了八具死尸。腥臭弥漫了院子，成群的苍蝇随之
而来。对墙投下的明亮，强烈的光线斜射在潮湿窄小的渗井坑中。
人们全恐惧地睁大了眼睛，用席要掩盖了那坑时，同时又发现坑
底还有一条胳膊。

八个半? 刑警脸皮上都生了鸡皮疙瘩。

the greener as the sun grew brighter, and although there was no
wind, your armpits still felt cool. A bamboo stalk rose from a hole for
the water course in the fence. In a matter of five days, it had reached
the foot of a flight of steps and lay prone like a yellow snake among
the fungi and grass in a crevice between the bricks. A sparrow with
wet feet walked over the rows of roof tiles, weaving the character
"个" as its claws met with scattered bamboo leaves. You Yiren stood
staring blankly. His brief feeling of happiness suddenly turned to
apathy like dying embers. There was an emptiness to the heat, and
the only audible sounds were that of digging—loud, jarring, angry
noises of stones being dug out or of hoes being thrown down. The
millstone in the corner of the courtyard on the western side was
overturned. Since the ox died three years ago, the pair of blinders
it wore its whole life spent treading the millstone path were now
uselessly hung in the corner of the mud wall. Every small hole in the
wall was filled with hair. . . . You Yiren stood motionless in the yard
watching the perspiring workers who were hired to dig. They dug as
if they were searching in silence for some pot of gold. Nervous, his
hands were once again clammy.

"Can I say something?" He finally broke the unbearable silence
like that before a bomb detonates.

"Go ahead!" said the policeman who was handling the criminal,
looking at him.

"You're digging in all the wrong spots." Pointing to the washing
stone at the foot of the flight of steps, he said, "They're all there,
under the washing stone. There was a seepage pit there once; later,
dirty water had to be dumped outside."

So eight bodies were dug up. The courtyard was filled with a
stench that attracted hordes of flies. The bright and strong light shone
down obliquely into the small, damp seepage pit. All eyes were open
wide in terror. As they were covering the bodies with mats, they
discovered an arm in the bottom of the seepage pit.

Eight and a half? The policeman had gooseflesh all over.

"那胳膊是什么人的?"

"神秘人的?"

"还杀了多少人呢?"

他真的记不起来了,这能是谁的胳膊? 仰起球头,嘴陷进去的一个深深的黑洞。有个时期,汉江北岸有许多收废品的。"谁有烂铜烂铁头发窝子酒瓶破纸喽——!"一吆喝,他就提一把斧头做刚刚劈了柴的姿势在门口应,我家有! 收买者遂进了屋,接住了递过来的香烟,点燃上。"酒瓶都在柜底下。"头刚一弯下,斧头脑儿轻轻一敲那后脑勺,就倒了。他过去从死者的口里取了燃着的香烟。

收废品的都是男的。尤佚人端详起胳膊,胳膊腕上戴有绿塑料环,这是女人的胳膊,戴不起手表,也没有银镯子,丑美人!

是黄昏吧,晚霞十分好看,他是去过十八个石磙子碌碡的桥上的,让柔柔的风拂在脸上想像到一种受活。看桥那边远处的县城,看到了微尘浮动。有三个女子就从霞光里走过来了。她们都胖乎乎的身体。他身上的肌肉就勃动起来,又恨起来,听她们谈论着编草袋的生意,咒骂草价高涨又货物奇缺。"我家有稻草!"他主动地说。"有多少?""不多,七十多斤,够一个人用的!"三个女子却互相看看,走了。第二天竟来了那个最胖的,说她们都想买了又害怕对方买去所以前一日么有应承,要求他替她守秘密。胖女子死了。他将她白日放在柜里黑夜抱到炕上,后来腐烂生蛆

"Whose arm is it?"

"Whose?"

"How many more did you kill?"

Was he really unable to remember whose arm it was? The round head faced upward, the mouth sank into a deep dark hole. There was a time when many people collected scrap. "Who has scrap iron, bronze, shocks of hair, wine bottles, waste paper?" the man shouted. "We do!" he replied at the door, lifting an axe as if he had just finished chopping firewood. The man who came into the house to buy the scrap took the cigarette that was handed to him and lit it. "All the wine bottles are under the cabinet." As soon as the man bent down, he hit the back of his head ever so deftly with his axe. The man fell, and he stepped over to remove the burning cigarette from his mouth.

The people who collected scrap were all men. You Yiren scrutinized the arm that wore a green plastic bracelet. The arm belonged to a woman who couldn't afford to wear a watch or a silver bracelet, an ugly beauty!

It was dusk, and the sunset clouds were very beautiful. He went to 18 Stone Roller Bridge and let the gentle breeze caress his face and imagined a kind of living. He looked at the county town in the distance and saw the dust floating in the air. Three women walked in his direction in the evening sunlight. Their plump bodies made his muscle stir and also made him mad. He listened to them talking about the business of weaving straw bags and bitching about the high price and shortage of straw. "I have straw at home!" he volunteered. "How much do you have?" "Not much, seventy odd *jin*, just enough for one person to use!" The three of them looked at one another and then walked away. The following day the fattest woman came and told him that they all wanted to buy it and were afraid that the others might get it; that's why no one had said anything the previous day. She asked him to keep it a secret. The fat woman died. That day, he kept her dead body in the cabinet and carried it to the pit at night. Later her body became rotten and filled with maggots,

只好割碎去。但他却是为他守了秘密。

"你奸尸碎尸?!"

一个耳光打得尤佚人口鼻出血,又被三轮摩托车带回县城去了。尤佚人有生以来已经是第二次坐摩托车了,铐了双手,头塞在斗壳下,汗如滚豆子一样下来。他所遗憾的是没能看到十八个石磙子碌磗桥。这一个傍晚云烧得越来越红,漆水河上湉湉的水,与汉江交汇处漂浮的鸭梢子船,已经被腐蚀得通体金黄。

父亲靠着勇敢,当了武斗队长。队长可以背盒子枪,可以有一个穿一身黄上衣系着宽皮带的女秘书。女秘书有一双吊梢子眼。爹就不要娘了。

"你败兴了我的人!"爹拿烟头烧娘的脸,揪下娘头上一把一把头发。砸浆水瓮,砸炕背墙,疯得像一头狼,爹顺门走了。尤佚人扑出去抱住爹的大腿咬,他腮帮子上挨了一巴掌眼冒火星倒在尘埃中。

"你要是我的儿子!"火星中爹在说,"跟我造反去!造反了什么都有了!"

他说:"我要杀了你!"一口唾沫连血连牙吐出来。

爹嘿嘿笑着,捡了他的牙撂在高高的屋檐上,说:"落了呀撂在高处着好,你能杀了我就是我儿子!"

尤佚人和娘住在三间土屋里,娘常常惊起说有人进了院,吓瘫,下身就汪出一摊血来。天一黑,外边劈劈啪啪枪声响,娘又

and he had to cut it into pieces. But he did keep that secret of hers.

"You raped the dead body and then cut it into pieces?!"

A box to his ears made You Yiren bleed from his mouth and nose, and then he was taken back to the county town by three-wheeled motorcycle. It was the second time in his life that You Yiren had ridden a motorcycle; his hands were chained and his head crammed in a round helmet from which beads of sweat rolled like peas. What he really regretted was that he could no longer see the 18 Stone Roller Bridge. At dusk that day the clouds glowed ever redder. The slowly flowing water of the Qishui River and the boats floating at the confluence of the Han River were corroded a golden yellow.

His dad became the leader of the group that resorted to violence because he was very brave. As the leader, he carried a Mauser rifle on his back and had a female secretary in a khaki shirt and wide leather belt. She had slanting eyes, for which his dad abandoned his ma.

"You're the one who has ruined my mood!" His dad burned his ma's face with his cigarette butt and yanked out handfuls of her hair. He smashed an earthen water jar against the wall behind the *kang*, raving like a wolf before stalking out the door. You Yiren pounced on him, grabbed his thigh, and bit. His dad slapped his face with the palm of his hand, making his head swim. He fell in the dirt.

"If you're my son," he heard his dad say out of the blue, "come and make revolution with me! You can have everything through revolution!"

"I want to kill you!" he said, spitting blood along with a tooth.

"Ha-ha!" he laughed, picking up his tooth and throwing it high up on the roof. "Your tooth is way up high there. If you can kill me, you are my son!"

You Yiren and his mom lived in a three-room earthen house. She often woke up in alarm saying someone was in their courtyard. When she got scared, she couldn't move at all, and a pool of blood would come out of her lower body. As soon as night fell the sound of gunfire would crackle outside. His mom

要于黑暗中和衣下炕迈着干瘦如柴的腿去摸窗子关了没有。门关了，且横一根粗木。

每一夜都清冷漫长。风吹动着院东边竹林，惶惶不宁。竹在这年月长得特别旺，衍过墙头，黑黝黝的浓重之影压在窗上如鬼如魅。尤佚人悄然下炕，夜行到汉江边的一个村子去找驻扎的一派。"谁？""我！""你是狗！""你娘是母狗！"黑暗处一个持枪人近来拉动了枪栓。"你动我，我爹杀了你！"那人不动了，扭头追撵绰绰约约一行人。他看清那里八个人押着五个俘房，俘房五花大绑且背上皆有一小石磨盘。是去汉江里"煮饺子"。他钻进村子，寻着了爹住的房。门关着，灯还在亮，窗缝里看去，一面大炕上铺了豌豆放了木板载着一男一女悠来晃去地畅美。夜风里，他将门前一垛包谷秆点燃了。

他逃坐在汉江边的弯脖子枯柳上，看熊熊的火光烧得半边天红，却奇怪地闻见了一种幽香，河岸石丛中的狼牙刺花的气味刺激着他大口吸了一嘴空气，而失身跌进河里去。第二天早晨冲在一片沙滩上，泥里水拱出来，第一次捉住了鱼生吞活吃。

瘪家沟里惟独尤佚人个头太矮，七分像人，三分如鬼。家空

got up in her clothes in the dark and stepped with her bony legs, feeling to make sure the windows were closed. She closed the door and barred it with a piece of wood.

The nights were long and cold. The wind shook the bamboo grove on the eastern side of the courtyard, causing fear and anxiety. The vigorous bamboo grew over the walls, casting dense shadows to the window like ghosts and goblins. One night, You Yiren quietly slipped off the *kang* and walked in the dark to a village on the shore of the Han River, where one faction was stationed. "Who's there?" "Me!" "You're a dog!" "Your ma is a bitch!" In the dark, a man with a rifle approached him, working the rifle bolt. "You touch me and my dad will kill you!" The man stopped and turned back to catch up with a group of people. He saw that there were eight of them to escort five captives who were tightly trussed up, each with a small millstone on his back. They were going to drop them into the Han River as if they were cooking dumplings. Making his way into the village, he located the house where his dad lived. The door was closed, but the light was on. He peeked through a crack in the window. He saw a man and a woman who looked quite pleased with themselves. They sat on a board that shifted on the peas spread on a big *kang*. The night wind blowing, he put a match to a pile of cornstalks in front of the door.

He ran and sat on the crooked trunk of a withered willow by the Han River, watching the raging fire that turned half the sky red. He then smelled a faint fragrance that seemed strange to him. The smell of the pagoda shrubs that grew among the rocks by the riverbank irritated him, and, as he opened his mouth wide to gulp down the air, he lost his balance and fell into the river. The next day he found himself washed up on a beach, where for the first time in his life he caught a fish in the muddy water and swallowed it raw.

You Yiren was considered too short in Biejia Gully, more like a devil than a man. His home

空无物贫困似洗。娘得知丈夫已同女秘书同床卧枕,一夜里将老鼠药喝下七窍流血闭目而去。一条破板柜锯了四个腿儿将娘下葬后,白天吃稀粥糠菜,夜里玩弄那一根筋肉竟修长巨大,与身子失去比例。夏日之夜月明星稀,天地银辉,他浮游于汉江浅水之潭,那物勃起,竟划出水底淤泥如犁沟一般的渠痕,将河柳红细根须纠缠一团。遂碰见岸边一妇人经过,"我和你那个!"指着案头两只狗在交媾。妇人扇他一个耳光。这耳光便从此扇去了他的正常勇敢,被村人嘲笑其父在革命中多享了几份女人,致使儿子见不上肉也喝不上汤。世界原本是大的,这年月使世界更空旷荒阔,于是他在瘟家沟无足轻重,走了并不显得宽松,回来亦不怎么拥挤。

偶然有人发觉他做贩肉的生意了。

"要赚钱呀?"

"……"

"挣女人呀?"

"……"

有人将他的肉全部买去,在十八个石磙子碌碡桥上,并约定他贩了肉专门卖他。他的肉很便宜。再挑着肉到桥上去,叫天子叫得生欢,往年冲垮了桥墩碌碡的洪水,吃水线高高地残留在半崖保存下记录,他脑子在游荡。

was absolutely bare, poor, as if everything had been washed away by a flood. Upon learning that her husband was sleeping with his secretary, his mom swallowed rat poison, which caused all the orifices of her head to bleed, and she died. He cut off four legs from a shabby wooden cabinet and used them to make a coffin in which to bury his mom. After that, he ate watery porridge during the day and played with that stiff "muscle" of his at night, which unexpectedly had grown so big that it was out of proportion with the rest of his body. On summer nights when the moon was bright and the stars were few and heaven and the earth were bathed in silver light, he would swim in a shallow pool in the Han River. His erect member would cut a furrow like a plow in the sand where the fine, red willow roots would collect and ball together. One time he saw a woman pass by. Pointing at a pair of humping dogs, he said to her, "Let's do it." The woman slapped his face. The slap sapped his courage after that. All the villagers joked about him, saying that because his father had enjoyed so many women during the revolution he had left nothing for his son. The world was a big place, and the times made it even bigger and more spacious. He was so insignificant in Biejia Gully that if he had left, there wouldn't have been any more space, and if he'd come back, it wouldn't have been any more crowded.

Someone chanced to find him selling meat.

"Making money?"

"..."

"To get a woman?"

"..."

Someone bought all of his meat on 18 Stone Roller Bridge and made him promise to sell only to him. His meat was cheap, and when he shouldered it and carried it to the bridge again, the skylark sang even more joyfully. The flood that had washed away the stone rollers of the bridge years ago had left a mark halfway up the cliff. His mind wandered.

往东，是繁华的县城，南城门外的渡口上成群的女子捣着棒槌洗衣，裙子之下也是没穿裤衩的吗？往西，一漫是山区，田野上的吐露纠结，争取着三五日暮归人，女人直面走过来，奶头子抖得像揣了两个水袋……他计算着自己的年龄，还要活着三十年和四十年……

拣着天高云淡的日子到县城去，县城人鄙视着他，他也更仇恨起县城的人。听说城关一家饺子店做食极美，趄进去买了坐吃，就认识了一位还看得上与他说话的老太太。她胖如球类，坐下和站着一样高，睡下也一定和坐下一样高，每一次总夸说这饺馅特别油，特别香。

"你也常在这吃吗？"

"不多。"

老太太健谈，对他夸说自己的丈夫在县政府任一个主任。说她的儿子在县公安局工作。说她年纪大了还能吃下四两饺子。然后问他身世，哀叹他没有媳妇。由没媳妇又说到没媳妇的可怜。

"中街扣的那个寡妇告隔壁的一个男人强奸了她，你认为这可能吗？"

"……"

"这怎么会可能呢？你拿着这个吧，你往笔帽里捅！"老太太兴致倒高，把口袋里一支钢笔拔出来卸了笔帽，她拿了笔帽让他把笔尖往里捅。他莫名其妙，左捅她偏右，右捅她偏左。

To the east was the bustling county town. At the ferry outside the southern gate, a group of women washed clothes. Did they wear underpants under their skirts? To the west were a flooded area and the mountains. The dirt roads banded together in the open country, over which several old women walked straight toward him, their breasts shaking like two water bags. . . . He took stock of his age and saw he had another thirty or forty years ahead of him. . . .

To go to the county town, he chose a day when the sky was high and the clouds were pale. The city people despised him, and he hated the city people. He heard that there was a restaurant that made delicious dumplings, so he went inside to sample them. There he met an older woman whom he didn't mind and who talked with him. She was as round as a ball and was as tall standing as she was sitting. Sleeping, she was no doubt as tall as she was when sitting. She praised the stuffing of the dumplings as especially oily and fragrant.

"Do you often come here to eat, too?"

"Not very often."

The old woman was a brilliant conversationalist. She told him her husband was a director in the county government and her son worked for the public security bureau. She told him that even though she was old, she could still eat two hundred grams of dumplings. Then she asked about his life and took pity on him for being a bachelor. She talked about how pitiful it was for a man not to have a wife.

"The widow at the mouth of Central Street accused her neighbor of raping her, do you believe her?"

". . ."

"Do you buy that? Take this pen and shove it inside the cap!" Filled with excitement, the old woman handed him a pen she took from her pocket and removed the cap. Holding the cap she had him try to insert the pen in the cap. As he poked left she moved to the right, and as he poked to the right she moved to the left. He was unable to make heads or tails of it.

"瞧瞧,这能行吗?一定是通奸,或许就是男人用刀子逼着她,把她杀了!"

尤佚人默然同意,但脸变得铁青。

这一次在饭店里又碰着老太太了,她带了小孙女来吃,吃得满嘴流油。

"奶奶,我不吃这漂着的油珠花儿。"外孙女嚷着。

"油珠花儿要吃的,一个油珠花儿多像一颗太阳啊!"

"奶奶,太阳是圆的,油珠花儿是半圆的。"

"半圆?那就是月亮了!"

"啊啊,油月亮!"

孩子在喜欢地叫着,尤佚人猛然才发觉满碗的油珠花儿皆半圆如小月。脑子里针扎地一疼,放下筷子逃走了,再不到这家饺子店用饭。

烈烈大伙烧毁了包谷秆垛,烧毁了一明两暗的三间瓦房。但队长和他的秘书逃出来及时,仅将上衣和裤子化成灰烬。尤佚人知道了爹没有死,也就"革命"了,参加到另一派。虽然没能够在武斗中杀人,别人却把人杀了让他去用树棍捅那裂开的脑袋,用石头砸那补镶的金黄铜门牙。

枪很长,背在肩上磕打膝盖。两派对垒在汉江,落日在河心大圆的黄昏里,风鸟啁啾,流水咽咽,河堤上的工事上架起乌黑的枪管。战壕里说着"革命",又说杀人和女人,说的浑身燥热了枪放下都解了裤子手淫。他说:"我没孩子?哼,我要是不槽蹋这东西,十个二十个孩子都站成排了!"说罢,孤独和冷寂并没有

"See, can it be done? They must have committed adultery or else the man used a knife to force her and kill her!"

You Yiren agreed in silence, but his face turned ashen.

He ran into her again at the restaurant. She had her granddaughter with her, and their mouths were dripping with grease.

"Grandma, I don't want to eat the floating pearls of grease," her granddaughter shouted.

"You have to eat them. They look so much like the sun."

"Grandma, the sun is round, but these pearl drops of oil are half round."

"Half round? Then they are like the moon!"

"Oh, greasy moons!"

The child shouted happily. You Yiren suddenly discovered that the floating pearl drops of grease filling the bowl were like little half moons. He felt a sharp pain, like a needle in his brain. Putting down his chopsticks, he ran out and never returned to the restaurant.

The raging fire burned the cornstalks and burned down the three tile-roofed rooms; one of which was lit and the other two dark. But the leader and his secretary escaped in time, though their jackets and pants were burned to ashes. When You Yiren learned that his dad was alive, he went to "make revolution," but with a different faction. Others did the killing, but he was told to break open their skulls with a club and knock out their gold- or bronze-filled teeth with a stone.

The long rifle he carried on his shoulder knocked against his knees. The two factions stood facing each other on either side of the Han River. As the huge sun set in the middle of the river at dusk, a bird twittered, and the water flowed hoarsely. The jet-black gun barrels were put up on the fortifications on the embankment. In the trench, someone said, "Revolution"; someone said, "Kill the men and the women." The words made him feel hot and dry. He put down his rifle, undid his pants, and masturbated. He said, "I don't have kids. Huh! If I didn't waste this stuff, I'd have ten or twenty kids lined up, standing in a row!" Thinking this, he felt lonely and cold.

解除，便等待天一染黑，将准星对准对岸某一目标。这时候他被一声枪响惊动了。

对岸一发冷弹将这边一个提灯笼送饭的伙夫击倒了。

"他活该用右手提灯笼?!"朝灯笼左边一尺的地方打当然是没命的。

"左手提就不会向右边打吗?"

"用树棍挑着!"

尤佚人默不作声，两眼死死盯住对岸就发现了一点红光，悠忽明灭，扳机就勾动了。那边有惊叫声："队长被打中了! 打中了上嘴唇了!"

爹从此上嘴唇开裂，如兔嘴。他不该在击中提灯笼的伙夫后得以抽纸烟。

翌日，一辆卡车拉着队长和秘书去县城医院做手术。车上装了钢板。汉江岸上两派拉锯攻占，形势紧张，刻不容缓，车行驶得疾速如风，长长的土路圣桑尘土飞扬，像点燃了巨大的导火索。在一个急弯，车上的钢板因惯性而错位滑动，两个人的脑袋，无声无息中从脖子处切除了。司机在反光镜中突然看见车角的两个木桩似的人身，瑟然惊悸，停下车看时果然没有了头。折身往来路回返，软乎乎的转弯处湿地上两颗无血的脑袋滚在一起，脸还是笑笑的。

He waited till it got dark and then took aim at a target on the opposite bank. At that moment there was a gunshot, which alarmed him.

A sniper had fired from the other side of the river and downed the mess cook, who was carrying a lantern to deliver food.

"It serves him right for carrying the lantern in his right hand!" He was as good as dead by simply shooting a third of a meter to the left of the lantern.

"If he carried the lantern in his left hand, wouldn't he be hit if they shot to the right?"

"He should have carried it on a stick!"

You Yiren kept silent, his eyes fixed at the other side of the river till he saw the red glow of a point of light. He pulled the trigger. "The leader has been shot! His lips were hit!" came the alarmed cries from across the river.

After that, his dad's upper lip was split, like a hare's lip. He shouldn't have acted so proud of himself by having a smoke after shooting the mess cook dead.

The following day, a truck armored with a steel plate took his dad and his secretary for treatment at the county hospital. The two factions on the banks of the Han River fought a seesaw battle, storming and capturing. The situation was tense and brooked no delay. The truck drove at high speed on the long dirt road, sending up dust as if a fuse had been ignited. When the truck made a sharp turn, the steel plate slid, due to the inertia, and quietly removed the heads from the necks of the two people. When the driver looked in the mirror and saw the two bodies piled like wood in the corner of the truck, he went cold from fright. He stopped the truck and saw that they were missing their heads. He turned and started back up the road he had come from, and at the bend in the road he came upon the two bloodless heads on the soft, wet ground, their faces still smiling.

"尤佚人!"

"有!"

"你为什么杀人?"

"……"

"杀人的动机和目的?"

"……"

一双手又湿漉漉的了。审讯室的地上铺着砖块,一群从砖缝里钻出来的蚂蚁在激战,为一块馍粒,结果死伤无数。

轻轻一敲,就那么倒下去,其实很简单。关上门,将灯芯点燃,四壁的漆黑的墙上却能映出他的黑影。那人脸上或许很痛苦,或者笑纹还在,看着,他要坐下来沉静静地吃一根烟卷。男人可以不管,女人则要剥脱衣服。全身凉硬脱不下来,用自己的肩膀扛起死者头,再努力用受去褪死者的两个袖子,这往往弄出他一头一身汗。

"你是图财害命,还是因奸杀人?"审讯员直逼着问。

这又该怎么老师坦白呢?判案总讲究个动机和目的,尤佚人否认自己是图财。"有钱人不可能到我家来的。"他想,只要能到家里来,他就产生着想杀的欲望,这如身上发现了虱子能不弄死吗?杀玩之后搜身子,虽然可以得十元二十元,甚至是一角或一角零五分。[1] 因奸杀人,自然只能是女性,"杀的不全是女人啊。

无意中又闻到一种幽香,如烧毁了爹和秘书的房子后的汉江边闻到的一样。他歪头看见窗外是一花圃,开许多芍药、牡丹。花是靠风传播着花粉而延续生命的,它将生殖器顶在了头上。瘪

"You Yiren!"

"Present!"

"Why did you kill?"

". . ."

"What was your motive and purpose?"

". . ."

His hands got clammy again. On the brick floor of the courtroom, a group of ants that had come out of the cracks were fighting fiercely over a crumb of steamed bread. Countless ants had died.

It was actually very simple. He just gave them a little tap and down they went. He closed the door and lit the lamp wick. His shadow was cast against the pitch-dark walls. The face of the person might look pained, or it might still reveal the lines of a smile. Looking at it, he would sit down and calmly smoke a cigarette. He didn't care if the person he killed was a man, but if it was a woman he would undress her. It was difficult to remove the clothes from a cold, stiff body. He'd have to rest her head on his shoulder and then forcibly pull off her sleeves, which always left him in a sweat.

"Did you murder for money or for sex?" the judge pressed him.

How to confess truthfully? The motive and the purpose were important elements in any murder case. You Yiren denied that he had killed for the money. "People with money wouldn't come to my place." If they did, he thought, the desire to kill them would arise, the same way it would when he found a louse on his body, right? After killing someone, he might find ten or twenty yuan, a *mao*, and a few *fen* after searching the dead body. As for sex, naturally he killed a woman for it, but he "didn't just kill women."

Unexpectedly he detected a delicate fragrance, like the one he smelled by the Han River after he burned down the house of his dad and secretary. He turned and saw a flower bed outside the window, where peonies were blooming. A flower, with its reproductive parts on top, relies on the wind to disperse its pollen in order to reproduce. Biejia

家沟那么大个瘊。他不知道自己杀人的目的，完成不了老实坦白。

"油月亮!"尤侠人突然嘟囔了一句。

"油月亮? 油月亮是什么意思?!"

他猛地清醒，想到他和娘在石洞的情景，想到爹打娘，便有了小小的心眼。不能不牵连和坑害了别的更多的人。他勾下脑袋手又是湿漉漉的了。

油月亮，成了办案人员兴奋而又颇为头痛的一条重要线索，他们开始软的硬的，轮番的审讯。但笔录本上一直是"油月亮"三个字。他被特别关押在一个号子里，饭菜端进来，屎尿端出去，不能打他。要喝酒还必须给他拿酒。

一日，他说要到十八个石磙子碌碡桥去。办案人认为这次去一定与油月亮有关了。囚车将他带去。他站在漆水河的上游，怎么也没高清那次断了桥后石磙子碌碡会冲到了上游泥沙里。他掬着水洗脸和脖子，搓下许多泥垢，拿着自己看还让办案人看。"你要坦白吗?""坦白什么?""油月亮!"他说:"我坦白我哄了你们，到这里来我想看看这桥的。"

尤侠人从来没有做过梦，当然更没有噩梦可言。但在一个冬天的正午，他睡在炕上似乎觉得做了一梦。梦到有许多女人，全来到他的炕上与他交媾，到后就阳痿了，见花不起，如垂泪蜡烛。沉沉睡下又复做梦，且经连续刚才，却又都是些男人，恍惚间骂

Gully was a big *bie*. He didn't know why he killed, so he couldn't truthfully confess.

"Greasy moon!" You Yiren suddenly blurted out.

"Greasy moon? What do you mean by that?"

His mind suddenly became clear as he thought of himself and his mom in the cave; of his dad, who beat his mom; the scenes when he and his ma were in the cave; thinking of his dad who beat his ma; then his mind narrowed. He couldn't implicate or frame anyone else. He lowered his head, and his hands got clammy again.

Greasy moon became a clue—both exciting and a headache— for the personnel handling the case. They used carrot and stick by turn as they questioned him, but all they ever got for their notebooks were the two words *greasy moon*. He was locked in a special room. Meals went in, and the slop bucket came out. They didn't beat him, and gave him wine whenever he asked for it.

One day he asked to go to 18 Stone Roller Bridge. The personnel handling the case assumed that it had to be related to the greasy moon. He was taken there in a prison van. Standing there at the upper reaches of the Qishui River, he still couldn't figure out how those stone rollers wound up in the sand farther upstream after the bridge collapsed. He scooped up some water to splash his face and neck, washing away a lot of dirt. Then he presented himself to the personnel handling the case for them to look. "Do you want to confess?" "Confess what?" "Greasy moon!" he said, "I confess I lied to you so that you'd bring me here. I wanted to see the bridge."

You Yiren never dreamed, much less had nightmares. But one winter at noon, as he slept on the *kang*, he seemed to have had a dream. He dreamed that women, lots of women, came to his *kang* to have sex with him, until he could no longer do it, his cock limp and dripping like a melting candle. He sank deeper into sleep and dreamed again, but this time it was all men who cursed him

他是狼。他就绰绰影影回忆起自己的娘在地里收割麦子，疲乏了睡倒在麦捆上，有一只狼就爬进来伏在娘的身上，娘把他血淋淋地生下来了。醒来，一头冷汗，屋里正寂空，晌午的太阳从瓦楞激射下注。他爬不起身，被肢解一般，腿不知是腿手不知是手。

"娘，娘！"他觉得娘还睡在炕的那一头轻轻叹息。"娘，我是你和狼生下的吗？"

娘没有言语。他作想刚才阳痿的事，摸摸果然蔫如绳头，又以为娘知道了他的一切。"娘，是这东西让我杀人吗？我不要它了！我割呀！"窸窸窣窣在炕头抓，抓到一把剃头的刀，将腿根那个东西割下，甩到炕地。

"娘，我真的割了！你不信吗？"

他坐起来，发现炕的那头并没有娘。娘早死了。炕地上那截东西竟还活着，一跳一跳的。

没有了想杀人的祸根，但尤佚人又常常冲动起杀人的欲望，他真不知道这是怎么啦？从瘪家沟走到县城，从县城走到瘪家沟。凡看见一个男人和女人，总觉地面熟。是他曾经杀掉的人？就怯怯地站定一边，等待着人家的讨伐。"这是阴鬼！"

他终于害怕了鬼。

他到山头上的寺院请求去当和尚。

住持却不接纳他。个矮丑陋，一脸杀相，文墨不识，住持立于山门的古柏古松之下，一番盘问之后将他撵下台阶去了。

and called him a wolf. He then dimly recalled his mom, who was working in the fields. She grew tired and slept on a pile of harvested wheat stalks. A wolf approached her and climbed on top of her and, as a result, his mom gave birth to him, dripping with blood. He woke up in a cold sweat. The house was empty and silent, and the noon sun shone through the cracks between the roof tiles. He was unable to get up, feeling as if he had been dismembered, unable to feel his hands and legs.

"Mom, Mom!" He thought his mom was still asleep and breathing softly at the other end of the *kang*. "Mom, am I the child of you and a wolf?"

His mom was silent. He recalled his limp cock and touched his soft penis. Then he felt that his ma knew everything about him. "Mom, is it on account of this thing that I kill people? I don't want it! I'm going to cut it off!" He felt around at the head of the *kang* and grabbed a razor with which he proceeded to slice off his cock and throw it onto the ground.

"Mom, I really cut it off! Don't you believe me?"

He got up and saw that his mom wasn't at the other end of the *kang*. His mom had died a long time ago. The thing on the ground was still alive and jumping.

Even without that "root" for killing, You Yiren still often had an impetuous desire to kill. He didn't know why. He walked from Biejia Gully to the county town and from county town to Biejia Gully. Every time he ran into a man or a woman, he felt they looked familiar. Were they the ones he killed? Then he stood there timidly waiting for them to come get him. "They're ghosts!"

He finally came to fear ghosts.

He went to the temple on the mountain peak and begged to be a monk.

Standing under an ancient cypress tree at the temple gate, the abbot, who was short, ugly, and looked like a killer, and was illiterate to boot, cross-examined him. The abbot refused to admit him and drove him down the flight of steps.

尤佚人开始在门前屋后的空地上烧焚香表，他每夜更深人静之后要在地上画一个圆圈，一个圆圈是给一个人的，画上依稀还记得的模样，就默默焚纸。这奇异的现象使瘪家沟的人惊讶。惊讶一次，再惊讶一次，就生了疑窦。一半年来，到处传说有人失踪。有人就将这半截人的怪异报告了公安局。公安局叫去他一逼问，他毫不抵赖地说他杀过人。

尤佚人终于有了罪名：歇斯底里杀人狂。法院判处他死刑。

宣判之后，问他有什么可讲的，他竟站过来对着麦克风说，我犯了个大错误，在我有生之年，我要为革命做出贡献。严肃的会场很是骚动，有人嘎地发笑了一声。

"你们知道油月亮吗?"他看着发笑的人说。

这正是一个夜晚，宣判室的门外夜空清净，半轮月亮一派银辉。

"油月亮就是人油珠花儿。"

"人油珠花儿?"

"菜油，花籽油，蓖麻油，豆油，猪油，羊油，油珠花儿都是圆圆的，人油是半个圆。"

宣判人不明白死囚犯话的意思，几乎忘记了追问下去。

"城关口的那一家饺子店是卖过人肉饺子的。店主也得判死

You Yiren started burning incense in the open spaces in front of the door and behind the house. In the quiet of the night, he traced a circle on the ground, drew inside the circle the image of the person he had killed as best he could remember, and then burnt spirit money for him or her. His strange behavior astounded the villagers of Biejia Gully, and, after it happened more than once, they eventually grew suspicious. News of people disappearing had been in the air for six months; finally someone reported the strange behavior of the half-pint to the public security bureau. He was called in and questioned and didn't deny killing anyone.

The court finally charged him as a homicidal maniac and sentenced him to death.

They asked him if he wanted to say anything after they'd pronounced judgment. Unexpectedly, he stood up and said into the microphone that he had made a great mistake. And that as long as he lived, he'd always wanted to make a contribution to the revolution. The people in the solemn courtroom became restless, and one of them even burst out laughing.

"Do you know what a greasy moon is?" he asked, staring at the person who laughed.

It happened to be night. Outside the courtroom, a half moon shone with a silvery brightness in the clear, clean sky.

"A greasy moon is a pearl of human fat."

"Human fat?"

"The blobs of grease from vegetable oil, rapeseed oil, castor seed oil, soybean oil, pork fat, lamb fat are all round in shape, but those from human fat are only half round."

The meaning of the accused, who had been sentenced to death, was so beyond the judge that he nearly forgot to ask for clarification.

"The dumpling restaurant at that key location in the county town sells dumplings made of human flesh. The shop owner should

刑。他害得人都去吃。你们可能都去吃过……”

　　宣判室里死寂了半晌，突然哗然了，宣判人脸色寡白地站起来发布纪律：此事谁也不能外传半点风声。遂让犯人在宣判书上按指印，便觉得胃里作呕，险些吐了什么出来。尤佚人终是坦白交待了一切，按指印很认真。但指印并不圆，半圆，一个红红的油月亮。

be sentenced to death. He has harmed those who have gone there to eat. Maybe you have eaten . . ."

The courtroom sank into dead silence, then exploded in an uproar. The judge, whose face had gone pale, pronounced that no one should utter a word about this. As they took the criminal's fingerprints, they felt sick to their stomachs to the point of nearly vomiting. You Yiren confessed everything, and his fingerprints were taken in all seriousness; however, his fingerprints were not round, but rather half round, red greasy moons.

Receiving the Precepts

受　戒[1]

Wang Zengqi

明海出家已经四年了。

他是十三岁来的。

这个地方的地名有点怪,叫庵赵莊。赵,是因为莊上大都姓赵。叫做莊,可是人家住得很分散,这里两三家,那里两三家。一出门,远远可以看到,走起来得走一会,因为没有大路,都是弯弯曲曲的田埂。庵,是因为有一个庵。庵叫菩提庵,[2] 可是大家叫讹了,叫成荸荠庵。[3] 连庵里的和尚也这样叫。"宝刹何处?"——"荸荠庵。"庵本来就是住尼姑的。"和尚庙"、"尼姑庵"嘛。可是荸荠庵住的是和尚。也许因为荸荠庵不大,大者为庙,小者为庵。

明海在家叫小明子。他是从小就确定要出家的。他的家乡不叫"出家",叫"当和尚"。他的家乡出和尚。就像有的地方出剿猪的,有的地方出织席子的,有的地方出箍桶的,有的地方出弹棉花的,有的地方出画匠,有的地方出婊子,他的家乡出和尚。人家弟兄多,就派一个出去当和尚。当和尚也要通过关系,也有帮。这地方的和尚有的走的很远。有的杭州灵隐寺的、上海静安寺的、镇江金山寺的,扬州天宁寺的。一般的就在本县的寺庙。明海家田少,老大、老二、老三,就足够种的了。他是老四。他七岁那年,他当和尚的舅舅回家,他爹、他娘就和舅舅商议,决定叫他当和尚。他当时就在旁边,觉得这实在是在情在理,没有理由反对。当和尚有很多好处。一是可以吃现成饭。

Minghai had been a monk for four years. He came here when he was thirteen. The name of this place is a bit strange. It's called Nunnery Zhao Village. Zhao, because most of the folks in the village were surnamed Zhao. It's called a village, but people lived scattered all over—two or three families here, two or three families there. Stepping outside, the houses could be seen in the distance, but it took some time to reach them on foot because there were no roads, and a person had to follow the winding field ridges. Nunnery, because there was a nunnery there. It was called Bodhi Nunnery, but most people pronounced it Biqi Nunnery. The monks who lived there did the same. "Where is your temple?" "Biqi Nunnery." A nunnery was originally a place where nuns resided; monks lived in temples and nuns in nunneries. But monks lived at Biqi Nunnery. Perhaps it was because Biqi Nunnery was small—temples are big and nunneries are small.

When Minghai lived at home, he was called Little Mingzi. From an early age, he was determined to leave the home life. They didn't call it leaving the home life where he came from; they called it being a monk. His hometown produced monks the way other places produced pig gelders, mat weavers, bucket makers, cotton fluffers, artisans, and prostitutes. His hometown produced monks. If a family had a lot of boys, one would be sent to be a monk. In order to be a monk, one had to rely on connections or groups. Some monks in this place ended up far away; some went to Lingyin Temple in Hangzhou, Ji'an Temple in Shanghai, Jinshan Temple in Zhenjiang, and Tianming Temple in Yangzhou. Most, though, ended up in local temples in the county. Minghai's family didn't have a large amount of farmland, and his three older brothers were enough to farm the land they had. He was the fourth son. The year he turned seven, his uncle, who was a monk, returned home for a visit. After his parents conferred with his uncle, it was decided that he would become a monk. He was present at the time and decided that it made sense and that there was no reason to oppose. Being a monk had its advantages. One didn't have to cook—every temple

哪个庙里都是管饭的。二是可以攒钱。只要学会了放瑜伽焰口，拜梁皇忏，[4] 可以按例分到辛苦钱。积攒起来，将来还俗娶亲也可以；不想还俗，买几亩田也可以。当和尚也不容易，医药面如朗月，二要声如钟磬，三要聪明记性好。他舅舅给他相了面，叫他前走几步，后走几步，又叫他喊了一声赶牛打场的号子："格磴嘚——"，说是"明子准能 个好和尚，我包了！"要当和尚，得下点本，——念几年书。哪有不认字的和尚呢！于是明子就开蒙入学，读了《三字经》、《百家姓》、《四言杂字》、《幼学琼林》、《上论、下论》、《上孟、下孟》，[5] 每天还写一张仿。村里都夸他字写得好，很黑。

舅舅按照约定的日期又回了家，带了一间他自己穿的和尚领的短衫，叫明子娘改小一点，给明子穿上。明子穿了这件和尚短衫，下身还是在家穿的紫花裤子，赤脚穿了一双新布鞋，跟他爹、他娘磕了一个头，就随舅舅走了。

他上学时起了个学名，叫明海。舅舅说，不用改了。于是"明海"就从学名变成了法名。

过了一个湖。好大的一个湖！穿过一个县城。县城真热闹：官盐店，税务局，肉铺里挂着成片的猪肉，一个驴子在磨芝麻，满街都是小磨香油的香味，布店，卖茉莉粉、梳头油的什么齐，

had someone who was in charge of the meals. One could also save money. As long as one learned to relieve the hunger of hungry ghosts and release their souls, and to chant the Litany of Liang Wu Di for the dead, he normally shared some money, and by saving it up, he could resume secular life by taking a wife. If he didn't resume secular life, he could buy several *mu* of land. But being a monk wasn't that easy. One had to have a face like a bright moon, a bell-like voice, and be smart and have a good memory. His uncle examined his physiognomy and had him take a few steps forward and then back. He had him shout as if he were driving an ox on a threshing ground: "*gedangde . . .*" His conclusion was: "Mingzi has what it takes to be a good monk. I guarantee it!" But to be a monk, one had to invest a little by studying for several years. There was no such thing as an illiterate monk. Thus Mingzi began to study. He read *The Three-Character Classic, The Hundred Surnames, The Four Characters and Mixed Words, The Elegant Valuable Collection for Young Learners, The Analects* in two volumes, and *The Mengzi* in two volumes. Every day he wrote a page of characters, which the villagers praised as good and solid.

His uncle returned home on the appointed day. He brought with him a short monk's smock of his own and had Mingzi's mother alter it for him to wear. Mingzi wore the short monk's smock along with a pair of colorful pants he wore at home. He put a pair of new cotton shoes on his bare feet. Then he kowtowed to his parents and left with his uncle.

When he started to go to school, he took on a study name, Minghai. His uncle told him to keep it, so thus Minghai became his monastic name.

They crossed a lake, a huge lake. Then they passed through the bustling county town: there was a salt office, a tax office, a butcher's shop where hunks of pork hung. A donkey turned a sesame mill, filling the street with the aroma of sesame oil. There was a fabric store and shops selling jasmine powder and hair oil

卖绒花的，卖丝线的，打把式卖膏药的，吹糖人的，耍蛇的，
……他什么都想看看。舅舅一劲地推他："快走！快走！"

到了一个河边，有一双船在等着他们。船上有一个五十来岁
的瘦长瘦长的大伯，船头蹲着一个跟明子差不多大的女孩子，在
剥一个莲蓬吃。明子和舅舅坐到舱里，船就开了。

明子听见有人跟他说话，是那个女孩子。

"是你要到荸荠庵当和尚吗？"

明子点点头。

"当和尚要烧戒疤[6]呕！你不怕？"

明子不知道怎么回答，就含含糊糊地摇了摇头。

"你叫什么？"

"明海。"

"在家的时候？"

"叫明子。"

"明子！我叫小英子！我们是邻居。我家挨着荸荠庵。——给
你！"

小英子把吃剩的半个莲蓬扔给明海，小明子就剥开莲蓬壳，
一颗一颗吃起来。

大伯一桨一桨地划着，只听见桨拨水的声音：

"哗——许！哗——许！"

荸荠庵的地势很好，在一片高地上。这一代就数这片地势高，

along with velvet flowers and silk thread. There were peddlers of medicinal plasters, malt sugar blowers, and snake charmers. He wanted to look at everything, but his uncle kept pushing him along, saying, "Hurry up, hurry up!"

There was a boat waiting when they got to the riverside. A tall thin ferryman of about fifty years of age was on board, and squatting at the prow was a girl about Mingzi's age. She was peeling and eating a lotus seedpod. Mingzi and his uncle took a seat inside the cabin, and the boat departed.

Mingzi heard someone address him. It was the girl.

"Are you going to Biqi Nunnery to be a monk?"

Mingzi nodded.

"To be a monk you have to have the precept scars burned on your head. Aren't you afraid?"

Mingzi wasn't quite sure how to answer so just vaguely shook his head.

"What's your name?"

"Minghai."

"What were you called at home?"

"I was called Mingzi."

"Mingzi! My name's Little Yingzi! We're neighbors. My house is next to Biqi Nunnery. Here, these are for you."

Little Yingzi threw the remaining half of the lotus seedpod to Minghai. Little Mingzi picked apart the lotus seedpod and ate the seeds one by one.

As the ferryman rowed, all that could be heard was the oar in the water: *Hua . . . xu, hua . . . xu.*

Biqi Nunnery was well situated on a patch of high ground. It was the one piece of high ground in the area,

当初建庵的人很会选地方。门前是一条河。门外是一排你很大的打谷场。三面都是高大的柳树。山门里是一个穿堂。迎门供着弥勒佛。不知是哪一位名士撰写了一副对联：

大肚能容容天下难容之事
开颜一笑笑世间可笑之人

弥勒佛背后，是韦驮。过穿堂，是一个不小的天井，种着两棵白果树。天井两边各有三间厢房。走过天井，便是大殿，供着三世佛。佛像连龛才四尺来高。大殿东边是方丈，西边是库房。大殿东侧，有一个小小的六角门，白门绿字，刻着一副对联：

一花一世界
三藐三菩提

进门有一个狭长的天井，几块假山石，几盆花，有三间小房。小和尚的日子清闲得很。一早起来，开山门，扫地。庵里的地铺的都是箩空方砖，好扫得很，给弥勒佛、韦驮烧一炷香，正

and the people who had started construction on the nunnery had made a good choice. A river ran in front of the place. Just outside the door was a large threshing ground. Large willows surrounded the place on three sides. Inside the nunnery was a hallway at the end of which was a Maitreya Buddha. An unknown literary celebrity had written a couplet:

A big belly bears the unbearable matters of the world
Laughing at all the laughable people in the world

Behind Maitreya stood the Deva Protector Wei Tuo. The hallway opened out onto a fairly good size courtyard in which two gingko trees were planted. There were three wing-rooms on either side of the courtyard. Across the courtyard stood the main hall of the nunnery, housing the three Buddhas of the past, present, and future—Kasyapa, Shakyamuni, and Maitreya. The images and niches together were only slightly more than a meter in height. The abbot's room was located on the east side of the main hall, and a storage room on the west. On the east side there was a small hexagonal white side door on either side of which was carved a couplet in green characters:

A single flower is one world
Three motes of dust are perfect enlightenment

Inside was a long, narrow courtyard with several artificial stone mountains and several pots of flowers. There were also three small rooms.

The young monks lived a somewhat leisurely life. They rose early in the morning and opened the front gate and swept the grounds, which were paved with square bricks, making for easy sweeping. In the main hall they would burn a stick of incense for Maitreya and Wei Tuo and

殿的三世佛面前也烧一炷香、磕三个头，念三声"南无阿弥陀佛"，[7] 敲三声磬。这庵里和尚不兴做什么早课、晚课，明子这三声磬就全都代替了。然后，挑水，喂猪。然后等当家和尚，即明子的舅舅起来，教他念经。

　　教念经也跟教书一样，师父面前一本经，徒弟面前一本经，师父唱一句，徒弟跟着唱一句。是唱哎。舅舅一边唱，一边还用手在桌上拍板。一板一眼，拍的很响，就跟教唱戏一样。是跟教唱戏一样，完全一样哎。连用的名词都一样。舅舅说，念经：一要板眼准，二要合工尺。说：当一个好和尚，得有条好嗓子。说：民国二十年闹大水，运河倒了堤，最后在清水潭合拢，因为大水淹死的人很多，放了一台大焰口，十三大师——十三个正座和尚，各大庙的方丈都来了，下面的和尚上百。谁当这个首座？推来推去，还是石桥——善因寺的方丈！他往上一坐，就跟地藏王菩萨[8]一样，着就不用说了；那一声"开香赞"，围看的上千人立时鸦雀无声。说：嗓子要练，夏练三伏，冬练三九，要练丹田气！说：要吃得苦中苦，方为人上人！说：和尚里也有状元、榜眼、探花！要用心，不要贪玩！舅舅这一番大法要说得明海和尚实在是五股

also a stick of incense for the Buddhas of the past, present, and future. They would bow three times, recite "Namo Amitofo" three times, and then bang an inverted bell three times. The monks had no reason to have any classes in the morning or evening. Mingzi's banging three times of the inverted bell would substitute for everything. Afterward, he would carry water and feed the pigs, after which he would wait for the monk who managed the household, his uncle, to get up and teach him to recite the sutras.

Teaching sutra recitation was like teaching a class at school. There was one sutra in front of the master and one in front of the disciple; the master would sing one line followed by the disciple. It was singing. His uncle kept time by tapping on the table as he sang. Scrupulous and methodical, he tapped resonantly. Teaching the sutra was identical to the teaching of opera. Even the words used were the same. His uncle said that when it came to reciting sutras, one first had to be precise and second had to follow the musical notation. He said that to be a good monk one had to have a good voice. He said that in the twentieth year of the Republic (1931) there had been a flood, and the canal dikes had collapsed and the water had converged on the Qingshui Reservoir. Since so many people had died in the flood, a platform for reciting prayers for the spirits had been erected. Thirteen masters—thirteen senior monks, the abbots of temples—had all arrived with around a hundred monks. Who was going to take the highest seat? After a good deal of declining back and forth, Shi Qiao, the abbot of Shanyin Temple, was chosen. Taking the highest seat, it goes without saying that he resembled the Earth Store Bodhisattva. With the words "Sing the hymn in Praise for Lighting the Incense," the assembled multitudes, amounting to about one thousand, fell silent. His uncle said the voice had to be trained, which meant practicing through the hottest days of summer and through the coldest days of winter, exercising the *qi* in the lower abdomen. He said only those who endure the most will rise the highest. Among monks there were the very best, the second best, and the third rate. One had to be diligent and not fool around. The monk Minghai greatly admired this exhortation of his uncle's, so he scrupulously

投地，于是就一板一眼地跟着舅舅唱起来：

炉香乍爇——

炉香乍爇——

法界蒙薰——

法界蒙薰——

诸佛现金身——

诸佛现金身——

等明海学完了早经，——他晚上临睡钱还要学一段，叫做晚经，——荸荠庵的师父们就都陆续起休了。

这庵里人口简单，一共六个人。连明海在内，五个和尚。

有一个老和尚，六十岁了，是舅舅的师叔，法名普照，但是知道的人很少，因为很少人叫他法名，都称之为老和尚或老师父，明海叫他师爷爷。这是个很枯寂的人，一天关在房里，就是那"一花一世界"里。也看不见他念佛，之事那么一声不响地坐着。他是吃斋的，过年时除外。

下面就是师兄弟三个，仁字排行：仁山、仁海、仁渡。庵里庵外，有的称他们为大师父、二师父；有的称之为山师父、海师父。只有仁渡，没有叫他"渡师父"的，因为听起来不像话，大都直呼之为仁渡。他也只配如此，因为他还年轻，才二十多岁。

仁山，即明子的舅舅，是当家的。不叫"方丈"，也不叫"住持"，欲叫"当家的"，是很有道理的，因为他确确实实干的是当家的职务。他屋里摆的是一张帐桌，桌子上放的是帐簿和算盘。

and meticulously followed his uncle in singing:

> The fragrance of the incense burner is spreading . . .
> The fragrance of the incense burner is spreading . . .
> The Dharma world is filled with fragrance . . .
> The Dharma world is filled with fragrance . . .
> In golden bodies the Buddhas reveal themselves . . .
> In golden bodies the Buddhas reveal themselves. . . .

By the time Minghai had learned the morning sutra—he had to learn another passage that evening before going to bed, which was referred to as the evening sutra—the older monks had all arisen.

There were only six people living in the nunnery, five monks and Minghai.

An old monk, who was over sixty years old, was master to his uncle. His monastic name was Puzhao, but very few people knew this; few were aware of his monastic name. Everyone called him Old Monk or Old Master. Minghai called him Master's master. He was a very solitary individual and spent most of his time in his room, exactly as in the verse "A single flower is one world." He was never seen reciting the Buddha's name; he simply sat there in silence. He was a vegetarian, except when the New Year rolled around.

Next came three monks of one and the same master whose monastic names included the character *ren* in seniority: Renshan, Renhai, and Rendu. Inside and outside the nunnery, some referred to them as great master or second master; some referred to them as Master Shan or Master Hai. But no one called Rendu Master Du, because it didn't sound appropriate. Most people just called him Rendu. He went along with this because he was only in his twenties, still young.

Renshan was Mingzi's uncle and was the monk who managed household affairs. He was not referred to as "abbot," but rather as "manager." This was reasonable because he did indeed work in the capacity of a manager. In his room was an accounting table on which lay the account books and an abacus.

账簿共有三本。一本是经帐，一本是组帐。和尚要做法事，做法事要收钱，——要不，当和尚干什么？常做的法事是放焰口。正规的焰口是十个人。一个正座，一个敲鼓的，两边一边四个。人少了，八个，一边三个，也凑合了。荸荠庵只有四个和尚，要放整焰口就得和别的庙里合移。这样的时候也有过。通常只是放半台焰口。一个正座，一个敲鼓，另外一边一个。一来找别的庙里合移费事；二来这一带放得起整焰口的人家也不多。有的时候，谁家死了人，就只请两个，甚至一个和尚咕噜咕噜念一通经，敲打几声法器就算完事。很多人家的经钱不是当时就给，往往要等秋后才还。这就得记账。另外，和尚放焰口的辛苦钱是不一样的。就像唱戏一样，有份子。正座第一份。因为他要领唱，而且还要独唱。当中有一大段"欢骷髅"，别的和尚都放下法器休息，只有首座一个人有板有眼地曼声吟唱。第二份是敲鼓的。你以为这容易呀？哼，但是一开头的"发擂"，手上没功夫就敲不出迟疾顿挫！其余的，就一样了。这也得记上：某月某日、谁家焰口半台，谁正座，谁敲鼓……省的到年底结账时诅咒骂娘。……这庵里有

There were three account books: one for income from ceremonies, one for rents, and one for money debts. Monks had religious duties, and such services had to be paid for; otherwise, why be a monk? The most common religious service was that for releasing the souls of hungry ghosts. A standard ceremony for hungry ghosts required ten persons: one officiating monk, one to drum, and then four on either side. Fewer, say, eight, would mean three on either side, which could be done. There were only four monks in Biqi Nunnery, so for a complete litany for releasing the souls of hungry ghosts they would have to partner with another temple. Such occasions had arisen in the past. Normally, they would just hold half a litany, with one officiating, one drumming, and two on either side. On the one hand, looking for another temple with which to partner was a lot of trouble; on the other hand, few households held a full litany. Sometimes, when there was a death in a family, two monks or even one was called to chant the sutras and tap a few times on a religious instrument and have done with it. In many cases, the fees were not paid at the time, and would usually be paid back only after autumn. In such cases, outstanding debts had to be recorded. Moreover, the money shared by the monks who served in the ceremonies for the hungry ghost was not shared equally, just like opera performers. The first part went to the officiating monk, because he had to lead the singing as well as sing solo. In the middle of the ceremony was a long passage referred to as "Death's Head Lament," when all the monks would lay aside their instruments and take a break save the officiating monk; the officiating monk would chant rhythmically. The second part went to the percussionist. Do you think that it's easy? Huh, even with the "opening beat" one had to have the skill for the pause and transition in rhythm. The rest of the monks got the same shares. It all had to be recorded: in what month, on what day, whose family held half a ceremony, who officiated, who was the percussionist . . . This would prevent anyone swearing at the end of the year when the accounts were settled. The nunnery

几十田庙产，租给人种，到时候要收租。庵里还放债。租、债一
向倒很少亏欠，因为租天借钱的人怕菩萨不高兴。这三本帐就够
仁山忙的了。另外香烛、打火、油盐"福食"，这也得随时记记帐
呀。除了帐簿之外，山师父的方丈的墙上还挂着一块水牌，上漆
四个红字："勤笔免思"。

　　仁山所说当一个好和圣桑的三个条件，他自己其实一条也不
具备。他的相貌只要用两个字就说清楚了：黄，胖。声音也不想
钟磬，倒像母猪。聪明么？难说，打牌老输。他在庵里从不穿袈
裟，[9]连海青直裰也免了。经常是披着件短僧衣，袒露着一个黄
色的肚子。下面是光脚趿拉一双僧鞋，——新鞋他也是趿拉着。
他一天就是这样不衫不履地这里走走，那里走走，发出母猪一样
的声音："呣——呣——"。

　　二师父仁海。他是有老婆的。他老婆每年夏秋之间来往几个
月，以为庵里凉快。庵里有六个人，其中之一，就是这位和尚的
家眷。仁山，仁渡叫她嫂子，明海叫她师娘。这两口子都很爱干
净，整天的洗刷。傍晚的时候，坐在天井里乘凉。白天，闷在屋
里不出来。

　　三师父是个很聪明精干的人。有时一笔账大师兄扒了半天算
也算不清，他眼柱子转两转，早算得一清二楚。他打牌赢的时候

had dozens of fields that were rented out for people to sow, from which rents had to be collected at season's end. The nunnery also lent money at interest. But rents and loans usually never went unpaid, because people were afraid of displeasing the bodhisattvas. These three account books were enough to keep Renshan busy. From time to time, expenses for incense, candles, firewood, oil, salt, non-staple foods—all had to be recorded. In addition to account books, Master Shan also had a lacquered board on which the following maxim was written in red on the black: "Being assiduous with the writing brush today, one can avoid headaches tomorrow."

Renshan said that there were three qualities necessary for a good monk, none of which he himself possessed. Two words could sum up his appearance: yellow and fat. Nor did his voice resemble a bell; it was more like that of a sow. Intelligent? That's hard to say—he always lost when he played mah-jongg. He never wore a monk's kasaya in the nunnery or even a simple robe. Normally he wore a short monk's smock, from which his big yellow belly protruded. He shuffled about in a pair of old monk's cloth shoes, and would do the same in a new pair. All day long he would go about from here to there and from there to here, slovenly in dress, grunting like a sow.

Second Master Renhai had a wife. She would come and spend several months from summer to fall because the nunnery was cool. One of the six residents of the nunnery was the monk's wife. Renshan and Rendu called her "aunt"; Minghai called her "Master's wife." The two of them were scrupulously clean and spent all day cleaning. Toward evening, they would sit in the courtyard enjoying the cool. During the day, they stayed in their room and didn't appear.

Third Master was smart and capable. Once, the senior monk had spent all day with an abacus trying to figure a large account, but couldn't get it right. Rolling his eyes a couple of times, he had it clear as a bell. Playing mah-jongg,

多，二三十张牌落地，上下家手里有些什么牌，他就差不多都知道了。他打牌时，总偶人爱在他后面看歪头胡。谁家约他打牌，就说"想送两个钱给你。"他不但经忏惧通（小庙的和尚能够拜忏的不多），而且身怀绝技，会"飞铙"。七月间有些地方做盂兰会，在旷地上放大焰口，几十个和尚，穿绣花袈裟，飞铙。飞铙就是把十多斤重的大铙钹飞起来。到了一定的时候，全部法器皆停，只几十副大铙紧张急促地敲起来。忽然起手，大铙向半空中飞去，一面飞，一面旋转。然后，又落下来，接住。接住不是平平常常接住，有各种架势，"犀牛望月"，"苏秦揹剑"……这哪是念经，这是要杂技。也许是地藏王菩萨爱看这个，但真正因此快乐起来的是人，由其是父女和孩子。这是年轻漂亮的和尚出风头的机会。一场大焰口过后，也像一个好戏班子过后一样，会有一个两个大姑娘、小媳妇失踪，——跟和尚跑了。他还还会放"花焰口"。有的人家，亲戚中多风流子弟，在不是很哀伤的佛事——如做冥寿时，就会提出放花焰口。所谓"花焰口"就是在正焰口之后，叫和尚唱小调，拉丝弦，吹管笛，敲鼓板，而且可以点唱。仁渡一个人可以唱一夜不重头。仁渡前几年一直在外面，近二年才常住在庵里。据说他有想好的，而且不止一个。他平常可是很规矩，

he usually won. With twenty or thirty pieces showing, he more or less
knew who had what hand. When he played, someone always liked to
watch, peeking from the side. Whenever someone wanted him to join
a game, they'd say, "Come on, I want to give you a couple of coins."
Not only did he have all the sutras and confessional litanies down pat
(few monks in small temples did confessional litanies), but he was
also physically adept and could perform "flying cymbals." During the
seventh lunar month, many places held a Feast of All Souls. In a large
open space, several dozen monks dressed in embroidered kasayas
would perform a ceremony for the hungry ghosts involving flying
cymbals. Flying cymbals was just that: large cymbals of several kilos
in weight would be sent sailing through the air. At a certain point,
all religious instruments would cease save for a dozen or so rapidly
clanging cymbals. Suddenly the hands would go up and the cymbals
would be sent soaring into the air, spinning as they flew. Then they
would fall where they would be caught, not in the ordinary way, but
in interesting moves, such as "the rhinoceros looks at the moon"
or "Su Qin shoulders his sword." It was more acrobatics than sutra
recitation. Perhaps it was the Earth Store Bodhisattva who liked
watching this, but it really made people happy, especially the women
and children. It was an opportunity for the young handsome monks
to show off. The large-scale ceremony would end the same way a good
theatrical troupe/opera performance did, with the disappearance of
one or two older daughters or young wife running off with a monk.
He could also perform a "sidelight ceremony." There were times
when the dissolute youngsters would propose a sidelight litany,
when a sad Buddhist affair such as the anniversary of a death wasn't
involved. A so-called sidelight ceremony came after the completion
of a religious litany. The monks would be asked to sing a ditty, play
stringed instruments and flutes, and beat clappers and they could also
perform. Rendu could sing all night without tiring. In previous years,
Rendu had spent much time away from the nunnery, but only in the
last two years had he resided at the nunnery. It was

看到姑娘媳妇总是老老实实的，连一句玩笑都不说，一句小调山
歌都不唱。有一回，在打谷场上乘凉的时候，一伙人把他围起来，
非叫他唱两个不可。他却情不过，说："好，唱一个。不唱家乡的。
家乡的你们都熟，唱个安徽的。"

> 姐和小郎打大麦，
>
> 一转子讲得听不得。
>
> 听不得就听不得，
>
> 打完了大麦打小麦。

唱完了，大家还嫌不够，他就又唱了一个：

> 姐儿生得漂漂的，
>
> 两个奶子翘翘的。
>
> 有心上去摸一把，
>
> 心里有点跳跳的。

这个庵里五所谓清规，连两个字也没人提起。

仁山吃水烟，连出门做法事也带着他的水烟袋。

他们经常打牌。这是个打牌的好地方。把大殿上吃饭的方桌
往门口一搭，斜放着，就是牌桌。桌子一放好，仁山就从他的方
丈里把筹码拿出来，哗啦一声倒在桌上。门纸牌的时候多，搓麻

said that he had a woman with whom he was on intimate terms, and not just one. Normally he was very well behaved, and was always proper in the presence of the ladies. He wouldn't joke or sing even a ditty or a folk song. One time, when he was relaxing at the threshing ground, a group of people surrounded him and insisted that he sing a couple of songs. He was unable to refuse and replied, "Okay, I'll sing one. But I won't sing one from here, because you know them all. I'll sing one from Anhui."

> Sister and the young man threshed barley
> Soon they were unable to hear a word that was said
> Unable to hear, just unable to hear
> They threshed the wheat after they finished the barley

When he finished singing, folks complained that it wasn't enough. So he sang another:

> Sister was quite a beauty
> Pert were her breasts
> I wanted to touch them
> But my heart was all atremble

They were not too particular about monastic rules at the nunnery, and rarely mentioned the words.

Renshan smoked a water pipe. Even when he went out for some religious function, he carried his water pipe.

They often played cards or mah-jongg. It was a good place to play. They would place the dining table in the main hall by the door for a mah-jongg table. As soon as the table was positioned, Renshan would take out chips from his abbot's room and dump them noisily on the table. They played cards more often than they played

将的时候少。牌客除了师兄弟三人，常来的是一个收鸭毛的，一个打兔子兼偷鹅的，都是正经人。收鸭毛的担一副竹筐，串乡串镇，拉长了沙哑的声音喊叫：

"鸭毛卖钱——！"

偷鹅的有意见家什——铜蜻蜓。看准了一双老母鹅，把铜蜻蜓一丢，鹅婆子上去就是一口。这一啄，铜蜻蜓的硬簧绷开，鹅嘴撑住了，叫不出来了。正在这鹅十分纳闷的时候，上去一把薅住。

明子会经跟这位正经人要过铜蜻蜓看看。他拿到小英子家门前试一试，果然！小英的娘知道了，骂明子：

"要死了！儿子！你怎么到我家来玩铜蜻蜓了！"

小英子跑过来：

"给我！给我！"

她也试了试，真灵，一个黑母鹅一小子就把嘴撑住，傻了眼了！

下雨阴天，这二位就光临荸荠庵，消磨一天。

有时没有外客，就把老师叔也拉出来，打牌的结局，大都是当家和尚气得鼓鼓的："× 妈妈的！又输了！下回不来了！"

他们吃肉不瞒人。年下也杀猪。杀猪就在大殿上。一切都和在家人一样，开水、木桶、尖刀。捆猪的时候，猪也是没命地叫。跟在家人不同的，是多一道仪式，要给即将升天的猪念一道"往生咒"，并且总是老师叔念，神情很庄重：

mah-jongg. In addition to the three monks, those who came to play most frequently included a guy who bought duck down and a petty thief who also killed rabbits. They were both decent people. The guy who bought the down carried a pair of baskets on his shoulder, going from one village to town, calling out hoarsely:

"Money paid for duck down!"

The petty thief had a special tool: a copper dragonfly. Spotting a hen, he'd toss the copper dragonfly. The hen would come forward, beak open. With one peck, the dragonfly would spring shut, clasping the hen's bill so that it couldn't utter a sound. With the hen thus vexed, he would step forward and grab her.

Mingzi had once asked this decent fellow to see the copper dragonfly. He took it to Little Yingzi's house to try out in the front of her door. But Little Yingzi's mother found out what it was and scolded Mingzi:

"Damn it, son, why are you playing with a copper dragonfly at my house?"

Little Yingzi came running up:

"Give it to me, give it to me."

She tried it out and was quick and clever. Soon a black hen's bill was clasped shut, stunned.

On rainy days, the two fellows would come to Biqi Nunnery to pass the day.

Sometimes, when no one showed up, they'd drag the old master's uncle out to play, as a result of which, the managing monk would usually end up in a fit: "X your mother! I lost again! I won't play next time."

They openly ate meat. At year's end, they'd butcher a pig. This would take place above the main hall. Everything was like at home: they'd boil water, prepare buckets, and sharpen knives. While they trussed up the pig, it would squeal desperately. What was different from at home was one extra step: they would recite a Mantra of Rebirth for the pig. The prayer was always recited by the old master's uncle, his expression solemn:

……一切胎生、卵生、息生，来从虚空来，还归
虚空去，往生再世，皆当欢喜。南无阿弥陀佛！

三师父仁渡一刀子下去，鲜红的猪血就带着很多沫子喷
出来。

明子老往小英子家里跑。

小英子的家像一个小岛，三面都是河，西面有一条小路通到
荸荠庵。独门独户，岛上只有这一家。岛上有六棵大桑树，夏天
都结大桑椹，三棵结白的，三棵结紫的；一个菜园子，瓜豆蔬菜，
四时不缺。院墙下半截是砖砌的，上半截是泥夯的。大门是桐油
油过的，贴着一副万年红的春联：

　　　　　　　向阳门第春常在
　　　　　　　积善人家庆有余

门里是一个很宽的院子。院子里一边是牛屋、碓棚；一边
是猪圈、鹅窠，还有个关鸭子的栅栏。露天地放着一具石磨。正
北面是住房，也是砖基土筑，圣桑卖弄盖的一半是瓦，一半是草。
房子翻修了才三年，木料还露着白茬。正中是堂屋，家神菩萨的
画像上贴的金还没有发黑。两边是卧房。隔扇窗上各嵌了一块一
尺见方的玻璃，明亮亮的打，——这在乡下是不多见的。房檐下

. . . those born from wombs, those born from eggs, those
born of breath, all come from emptiness, and to emptiness
return. May they be born in happiness in the next life.
Namo Amitofo.

Third Master Rendu wielded the knife, and the foaming blood
would shoot out.

Mingzi always visited Little Yingzi's house.

Little Yingzi's house was like an island, surrounded as it was
on three sides by the river. On the western side there was a small
path that led to Biqi Nunnery. A house with a private entrance, it
stood alone on its island. Also on the island were six mulberry trees:
three with white mulberries and three with purple mulberries, and
a garden with squash, beans, and vegetables growing all year round.
As for the courtyard wall, the lower half was made of brick, while
the top half was made of tamped earth. On the main gate, which had
been painted with tong oil, there was a spring couplet that read:

> Facing south, it is always spring at the house
> Accumulating virtue, people have more than enough

Inside the gate was a very wide courtyard, on one side of which
was a cowshed and a shed for hulling rice; on the other side was a
pigpen, a chicken coop, and a pen for the ducks. In the open was a
stone mill. On the north was the house, which was made of tamped
earth on a base of bricks. The roof was half tile and half thatch. The
house had been rebuilt just three years before. The timber was still
white. The gilt on the painted household gods and bodhisattvas in the
main room had not turned black with age. There were two bedrooms
on either side of the main room. The windows of bright, clear glass
were rare in the countryside. A persimmon tree was planted under

一边种着一棵石榴树，一边种着一棵栀子花，都齐房檐高了。夏天开了花，一红一白，好看得很。栀子花香得冲鼻子。顺风的时候，在荸荠庵都闻得见。

这家人口不多。他家当然是姓赵。一共四口人：赵大伯、赵大妈，两个女儿，大英子、小英子。老两口没得儿子。因为这些年人不得病，牛不生灾，也没有大旱大水闹蝗虫，日子过得很兴旺。他们家自己有天本来够吃的了，有租种了庵上的十亩田。自己的田里，一亩种了荸荠，——这一般是小英子的主意，她爱吃荸荠，一亩种了茨菇。家里喂了一群鹅鸭，单是鹅蛋鸭毛就够一年的油盐了。赵大伯是个能干人。他是一个"全把式"，不但田里场上样样精通，还会罩鱼、洗磨、凿砻、修水车、修船、砌墙、烧砖、箍桶、劈篾、绞麻绳。他不咳嗽、不腰疼，结结实实，像一棵榆树。人很和气，一天不声不响。赵大伯是一棵摇钱树，赵大娘就是个聚宝盆。大娘精神得出奇。五十岁了，两个眼镜还是清亮亮的。不论什么时候，头都是梳得滑滴滴的，身上衣服都是格挣挣的。像老头子一样，她一天不闷着。煮猪食，喂猪，腌咸菜，——她腌的咸萝卜干非常好吃，舂粉子，磨小豆腐，编蓑衣，织芦篚。她还会剪花样子。这里嫁闺女，陪嫁妆，磁坛子、锡罐子，都要用梅红纸剪出吉祥花样，贴在杀死那个面，讨个吉利，也才

the eaves on one side and a gardenia on the other side, both of which stood as high as the eaves. They bloomed in summer—one red and one white, and both quite lovely. The strong fragrance of gardenia assailed the nostrils, which wafted all the way to the Biqi Nunnery when the wind blew in that direction.

The family was small and, of course, surnamed Zhao. They were four, Old Uncle and Auntie Zhao and their two daughters, Big Yingzi and Little Yingzi. The couple had no sons. They lived quite well, because in those years people didn't get sick, the cows didn't come down with the plague, and there was neither drought nor flood nor plagues of locusts. They had their own lands; in addition to what they had, they also rented ten *mu* of land from Biqi Nunnery to farm. On their own lands they planted one *mu* of water chestnuts, which was the idea of Little Yingzi, because she loved to eat water chestnuts, and one mu of arrowhead root. They raised many chickens and ducks; the money from chicken eggs and duck down alone could pay for their oil and salt. Old Uncle Zhao was very capable, a kind of "all-rounder"; not only had he mastered farming, but he also knew how to trap fish with bamboo, wash a mill, carve out a rice huller, repair a waterwheel and boat, build tamped-earth walls, bake bricks, bind a bucket, cut bamboo strips, and twist hemp cords.

He was strong like an elm tree; he never coughed or was pained in the waist; he was very kind and quiet. While Old Uncle Zhao was a ready source of money, Old Auntie Zhao was a treasure trove. She was extraordinarily energetic, and her eyes were still bright even though she was already fifty years old. Her hair was always brushed and shiny and her clothes neat. She was never idle and, like her husband, kept busy all day long, cooking pig feed, feeding pigs, pickling vegetables—her dry salted turnips were delicious—pounding flour, grinding soybeans for tofu, plaiting straw rain gear and reed baskets. She was also accomplished at cutting paper flowers. When a girl was ready to get married, her trousseau, porcelain jars, and tin cans had to be decorated by pasting on flowers cut from plum red paper. In addition to being

好看:"丹凤朝阳"呀、"白头到老"呀、"子孙万代"呀、"福寿绵长"呀。二三十里的人间爱都来请她:"大娘,好日子是十六,你那天去呀?"——"十五,我一大清早就来!"

"一定呀!"——"一定!一定!"

两个女儿,长得跟他娘像一个模子里托出来的。眼镜长得由其像,白眼珠鸭蛋青,黑眼珠棋子黑,定神时如清水,闪动时像星星。浑身是桑下,头是头,脚是脚。头发滑滴滴的,衣服格挣挣的。——这里的风俗,十五六岁的姑娘就都梳上头了。这两个丫头,这一头的好头发!通红的发根,雪白的簪子!娘女三个去赶集,一集的人都朝她们望。

姐妹俩长得很像,性格不同。大姑娘很文静,话很少,像父亲。小英子比她娘还会说,一天叽叽呱呱地不停。大姐说:

"你一天到晚叽叽呱呱——"

"像个喜鹊!"

"你自己说的!——吵得人心乱!"

"心乱?"

"心乱!"

"你心乱怪我呀!"

二姑娘话里有话。大英子已经有了人家。小人她偷偷地看过,人很敦厚,也不难看,家道也殷实,她满意。已经下过小定,日子还没有定下来。她这二年,很少出房门,整天赶她的嫁妆。大

auspicious, they were also pretty. "The red Phoenix faces the morning sun," "Live to a ripe old age in conjugal bliss," "Ten thousand generations of descendants," and "Prosperity and longevity." People from twenty or thirty *li* around would ask her, "Auntie, the sixteenth is an auspicious day. What day will you go?" "I'll come over early on the fifteenth."

"You must! You must!" "Sure! Sure!"

The two daughters were from the same mold as their mother. Their eyes were especially alike: the whites were a duck's egg blue; the blacks as black as chess pieces. When they concentrated they were as limpid as clear water, and when they twinkled they were like stars. They were well shaped from head to toe. Their hair was shiny and their clothes neat. According to custom, girls of fifteen or sixteen had to wear their hair up. These two girls had heads of beautiful hair, dark hair with white hairpins. When the mother and daughters went to market together, everyone's eyes would turn in their direction.

The two sisters looked alike, but they were unalike in temperament. The older girl was gentle and quiet and not very talkative, much like her father. Little Yingzi was more talkative than her mother and chattered nonstop all day long. Her sister said:

"You chatter all day long. . . ."

"Like a magpie."

"So you admit it! You upset everyone with all your noise."

"Upset?"

"Upset!"

"Don't blame me if you are upset!"

The younger girl was hinting at something. Big Yingzi was already spoken for. She had stolen a glimpse of him before—he was honest and sincere and not at all bad looking. His family was well off, and she was in all quite satisfied. The match was arranged and she was betrothed, but the date had not been set. For the last two years she seldom went out, and spent most of her time working on her dowry.

裁大剪，她都会。挑花绣花，不如娘。她课又嫌娘出的样子太老了。她到城里看过新娘子，说人家现在 的都是活花活草。这可把娘难住了。最后是喜鹊忽然一拍屁股："我给你保举一个人!"

这人是谁？是明子。明子念"上孟下孟"的时候，不知怎么得了半套《芥子园》,[10] 他喜欢得很。到了荸荠庵，他还常翻出来看，有时还吧旧账簿子翻过来，照着描。小英子说：

"他会画！画得跟活的一样!"

小英子把明海请到家里来，给他磨墨铺纸，小和尚画了几张，大英子喜欢得了不得：

"就是这样！就是这样！这就可以乱孱!"[11]——所谓"乱孱"是绣花的一种针法：绣了第一层，第二层的针脚插进第一层的针缝，这样颜色就可由深到淡，不露痕迹，不像娘那一代 的花是平针，深浅之间，界限分明，一道一道的。小英子就像个画童，又像个参谋：

"画一朵石榴花!"

"画一朵栀子花!"

她把花掐来，明海就照着画。

到后来，凤仙花、石竹子、水蓼、淡竹叶、天竺果子、腊梅花，他都能画。

大娘看着也喜欢，搂住明海的和尚头：

She could cut out fabric and sew; her embroidery, though, was not as good as her mother's, but she complained that her mother's was too old-fashioned. Having been to the city and seen a bride, she said that everyone was embroidering living flowers and grasses. This stumped her mother. In the end, the magpie suddenly slapped her butt and said, "I can recommend someone."

Whom was she referring to? Mingzi. When Mingzi was studying the two volumes of *The Mengzi*, he had got hold of half a set of *The Mustard Seed Garden*, which he liked enormously. After arriving at Biqi Nunnery, he often took it out and flipped through it. Sometimes he would turn over the old account book and copy on it. Little Yingzi said:

"He can paint! His painting is very lifelike."

Little Yingzi invited Minghai to her house, where she prepared ink and paper for him. The little monk painted several pieces, and Big Yingzi was overjoyed.

"That's it! That's it! Now I can embroider mixed stitches! So-called mixed stitches was a needlework technique in which one layer was embroidered onto a piece of cloth and then a second layer was embroidered directly onto the first layer so as to provide smooth shading. There are no obvious stitches, which was very much different from her mother's generation, who used simple straight stitches to embroider flowers, in which all lines were clear and separate. Little Yingzi was like a scholar's young attendant but also like an adviser:

"Paint a pomegranate flower."

"Paint a gardenia flower."

She would pluck a blossom so that Minghai could use it as a model.

Later, he was able to paint garden balsam, China pinks, knotweed, henon bamboo leaves, Chinese holly berries, and plum blossoms.

Auntie also liked what she saw and clasped the monk's head and said:

"你真聪明！你给我当一个干儿子吧！"

小英子捺住他的肩膀，说：

"快叫！快叫！"

小明子跪在地下磕了一个头，从此就叫小英子的娘做干娘。

大英子绣的三双鞋，三十里方圆都传遍了。很多姑娘都走路坐船来看。看完了，就说："啧啧啧，真好看！这哪里是绣的，这是一朵鲜花！"她们就拿了纸来央大娘求了小和尚来画。有求画帐檐的，有求画门帘飘带的，有求画鞋头花的。每回明子来画花，小英子就给他做点好吃的，煮两个鹅蛋，蒸一碗芋头，煎几个藕团子。

因为照顾姐姐赶嫁妆，田里的零碎生活小英子就全包了。她的帮手，是明子。

这地方的忙活是栽秧、车高田水、薅头遍草，再就是割稻子、打场了。这几茬重活，自己一家是忙不过来的。这地方兴换工。排好了日期，几家顾一家，轮流转。不收工钱，但是吃好的。一天吃六顿，两头见肉，顿顿有酒。干活时，敲着锣鼓，唱着歌，热闹得很。其余的时候，各顾各，不显得紧张。

薅三遍草的时候，秧已经很高了，低下头看不见人。一听见非常脆亮的嗓子在一片浓绿里唱：

> 栀子哎开花哎六瓣头哎……
>
> 姐家哎门前哎一道桥哎……

"You are so clever. Why not become my godson!"

Little Yingzi pressed his shoulders and said:

"Quick! Quick, call her Godmother!"

Little Mingzi knelt and kowtowed, and from then on, he called Little Yingzi's mom Godmother.

Big Yingzi embroidered three pairs of shoes, and word got around within a thirty-*li* area. Many young women walked or took boats to have a look. After looking, they would say, clicking their tongues, "Wow! That is so beautiful. Those are real, not embroidered!" They would take paper to plead with Old Auntie Zhao for her to have the little monk paint for them. Some asked him to paint them for the eaves, some for the streamers on a door curtain and some for those on shoes. Each time Mingzi painted flowers, Little Yingzi would cook something nice for him: a couple of eggs, a bowl of taro, or several dumplings made of lotus root flour.

In order to give her sister enough time to prepare her trousseau, Little Yingzi took over all of the farm chores. Her helper was Mingzi.

The work included planting rice seedlings, irrigating fields using a water wheel, pulling weeds, and cutting the rice at harvest time and threshing it. These tasks were too much for one family. Exchanging labor was a common practice in the area. Once the days were set, the families would rotate, helping one another. No money was exchanged, but they ate well. They would eat six times in one day, with meat served at least twice and liquor at each meal. As they worked, drum and gong sounded and everyone sang. It was quite boisterous. The rest of the time, they each did what they wanted and never appeared anxious.

By the time they had weeded the fields three times, the rice sprouts were already high, so when they bent down, they couldn't see a soul. A clear, melodious voice was heard singing in the green:

> Oh! the gardenia blossoms, spreading six petals . . .
> Oh! in front of sister's door runs a bridge . . .

明海就知道小英子在哪里，三步两步就赶到，感到就低头薅起草来。傍晚牵牛"打汪"，是明子的事。——水牛怕蚊子。这里的习惯，牛卸了轭，饮了水，就牵到一口和好泥水的"汪"里，由它自己打滚扑腾，弄得全身都是泥浆，这样蚊子就咬不透了。低田上水，只要一柈十四轧的水车，两个人车半天就够了。明子和小英子就伏在车杠上，不紧不慢地踩着车轴上的拐子，轻轻地唱着明海向三师父学来的各处山歌。打场的时候，明子能替赵大伯一会，让他回家吃饭。——赵家自己没有场，每年都在荸荠庵外面的场上打谷子。他一扬鞭子，喊起了打场号子：

"格当嘚——"

这打场号子有音无字，可是九转十三弯，比什么山歌号子都好听。赵大娘在家，挺见明子的号子，就侧起耳朵：

"这孩子这条嗓子！"

连大英子也停下针线：

"真好听！"

小英子非常骄傲地说：

"一十三省数第一！"

晚上，他们一起看场。——荸荠庵收来的租稻也晒在场上。他们并肩坐在一个石磙子上，听青蛙打鼓，听寒蛇唱歌，——这个地方以为蝼蛄叫是蚯蚓叫，而且叫蚯蚓叫"寒蛇"，听纺纱婆子

Minghai knew Little Yingzi's whereabouts. He'd be beside her in two or three steps and then put his head down and pull weeds. Toward evening, it was Mingzi's job to take the water buffalo for a "bath." The water buffaloes didn't like mosquitoes. It was the custom in the area to yoke them and take them for a drink of water and then lead them to a muddy pool where they would roll around covering themselves with mud. Then the mosquitoes wouldn't be able to bite them. To raise the water level in a low field, a waterwheel of fourteen buckets was required. Two people working the waterwheel for half a day were enough. Mingzi and Little Yingzi would hunch over the bar on the waterwheel and tread the steps on the wheel's axle, neither too slowly nor too quickly, as they softly sang the folk songs from all over that Minghai had learned from the Third Master. At threshing time, Mingzi would spell Uncle Zhao for a while so that he could go home and eat. The Zhaos did not have a threshing ground of their own; they used the one at Biqi Nunnery every year. As he cracked the whip, he'd shout:

"*Gedangde!*"

This work chantey for the threshing ground was just a sound and not a word. But with a dozen turns around the threshing ground, it sounded better than any folk song. At home, Auntie Zhao would prick up her ears when she heard Mingzi:

"What a voice the youngster has!"

Even Big Yingzi would pause in her embroidering.

"So very pleasant to hear!"

Proudly, Little Yingzi would reply:

"He's the finest in thirteen provinces."

In the evening, they would watch the threshing ground together. The grain the nunnery had collected for rent was also drying on the threshing ground. They sat shoulder to shoulder atop a stone roller listening to the croaking frogs and the "cold snakes" singing—the people in these parts thought that the singing mole crickets were actually singing earthworms, and called them "cold snakes." They would listen to the longhorn grasshoppers

不停地纺纱，"哟——"，看萤火虫飞来飞去，看天上的流星。

"呀！我忘了在裤带上打一个结！"小英子说。

这里的人相信，在流星掉下来的时候在裤带上打一个结，心里想什么好事，就能如愿。

"捵"荸荠，这是小英最爱干的生活。秋天过去了，地净场光，荸荠的叶子枯了，——荸荠的壁纸的小葱一样的圆叶子里是一格一格的，用手一捋，哔哔地响，小英子最爱捋着玩，——荸荠藏在烂泥里。赤了脚，在凉净净滑溜溜的泥里踩着，——哎，一个硬疙瘩！伸手下去，一个红紫红紫的荸荠。她自己爱干这生活，还拉了明子一起去。她老是故意用自己的光脚去踩明子的脚。

她挎着一篮子荸荠回来了，在柔软的田埂上留了一串脚印。明海看着她的脚印，傻了。五个小小的趾头，脚掌平平的，脚跟细细的，脚弓部分缺了一块。明海身上有一种从来没有过的感觉，他觉得心里痒痒的。这一串美丽的脚印把小和尚的心搞乱了。

明子常搭赵家的船进城，给庵里卖香烛，卖油盐。闲时是赵大伯划船；忙时是小英子去，划船的是明子。

从庵赵庄到县城，当中要经过一片很大的芦花荡子。芦苇长

endlessly crying and watch the fireflies floating here and there or watch the shooting stars in the sky.

"Oh! I forgot to knot the belt of my pants," said Little Yingzi.

The people in these parts believed that if you tied a knot in your belt when you saw a shooting star, whatever you wished for would come true.

Picking water chestnuts by hand was work that Little Yingzi really liked. The autumn had gone, the fields were clean and bare, and the water chestnut leaves had dried up. Their hollow-stemmed, onion-like leaves would pop when squeezed, and Little Yingzi was fond of popping them for fun. The water chestnuts were hidden under the mud. She would step barefoot through the cool, slippery mud until she felt a hard lump. She'd reach down for the reddish purple water chestnut. She loved doing this, and dragged Mingzi along with her. With her bare feet, she'd often step on Mingzi's bare feet on purpose.

She'd return home carrying a basket of water chestnuts on her arm, leaving a trail of footprints in the soft soil of the field ridge. Mingzi would stare dumbly at her footprints. There were five little toes, the flat sole of her foot, the narrow heel, and where her arch was, a space was missing. Mingzi experienced something he had never felt before. His mind seemed to itch. The row of beautiful footprints had disturbed the little monk's mind.

Mingzi often took the Zhaos' boat to town to buy incense and candles as well as salt and oil for the nunnery. When Uncle Zhao was unoccupied, he'd row the boat; otherwise, Little Yingzi would go and Mingzi would row.

Between Nunnery Zhao Village and the county town, one had to pass through a large, shallow, reed-filled lake. A waterway cut through the reeds, which grew close together. All around, not a soul

得密密的，当中一条水路，四边不见人。划到这里，明子总是无端端地觉得心里很紧张，他就使劲地划桨。

小英子喊起来：

"明子！明子！你怎么啦？你发疯啦？为什么划得这么快？"

明海到善因寺去受戒。

"你真的要去烧戒疤呀？"

"真的。"

"好好的头皮杀死那个烧十二个洞，那不疼死啦？"

"咬咬牙。舅舅说这是当和尚的一大关，总要过的。"

"不受戒不行吗？"

"不受戒的是野和尚。"

"受了戒有啥好处？"

"受了戒就可以到处云游，逢寺挂褡。"

"什么叫'挂褡'？"

"就是在庙里住。有斋就吃。"

"不把钱？"

"不把钱。有法事，还得先尽外来的师父。"

"怪不得都说'远来的和尚会念经'。就凭头上这几个戒疤？"

"还要有一份戒牒。"

"闹半天，受戒就是领一张和尚的合格文凭呀！"

"就是！"

"我划船送你去。"

"好。"

was seen. Rowing to this point, Mingzi always felt nervous for no apparent reason, and rowed all the harder.

Little Yingzi would shout:

"Mingzi! Mingzi! What's the matter? Are you crazy? Why are you rowing so fast?"

Minghai went to Shanyin Temple to receive the precepts.

"Are you really going to have the precept scars burned?"

"Yes."

"Won't burning twelve holes in your beautiful scalp hurt?"

"I have to grit my teeth. My uncle says this is a critical point in becoming a monk, one that everyone must pass."

"Do you have to receive the precepts?"

"Without receiving the precepts, I'll never officially be a monk."

"What's so good about receiving the precepts?"

"After receiving the precepts, you can roam around, and coming to a temple, you can "hang up one's pouch.""

"What does 'hang up one's pouch' mean?"

"That means you can live in the temple and eat if there's food."

"Without paying?"

"Without paying. And if there is a religious service, the visiting monks have to be made use of."

"No wonder everyone says 'the monks from far away all recite the sutras.' And all it takes is those precept scars on your head?"

"You also need an official document certifying that you have received the precepts."

"So, for all the trouble of receiving the precepts, a monk gets a diploma!"

"Right."

"I'll row you there."

"Okay."

　　小英子早早就把船划到荸荠庵门前。不知是什么道理，她兴奋得很。她充满了好奇心，想去看看善因寺这座大庙，看看受戒是个啥样子。

　　善因寺是全县第一大庙，在东门外，面临一条水很深的护城河，三面都是大树，寺在树林子里，远处只能隐隐约约看到一点金碧辉煌的屋顶，不知道有多大。树上到处挂着"谨防恶犬"的牌子。这寺里的狗出名的厉害。平常不大有人进去。放戒期间，任人游看，恶狗都锁起来了。

　　好大一座庙！庙前的门坎比小英子的胳膝都高。迎门矗着两块大牌，一边一块，一块写着斗大两个大字："放戒"，一块是："禁止喧哗"。这庙里果然是气象庄严，到了这里谁也不敢大声咳嗽。明海自去报名办事，小英子就到处看看。好家伙，这哼哈二将、四大天王，有三丈多高，都是簇新，才装修了不久。天井有二亩地大，铺着青石，种着苍松翠柏。"大雄宝殿"，这才真是个"大殿"！一进去，凉嗖嗖的。到处都是金光耀眼。释迦牟尼佛坐在一个莲花座上，但是莲座，就比小英子还高。抬起头也看不全他的脸，只看到一个微微闭着的嘴唇和胖墩墩的下巴。两边的两根大红蜡烛，一搂多粗。佛像前的大供桌上供着鲜花、绒花、绢花，还有珊瑚树、玉如意、整棵的大象牙。香炉里烧着檀香。

Little Yingzi rowed the boat to the front door of the nunnery very early. For some reason she was very excited. Filled with curiosity, she wanted to go have a look at Shanyin Temple, which was a huge temple, and see what receiving the precepts was like.

Shanyin Temple was the biggest temple in the county. The eastern gate faced a deep city moat, and the temple was surrounded by trees on three sides. From a distance one could faintly make out the gold and blue roof of the temple amid the forest, but there was no way of saying how big it was. Signs that read "Beware of Guard Dogs" were hung on the trees. The temple was famous for its fierce guard dogs. People seldom entered the temple, except when the precepts were being conferred, and then the dogs were kept locked up.

It was a huge temple! The threshold was higher than Little Yingzi's knees. Two large stone steles stood on either side of the main gate. On one was written two huge words: "Conferring Precepts"; on the other, "Keep Silent." The atmosphere of the temple was solemn, so much so that no one would dare cough aloud. Minghai went to register by himself while Little Yingzi went to have a look around. Good God! There were two gods guarding the temple gate and the Four Heavenly Kings, all of which were ten meters in height and all were brand spanking new. The whole place had been recently renovated. The large courtyard was two *mu* in area and paved with black flagstones and planted with pines and cypresses. The "Great Temple Hall" was really a "great hall"! Once inside, it was cool and all about was gold to dazzle the eye. Shakyamuni Buddha was seated on a lotus, and although it was only a lotus, it stood higher than Little Yingzi. Looking up, she couldn't even see his whole face—all that was visible were his closed mouth and fat chin. On either side, there were two large red candles, so huge she couldn't have put her arms around them. On the large offering table before the statue were placed fresh flowers, velvet flowers, silk flowers, as well as coral trees, jade scepters, and a tusk of ivory. Sandalwood incense burned in the incense burner.

小英子出了庙，闻着自己的衣服都是香的。挂了好些幡。这里幡不知是什么缎子的，那么厚重，绣的花真细。这么大一口磬，里头能装五担水！这么大一个木鱼，有一头牛大，漆得通红的。她又去转了转罗汉堂，爬到千佛楼上看了看。真有一千个小佛！她还跟着一些人去看了看藏经楼。藏经楼没有什么看头，都是经书！妈吔！逛了这么一圈，腿都酸了。小英子想起还要给家里打油，替姐姐配丝线，给娘买鞋面布，给自己买两个坠围裙飘带的银蝴蝶，给爹买旱烟，就出庙了。

等把事情办齐，晌午了。她又到庙里看了看，和尚正在吃粥。好大一个"膳堂"，坐得下八百个和尚。吃粥也有这样多讲究：正面法座上摆着两个锡胆瓶，里面插着红绒花，后面盘膝坐着一个穿了大红满金绣袈裟的和尚，手里拿了戒尺。这戒尺是要打人的。哪个和尚吃粥吃出了声音，他下来就是一戒尺。不过他并不真的打人，知识做个样子。真稀奇，那么多的和尚吃粥，竟然不出一点声音！他看见明子也坐在里面，想跟他打个招呼又不好打。想了想，管他禁止不禁止喧哗，就大声喊了一句："我走啦!"她看见明子目不斜视地微微点了点头，就不管很多人都朝自己看，大摇大摆地走了。

第四天一大清早小英子就去看明子。她知道明子受戒是第三天半夜，——烧戒疤是不许人看的。她知道要请老剃头师父剃头，要剃头横摸顺摸都摸不出头发茬子，要不然一烧，就会"走"了

Coming out of the temple, Little Yingzi could smell the fragrance on her clothes. Pennants were hung all around. They were made of some sort of thick satin on which there were finely embroidered flowers. The inverted bell was so large that it could hold five loads of water. The wooden fish was as big as an ox, and was lacquered a deep red. She also went to have a look in the Hall of the Lohans and climbed the Tower of a Thousand Buddhas to take a look. There really were a thousand small Buddhas. She also accompanied a group of people to have a look at the Scripture Hall. There was nothing worth seeing; it was all sutras. Damn. After Yingzi had looked around, her legs were feeling tired. Then Little Yingzi recalled that she had to buy oil for home, thread for her sister, shoe fabric for her mom, tobacco for her dad, and two silver butterflies to hang from her skirt belt for herself, so she left the temple.

It was afternoon by the time she had taken care of everything. She returned to the temple to have another look around. The monks were eating rice porridge. The dining hall was huge and could seat eight hundred monks. They were very particular even when just eating porridge. At the main place setting in front stood two tin vases in which red velvet flowers were placed, behind which a monk sat cross-legged in a red-and-gold embroidered kasaya. He held a precept staff, with which he would strike people. If a monk slurped his porridge, he would descend from his seat and strike the guilty monk. But he didn't necessarily really strike anyone. It was more for show. Strange, for all the monks eating porridge, there was not an untoward sound. She saw Mingzi sitting among the other monks and wanted to greet him, but thought twice about it. Then, throwing caution to the wind with regard to the rule of silence, she shouted, "I'm leaving." She saw Mingzi nod without looking in her direction. She stomped out without regard for all the eyes that had turned toward her.

Early in the morning, four days later, Little Yingzi went to see Mingzi. She knew that Mingzi had received the precepts at midnight on the third night. No one was allowed to see the burning of the precept scars. She knew that the older monks had to shave the heads of the young supplicants so that there was no stubble. Otherwise, when the precept scars were burned, the burning would go too far

戒，烧成了一片。她知道是用枣泥子先点在头皮上，然后用香头子点着。她知道烧了戒疤就喝一碗蘑菇汤，让它"发"，还不能躺下，要不停地走动，叫做"散戒"。这些都是明子告诉她的。明子是听舅舅说的。

她一看，和尚真在那里"散戒"，在城墙根底下的荒地里。一个一个，穿了新海青，光光的头皮上都有十二个黑点子。——这黑疤掉了，才会露出白白的、圆圆的"戒疤"。和尚都笑嘻嘻的，好像很高兴。她一眼就看见了明子。隔着一条护城河，就喊他：

"明子！"

"小英子！"

"你受了戒啦？"

"受了。"

"疼吗？"

"疼。"

"现在还疼吗？"

"现在疼过去了。"

"你哪天回去？"

"后天。"

"上午？下午？"

"下午。"

"我来接你！"

"好！"

· · ·

and burn a large patch. She knew that the scalp was first smeared with date paste and then the burning incense was applied. She knew that after the precept scars were burned, he had to drink a bowl of mushroom soup to let them "set." The monks couldn't lie down and had to keep moving, which was called "spreading the precepts." Mingzi had told her all of this. He had heard it all from his uncle.

She could see that the monks were there "spreading the precepts" on the barren ground at the foot of the wall. One by one, dressed in monk's robes, each one exhibited the twelve black spots on their bald heads. Only after the dark spots had fallen off would the round, white precept scars appear. All the monks were smiling, as if very happy. She spotted Mingzi immediately. From the other side of the moat, she shouted:

"Mingzi!"

"Little Yingzi!"

"Have you received the precepts?"

"Yes."

"Did it hurt?"

"Yes."

"Does it still hurt?"

"It doesn't hurt anymore."

"When are you coming back?"

"Day after tomorrow."

"Morning or afternoon?"

"Afternoon."

"I'll come and meet you."

"Okay."

. . .

小英子把明海接上船。

小英子这天穿了意见细白夏布上衣，下边是黑洋纱的裤子，赤脚穿了一双龙须草的细草鞋，头上一边插着一朵栀子花，一边插着一朵石榴花。她看见明子穿了新海青，里面露出短褂子的白领子，就说："把你外面的一件脱了，你不热呀!"

他们一人一把桨。小英子在中舱，明子扳艄，在船尾。

她一路问了明子很多话，好像一年没有看见了。

她问，烧戒疤的时候，有人哭吗? 喊吗?

明子说，没有人哭，知识不住的念佛。有个山东和尚骂人："俺日你奶奶! 俺不烧了!"

她问善因寺的方丈石桥是相貌和声音都很出众吗?

"是的。"

"说他的方丈比小姐的绣房还讲究?"

"讲究。什么东西都是绣花的。"

"他屋里很香?"

"很香。他烧的是伽楠香，贵得很。"

"听说他会做诗，会画画的砖额上，都刻着他写的大字。"

"他是有个小老婆吗?"

"有一个。"

"才十九岁?"

"听说。"

Little Yingzi came in the boat to meet him.

That day she was wearing a white linen top and black muslin trousers. She also wore a pair of grass sandals made of Chinese alpine rushes. She also wore a gardenia on one side of her head and a pomegranate flower on the other. She saw that he was wearing new monk's robes, from which protruded the collar of a short monk's smock. She said:

"Take off your outer layer. Aren't you hot?"

Both of them rowed: Little Yingzi from the middle of the boat; Mingzi, the rudder from the stern.

The entire way, she kept asking him questions as if she hadn't seen him for a year.

She asked if anyone cried or shouted when they burned the precept scars.

Mingzi replied that no one cried and they just kept reciting the Buddha's name. He said there was a monk from Shandong who swore:

"Fuck your mother; I'm not taking this."

She then asked if Shiqiao, the abbot of Shanyin Temple, was exceptional in terms of appearance and voice.

"Yes."

"It's said that his room is more exquisite than a young girl's."

"Yes. Everything is embroidered."

"Is his room fragrant?"

"Very. He burns Jianan incense, which is really expensive."

"It's said he writes poetry and paints and writes calligraphy. Is that so?"

"Yes. In the brick at both ends of the hallway, his big characters are carved."

"Does he have a wife?"

"Yes."

"Is she only nineteen?"

"That's what they say."

“好看吗?”

“都说好看。”

“你没看见?”

“我怎么会看见? 我关在庙里。”

明子告诉他,善因寺一个老和尚告诉他,寺里有意选他当沙弥尾,[12] 不过还没有定,要等主事的和尚商议。

“什么叫‘沙弥尾’?”

“放一堂戒,要选出一个沙弥头,[13] 一个沙弥尾。沙弥头要老成,要会念很多经。沙弥尾要年轻,聪明,相貌好。”

“当了沙弥尾跟别的和尚有什么不同?”

“沙弥头,沙弥尾,将来都能当方丈。现在的方丈退居了,就当。石桥原来就是沙弥尾。”

“你当沙弥尾吗?”

“还不一定哪。”

“你当方丈,管善因寺? 管这么大一个庙?!”

“还早呐!”

划了一气,小英子说:“你不要当方丈!”

“好,不当。”

“你也不要当沙弥尾!”

“好,不当。”

又划了一气,看见那一片芦花荡子了。

小英子忽然把桨放下,走到船尾,趴在明子的耳朵旁边,小声地说:

"Is she pretty?"

"That's what they say."

"Didn't you see her?"

"How would I see her? I was locked in the temple."

Mingzi told her that an old monk at the temple had told him that the temple intended to select him as an assistant sramanera, but that they had remained undecided. They had to wait for the important monks to decide.

"What is a sramanera?"

"After conferring the precepts, they have to select a head sramanera and an assistant. The head sramanera has to be experienced and be able to recite a lot of sutras. The assistant has to be young, intelligent, and good looking.

"What's the difference between an assistant sramanera and other monks?"

"A sramanera and an assistant sramanera could one day serve as abbot. When the abbot retires, they fill the position. Shiqiao was originally an assistant sramanera."

"Are you going to be the assistant sramanera?"

"Not necessarily."

"If you become abbot, will you manage Shanyin Temple? Will you manage such a large temple?"

"It's too early to say."

After rowing a bit, Little Yingzi said, "Don't be an abbot."

"Okay. I won't."

"Don't be an assistant sramanera, either."

"Okay. I won't."

After rowing a bit more, she spotted the shallow lake filled with reeds.

Suddenly Little Yingzi put down the oars and walked to the stern. Bending to Mingzi's ear, she whispered:

"我给你当老婆，你要不要？"

明子眼睛鼓得大大的。

"你说话呀！"

明子说："嗯。"

"什么叫'嗯'呀！要不要，要不要？"

明子大声地说："要！"

"你喊什么！"

明子小小声说："要——！"

"快点划！"

英子跳到中舱，两双桨飞快地划起来，划进了芦花荡。

芦花才吐新穗。紫灰色的芦穗，发着银光，软软的，滑溜溜的，像一串丝线。有的地方结了蒲棒，通红的，像一枝一枝小蜡烛。青浮萍，紫浮萍。长脚蚊子，水蜘蛛。野菱角开着四瓣的小白花。惊起一双青椿（一种水鸟），擦着芦穗，扑鲁鲁飞远了。

1980 年 8 月 12 日，写 43 年前的一个梦

"I'll be your wife. How about it?"

Mingzi's eyes opened wide as saucers.

"Say something."

Mingzi said, "Huh."

"What does 'huh' mean? Do you want me to or not?"

Mingzi shouted, "Yes."

"What did you shout?"

Mingzi whispered, "Yes. . . ."

"Hurry up and row!"

Little Yingzi leapt to the middle of the boat and began rowing for all she was worth, and rowed into the shallow lake filled with reeds.

The reeds were just putting forth new tassels. The dull purplish tassels gave off a silvery glow, shining gently, like gossamer threads. Cattails had formed in some places, all red like candles. There were also green and purple duckweed, mosquitoes, and water striders. The little white flowers of wild water chestnut also bloomed. They scared a water bird that flapped off, brushing through the reed tassels.

August 12, 1980. A dream of thirty years before.

Notes on Chinese Texts

The Ancestor (Bi Feiyu)

1. 寿比南山福如东海 Common birthday wish for longevity.
2. 太湖石 Odd-shaped stones frequently seen in Chinese gardens.

Dog (Cao Naiqian)

1. 闹不机明 Local speech meaning not to understand.
2. 匹麻 Measure word + hemp. Hemp is used for making the soles of shoes.
3. 白头的 White-tipped matches.
4. 他的狗女妹妹 This is a reference to Dog's sister. We find out later in the collection that she is raped by her brother and commits suicide.
5. 喝西北风 Common idiom, meaning to go hungry.
6. 狗子家的斋斋苗儿没有了。别的可以没有，可斋斋苗儿不能没有。山药咸稀粥、莜面煮鱼鱼、凉拌山药丝还有调苦菜，要想有味道就离不开斋斋苗儿，斋斋苗儿是穷人的调料。 Reference here is to wild garlic flowers used for seasoning as well as to a variety of foods eaten by the poor inhabitants of rural Shanxi. Dough fish, for example, are simply fish-shaped pieces of dough boiled in water.
7. 公家的财产……我原根儿也不机明那是公家的还是母家的。 The words for "public" and "male" are homophonous in Chinese, hence Dog's confusion. He can relate to the male / female, but not to the idea of public property.
8. 要喜要喜 Phonetic representation of the Japanese *yoshi*, *yoshi*, "good, good."

Plow Ox (Li Rui)

1. The introductory sections to Li Rui's story come from a Ming dynasty text by Wang Zhen titled *Agricultural Implements*. The text quotes extensively from the Confucian classics such as *The Analects, The Book of Songs, The Book of Rites*, and from other classical texts such as *The Classic of Mountains and Seas*. References are made to China's legendary as well as historical rulers.

2. Reference here is to the cave dwellings found in Shanxi Province.

3. Chinese unit of length equal to one-half kilometer.

The Mistake (Ma Yuan)

1. 土火炕 Kang, heated brick bed common in parts of northern China.

2. 有人就是钻了这个空子。Ambiguous phrase typical of this story. It can be read as meaning someone who would make use of the light from someone else's candle, but more logically, someone took advantage of the dark to steal his hat.

3. 赵老屁和我最铁 Colloquial expression meaning they are best buddies, and not tough as might easily be assumed from the text.

4. 知青农场 The farms to which educated youth were sent during the Cultural Revolution.

5. 主要是那个贫农出身的田会计和那个下中农出身的李保管员两个人 Poor and middle peasant backgrounds. Class affiliation was important after the revolution. If, say, you had a grandfather who was a landlord, you would be suspect and treated so by the government, especially during political movements such as the Cultural Revolution.

Lanterns for the Dead (Jiang Yun)

1. 冥灯 Lanterns for the dead is a folk custom in which lanterns are set afloat on, say, a river during the Ghost Festival, which is celebrated on the fifteenth day of the seventh lunar month.

2. 《一无所有》 Cui Jian's rock classic.

3. 迟志强 He was born in Harbin in 1958 and began acting at an early age and was widely considered one of the up-and-coming young actors. In 1983 he was arrested for indecent behavior and sentenced to four years in prison. Due to model behavior, his sentence was commuted to two years. After his release from prison, he became a popular singer whose most popular songs dealt with his experience in prison.

Greasy Moon (Jia Pingwa)

1. 十元二十元，甚至是一角或一角零五分 Currency units: one yuan = ten mao = 100 fen.

Receiving the Precepts (Wang Zengqi)

1. 受戒 Receiving the precepts. The precepts are the ethical principles to which all Buddhists subscribe. There are five or eight for lay followers and ten for monastics.

2. 菩提庵 Transliteration for Bodhi, or "wisdom."

3. 荸荠庵 Biqi means "water chestnut."

4. 放瑜伽焰口，拜梁皇忏 Ceremonies for the dead and for freeing the souls of hungry ghosts.

5. 读了《三字经》、《百家姓》、《四言杂字》、《幼学琼林》、《上论、下论》、《上孟、下孟》 The standard curriculum for young people.

6. 戒疤 Precept scars. Points burned on the naked scalp of a monastic when he takes the precepts.

7. "南无阿弥陀佛" Standard invocation of the Buddha Amitabha.

8. 地藏王菩萨 Earth Store Bodhisattva. The bodhisattva who rescues beings from the underworld.

9. 袈裟 Monk's robes.

10. 《芥子园》 The Mustard Seed Garden, the Early Qing dynasty manual of painting.

11. 乱屏 Translated here as "mixed stitches"; an embroidery technique that became popular in the 1930s.

12. 沙弥尾 Sramanera, novice monk, who has taken the ten precepts.

13. 沙弥头 The monk in charge of the novices.

MORE FROM PENGUIN BY CONTEMPORARY CHINESE WRITERS

English
A Novel
Wang Gang
ISBN 978-0-14-311654-7

I Love Dollars
And Other Stories of China
Zhu Wen
ISBN 978-0-14-311327-0

Red Sorghum
A Novel of China
Mo Yan
ISBN 978-0-14-016854-9

Wolf Totem
A Novel
Jiang Rong
ISBN 978-0-14-311514-4

PENGUIN BOOKS